The Boreal Owl Murder

The Boreal Owl Murder

A Bob White Birder Murder Mystery

Jan Dunlap

North Star Press of St. Cloud, Inc.
St. Cloud, Minnesota

ISBN-10: 0-87839-277-7
ISBN-13: 978-0-87839-277-3

First Edition, July 2008

Printed in the United States of America

Published by
North Star Press of St. Cloud, Inc.
P.O. Box 451
St. Cloud, Minnesota 56302

northstarpress.com

info@northstarpress.com

Chapter One

I used to think that there was no such thing as a bad birding trip. I've been birding for almost twenty-six years—since I was eight years old—and I've always had a blast birding. Sure, it's Minnesota, and I get mauled by mosquitoes, soaked in the rain, sunburned in summer and frozen in the winter, but, hey, I get to travel all over this great state and eat all the prepackaged donuts I want from out-of-the-way gas stations. What's not to love about that? And it's a fairly inexpensive hobby, too. The birding, I mean, not the donut-eating. Of course, sometimes there are additional costs—like having to pay for speeding tickets when I try to get all over the state to see rare birds reported on the state birding hotline. But I've been working on reducing those costs. I just remind myself, "Bob, let someone *else* do the driving."

Anyway, I love to go birding. Unfortunately, though, I now know that there is such a thing as a bad birding trip. It starts when you find a dead body instead of the bird you're chasing, and, when someone starts shooting at you, it really goes downhill.

IT WAS GETTING CLOSE TO MIDNIGHT, and my buddy Mike and I were deep in the woods north of Duluth, listening for Boreal Owls.

I've been wanting to find a Boreal for years, but it's one of my nemesis birds—no matter how many times I've chased one, it's always given me the slip. Boreals are pretty rare, which, of course, makes finding one that much harder. But this time I was determined. Besides, I have a reputation to keep up. I'm one of the most successful birders in Minnesota—okay, maybe that's a dubious distinction for most people—but the fact that I still hadn't gotten a Boreal in almost twenty years of trying wasn't exactly boosting my self-confidence.

This year, though, I promised myself it was going to be different. This year, I not only had a strategy, I had a plan of attack. So to speak.

To begin with, I had determined the three most likely places to find the owls. Location, location, location, as my last realtor liked to say over and over and over. I had spent weeks researching where the owls had been observed over the past three years, which wasn't an easy job, since the only available information on the owls' location was in the annual reports by one Andrew Rahr, Ph.D., an ornithologist and field researcher based out of the University of Minnesota in Duluth.

It became pretty obvious to me, too, that Rahr really didn't want anyone else prowling around in the owls' vicinity. In his reports, which I basically had to dig out of the back of birding publications, he made it even more difficult to pin locations down by referring to places with vague directions, like "in the northwest quadrant of the upper third of the Superior

Forest," or "some miles from the Old Gunflint Trail," or "cut a lock of your hair and trace two circles in the moonlight." Just kidding. But he didn't exactly draw a road map, if you know what I mean.

But birders are nothing if not persistent. Hope springs eternal and all that. So I ignored the man's annoying ambiguity and painstakingly compared the annual reports to see which vague references recurred each year. Then I plotted the possible sites on a map.

At one point, I'd even tried talking with him on the phone to verify the locations. His reaction, however, wasn't exactly full of warm fuzzies—in fact, he was downright hostile. I'd never met the man, but he practically accused me of sabotaging his research. I mean, for crying out loud, all I wanted was a little affirmation that I was in the right neck of a very big woods to find the owl. I certainly wasn't trying to steal his job.

I've already got a job and it's a good one, and I like it. I'm a high school counselor at Savage Senior High, outside the Twin Cities. I spend my days helping kids navigate the often obscure and sometimes terrifying twists and turns of graduation requirements and teenage trauma. It may not be as impressive as being a world-renowned owl expert, but it works for me.

Anyway, after that phone call, I gave up on trying to get any help from Mr. Paranoid and focused on the map I'd drawn.

Location, location, location wasn't the only obstacle to finding a Boreal, however.

Timing is critical. As in *really* critical. As in "if you don't get this exactly right, you idiot, you are toast for at least another year. Ha ha ha."

So the first thing you have to remember is that the owls are nocturnal, which means they're only active at night. If you tried to look for them during the day, you could be standing right under one and never know it, because they're small and they blend right into the trees. At night, though, they're busy, hunting for food and doing whatever it is owls do with their free time. Remodeling nests, maybe. Making babies. Watching reruns of *Seinfeld*. I don't know. So the bottom line is, you have to hunt for them in the dark, and since they're still hard to see (it is dark, remember), instead of looking for them, you listen.

Fortunately, Boreal Owls have a very distinctive call, a series of rising flute-like notes. Once you hear it, you know it's a Boreal and not a Great Grey or a Barred Owl or a Great Horned Owl. And since your best bet to hear them is when they're calling during mating season, that narrows your window of opportunity even more for finding them. In fact, there are only about four weeks, from mid-March to mid-April, when the Boreals are mating in northern Minnesota.

As a result, my grand strategy to finally see a Boreal was simple: spend four weekends at three sites in the north woods of Minnesota in the freezing cold while listening for lusty owls.

A brilliant plan.

Cold, but brilliant.

Actually, make that damn cold.

And that was why Mike and I were hiking around in near-zero weather dressed in about ten layers of thermal clothing in the middle of the night in the forest north of Duluth.

After trying the first two of my chosen locations on Friday night and getting nothing, we headed for this last remaining site.

We followed an old logging trail most of the way in, so the path was pretty smooth. Here and there, though, patches of ice and some deep drifts made night walking a little hazardous.

"Are we having fun yet?" Mike asked, slogging through the snow behind me. "I could be home with my wife and daughter right now, you know. Warm, well-fed."

"And wishing you were here with me closing in on a Boreal," I added. "Come on, Mike, you know you want it. You get a Boreal, and you've got every possible bird in this county. A birder's delight. Tonight, we're the Canadian Mounties—we always get our man. Make that bird."

"I got news for you, Bob. We look like dough boys, not Mounties. Besides, I don't think we'll be getting anything to-night. I haven't heard even one owl cry, not even a Great Horned, and those guys are everywhere."

I had to admit that the absence of *any* owl calls was bothering me a little. It seemed like the deeper we got into the woods, the quieter it became. As Mike had pointed out, we should have been hearing some other owls calling by now. The Boreal wasn't the only species around here.

Instead, it was quiet, like the birds had been hushed. Like when they sensed humans.

Or danger.

Or both.

My boot slipped on something—a branch or root, I assumed—and as I caught my balance, it popped up in front of my knee.

Except it wasn't a branch.

It was an arm. A really stiff arm.

"Holy shit!" I yelled, jumping back at least a yard and right into Mike, who had apparently stopped to check out his new night vision binoculars and was looking beyond me.

At least that's what I figured he was doing because the edge of his binos nailed me hard in the neck, and I doubled over in pain.

Which put a hand directly into my face.

It was not, however, my hand.

Nor was it Mike's.

Which left only one very unattractive possibility: it belonged to the stiff arm.

"What? What?" Mike was still behind me, trying to keep his excitement in check, whispering loudly, swinging his binos from treetop to treetop. "Where is it? Where is it?"

"In front of me," I croaked, my stomach doing a double barrel roll. Even through my layers of winter gear, I could feel myself breaking into a sweat and shaking all over.

"The owl's in front of you?" Mike asked, pointing his binos into the trees ahead of us.

"No, the *hand* is in front of me."

I said it as clearly, as meaningfully, as I could, taking deep breaths and straightening back up. I took a step back and turned to look at Mike. "The hand that is attached to the arm that is, I assume, connected to a body that is, I'm thinking, probably dead."

Mike lowered the binos and peered at me in the darkness, totally non-plussed.

"What?"

"There's a dead body in front of me."

Mike leaned sideways to get a look around me. At six-foot-three, I'm a foot taller than Mike, so he hadn't yet seen the hand that now stuck upright a few feet away. I heard him make a gagging sound, and then, a moment later, he let out a low whistle.

"Yeah. Looks like a dead body, I'd say."

For a minute or two or three, it was—well—dead quiet. Then, somewhere in the distance, a hooting sound floated.

I froze, listening.

The Boreal?

I strained to hear it.

Another hoot.

I held my breath. Was I going to get the owl? Finally, after all these years? We had the location right, I was sure of that. I focused on the notes of the unseen bird's cry, willing it to be the flute-like call of the Boreal.

The hoots came closer. I held my breath, concentrating, waiting for the rest of the call that would unmistakably identify the bird.

Instead, I picked up another sound. A distant rumbling, almost like a motor, seemed to echo in the forest. I blocked it out. We were way too far into the woods from any roads to be hearing car engines.

The owl called again.

One hoot.

Two hoots.

Nothing more.

Silence returned to the forest.

"Damn," I whispered. "Not the Boreal. We didn't get him, Mike."

Mike was still staring at the body in front of us. Even in the night darkness, I could see that his face looked a few shades paler than his normal Minnesota white.

"We sure got something else instead," he muttered.

I looked down at the body, partly covered by branches, decaying leaves and drifted snow.

For just a few moments, I'd forgotten everything but the owl.

Including the frozen man at my feet.

Talk about being insensitive. Unfeeling. Cold. All of the above. Me, not the body.

Well, actually, the body, too.

And that's when it dawned on me that the dead man wasn't wearing a coat. Or a hat or gloves, either. No wonder he was frozen. It was damn cold out here. All he had on was a flannel shirt and jeans, which up north in March was hardly enough to even make a quick run out to the mailbox, let alone a hike in the woods miles away from anything. Mike and I were both bundled up in our serious winter gear, covering every bit of skin we could to avoid exposure to the cold: down parkas, wool hats, and thermal gloves. We'd had sub-zero temperatures with wind chill just the night before. The our breath frosted every time we spoke.

Now I wondered how long he had been there, since the corpse still looked fairly intact and definitely recognizable as a man. An older man, in fact. Even in death, his wrinkled face was tanned and weathered, like he'd spent a lot of time outdoors. I wondered where he'd come from, if he'd had Alzheimer's, or if, somewhere, right now, someone was looking for a grandfather or uncle who had wandered off. I figured he couldn't have been here long. There were a few scavengers and predators in these woods, and I would have thought they'd make short work of an available meal. Then again, it was still frigid in the forest. I supposed that the cold might have a preservative effect on a human body, and maybe the hungriest of the predators were still cozied up hibernating. Regardless of the corpse's length of residence here in the woods, though, we needed to get him home. Wherever that might be.

"So," I said to Mike. "What do we do with the stiff?"

"Not funny," Mike whispered.

I glanced again at the rigid body. The initial shock I'd experienced was wearing off, and instead, I was feeling numb. Mike was right, it wasn't funny. Not funny at all.

"Sorry, I didn't mean to make a joke," I mumbled. The intensity of the cold was obviously getting to my own brain cells. "Really. It just came out. We never covered this kind of thing in grad school. Eating disorders—yes. Frozen bodies—no. I'm totally lost here."

"You think I'm not? I'm a mailman, not a cop."

"You're a federal employee," I reminded him. "You get special training. You know what to do with a suspicious package, right? Well, this is suspicious, isn't it?"

"Look, all I do is take the mail, ask 'is there anything in this package that is liquid, fragile, flammable, or potentially able to blow up all forms of life as we know it?' I weigh it, stamp it and toss it in the bin. I don't do bodies." He rubbed his gloved hands together. "Do you have any bright ideas?"

I blew a frosted breath into the air. "Not at the moment, that's for sure."

Hoping for inspiration—divine or otherwise—I tipped my head back to look at the stars filling the sky. We needed to call the police, but my cell phone's battery had given out earlier in the night, so we didn't have any choices in the communications department. There wasn't anything to do but hike back to the car, drive to the nearest phone—probably about thirty minutes away—and call the police. Then we'd have to hike back here with them so they could locate the body. I'd been up since five-thirty this morning chasing birds all over the North Shore, and now, hitting the pillow was still going to be hours away.

Not to mention the Boreal had eluded me once again. Talk about birding gone bad.

I took a final glance at the dead man on the ground.

And then the bad got even worse.

About fifteen feet on the other side of the body, somebody else had decided to come to the party. I was pretty sure that we hadn't sent out any invitations, and yet, here he was, not even wearing a party hat or blowing a horn, but obviously ready for cake and ice cream. He did, however, bring his nice big teeth with him, which he was happy to display for us. I guessed he was five feet tall and weighed close to three hundred pounds. Overall, I'd say he was the most impressive party crasher I'd ever seen.

For a bear.

Hello, Smokey.

Chapter Two

So maybe I was wrong about that hibernating thing.

The bear growled low in its throat and took a step towards the corpse that lay between us. He kept his teeth bared.

From somewhere behind me, Mike spoke in a barely audible whisper. "I think it wants the body. You know . . . dinner?"

Thanks to a couple summers of employment with the state's Department of Natural Resources, I knew a little about black bears. They usually stay away from people, making me pretty confident that Mike was right—that it wasn't me being featured as the midnight special on tonight's menu. The corpse, though, was another matter. When bears are hungry enough, they'll eat garbage, so a week's worth of frozen meat all wrapped up in one package would probably entice even the shyest bear to make a bid for the checkout. But there was no way I was going to let Smokey past my cash register. Problem was, I wasn't sure what I could do about it without getting my arm ripped off in the process. I had a distinct feeling that the bear wasn't in the mood for accepting a rain check.

And then, lo and behold! I didn't have to do anything at all about it, because a bullet whizzed past my right ear and exploded on the ground right in front of Smokey's nose.

The bear started, blinked, turned tail and lumbered back into the forest. I spun around and found myself embarrassingly up close and personal with the business end of a rifle barrel aimed right at my crotch. On my unknown rescuer's other arm, hung a vicious-looking crossbow. That was pointed at Mike.

Well, hell, I thought. *Things just kept getting better and better tonight.*

Motionless, Commando Joe stared at me through his night vision goggles. In the distance, I heard an owl call.

"Great Grey," I said, without thinking.

Fortunately, Joe didn't respond by pulling the trigger and ending the family line before it even began. Instead, he lowered both weapons to the ground and peeled off his goggles. "White. Thought it might be you."

I knew this guy? I tried to see past the camouflage clothing and face paint, but without a flashlight, and under these circumstances, I was . . . well . . . in the dark. I couldn't recall any Rambo-types in my phone book.

And then it hit me.

It was Scary Stan.

Stan Miller.

The one birder in the state nobody liked to bird with because birding with Stan was like birding with a ghost. He rarely said a word, moved without making even the hint of a sound, could disappear in a heartbeat, and when he did look at you, it was like he looked right through you. Rumor had it he was either a free-lance sniper, a mob killer in the Witness Protection Program, a CIA operative on long-term medical (read "psychological rehab") leave, or just plain nuts.

And it was common knowledge in the Minnesota birding community that he hated my guts because I'd had the nerve to question one of his bird sightings a few years ago. But—come on—an Arctic Tern in downtown Minneapolis in June? Who wouldn't have questioned it?

Of course, when I went to see the bird myself and found that it was, indeed, an Arctic Tern (courtesy of a freak Alberta clipper cold front that had blown the poor bird thousands of miles off-course), I graciously ate a very large serving of crow and apologized to Stan, but as far as he was concerned, the damage to his credibility was done. Since then, we've had a running, but silent, competition to score the most unusual birds every season.

Which probably explained what he was doing up here tonight: he was chasing the Boreal, too.

Although that didn't explain the rifle and crossbow.

I blinked, and—naturally—he disappeared.

"You do this?" His voice came from behind me where he was squatting next to the frozen man.

I walked over to where he was studying the body.

"Right," I said. "I always bring bodies with me when I bird. It's the secret of my success."

Mike had recognized Stan, too. "How about you?" he asked.

Stan gave Mike his empty-eye stare.

"Just asking," Mike said.

Stan stood up. "Bears aren't the only predators in this forest."

And then he disappeared.

"Man, is he creepy." Mike shivered in his parka.

I shivered, too, but it wasn't from the cold. I could still feel Stan's stare through his night-vision goggles, watching me, and for the barest space of a moment, I wondered just how nuts Scary Stan was. If I'd been alone . . .

But I wasn't. Mike was with me. Reason number ninety-three to always bird with a buddy: to discourage scary people from killing you.

"Okay," I said to Mike. "We've got to get to a phone. We'll just have to hope the bear doesn't come back in the meantime."

"I doubt it will," he replied. He retied his parka hood to fit more snugly against his ears. "I expect Stan's gunshot convinced it to find a different buffet line for the night. I know I sure wouldn't hang around where someone was taking shots at me."

We started back down the trail, the moon beginning to rise above the treetops. Funny thing about someone taking shots at you, I realized. It could actually mean one of two different things. One: someone wanted to hurt you. Or two: someone wanted to scare you off so they wouldn't *have* to hurt you.

Without a doubt, Stan scared off the bear by shooting at it. And while I really didn't think Stan would shoot me—no matter how many times I might lock horns with him over birds—I couldn't help thinking a little bit about how close that

bullet had come to my ear, as well as his parting comment about predators in the woods. Was he trying to scare me out of the area so I wouldn't find a Boreal before he did?

That would be pretty low.

It would also be useless.

Because if he was so sure he'd find a Boreal in that particular location, then the last thing I was going to do was stay away from it.

Stan Miller might be scary, but he was also an exceptional birder, and I could certainly respect that. If finally getting a Boreal this season meant following in Stan's disappearing footsteps, then I was definitely willing to give it a try. I mean, really, if he didn't like me on his tail, what was the worst he could do to me?

Shoot me?

He'd already passed on that one tonight.

Leave me to freeze to death in his tracks?

I came to an abrupt halt on the trail. Now that I thought about it, Stan hadn't seemed particularly disturbed to see a frozen man in the middle of the forest. Of course, depending on which rumor about his real identity was true, finding dead men might be a big event on Stan's radar. Even so, if Stan had staked out the area for the Boreal, wouldn't he have noticed an underdressed man wandering around or have found the body before Mike and I did? And wouldn't he have done something about it? Instead, he'd just melted away into the woods tonight after shooting at the bear, like he'd never even been there.

And what was up with the rifle *and* crossbow? Not exactly standard birding equipment. Deer hunting, maybe. Boreal chasing, no. Bear hunting was a possibility, but he'd let Smokey go with only a warning shot. So what was Stan really hunting up here tonight?

Which only made me conclude that something weird was up with Scary Stan Miller. That, and the fact that all my finely-honed school counselor instincts were jangling. This guy had a secret, and I was going to find out what it was.

But first things first, and the first thing I had to do was get a police officer back up here in the woods to pick up a frozen body.

Yup, like I said, I love birding. And even when it goes bad—and at this point, I had no idea how bad it was really going to get there's always the possibility of getting something you hadn't planned on. Of course, you hope it's another bird.

Not a body.

Chapter Three

So then, like, you know, I told her she was being a lousy best friend because she knew I liked Brad, and he was starting to like me, too, and then she started flirting with him? I mean, Mr. White, how could she? And then . . ."

It was Monday morning. I was folded into my cubbyhole office at Savage Senior High, a good three hours south of where I'd spent the weekend chasing Boreals, not to mention finding a body and providing Stan Miller with the opportunity to practice his marksmanship. And, like every Monday morning, I already had a line of students waiting to talk with me as soon as I walked in.

Naturally, I like to think that students flock to me because I'm good at what I do. I feel their pain. I share their angst.

I get them out of class.

Bingo.

However, I also knew—and as my colleagues delighted in reminding me, frequently—that many of the girls I counseled had crushes on me, which seemed to be an occupational hazard for any single guy surrounded by masses of seething female teenage hormones.

Right now, it was one of those seething masses, by the name of Kim, who was taking a turn sitting in my office, venting about her upsetting weekend. Believe me, her upsetting weekend was nothing in comparison to *my* upsetting weekend, but, unfortunately, that wasn't what she wanted to talk about. No, at the moment, it was my turn, as her guidance counselor, not to unload my truckload of personal crap, but instead, to listen patiently while she unloaded hers.

Most of the time, that's not a problem for me. I really like kids. I want them to know I'm in their corner. I know that when I was growing up, I could have used a few more teachers' sympathetic ears. There were lots of times I was miserable, thanks to other kids. I got teased a lot, but with a name like Bob White, what did I expect? Once it got out that I was interested in birds—okay, make that practically obsessed with them—I got "bobwhite, bobwhite!" bird calls all the time and lots of mean-spirited remarks about bird brains, eating like a bird, and heading south for the winter.

Now, I figure all the harassment I put up with while I was growing up made me into the sensitive and understanding kind of guy I am, which is one of the reasons I chose counseling for my career path. God knows it wasn't for the money. And it sure wasn't for the non-existent luxury office space, either. Or the mandatory lunchroom duty assignment.

Talk about human misery.

Don't get me wrong—I love what I do. There's nothing better than working with teenagers. Hormones notwithstanding.

Plus, you get the same schedule they get—almost three months of summer off every year. And don't forget winter break, spring break, and the occasional long weekend, too, thanks to a couple dead presidents and Martin Luther King, Jr. *Hail to the Chief* and *I Have a Dream*. I can always find a bird to chase.

This morning, though, my counseling skills were being sorely tested. I was having my own "issues"—that's a code word we counselors like to use. It's shorter than "self-indulgent bull crap." I didn't want to listen to Kim, the drama queen of the hour. For one thing, she kept repeating herself, and I'd gotten the highly complex concept the first time around: she was angry with her best friend over a boy. Big surprise. What I really wanted to say was, "Hey! Just get over it! Get your little caboose outta here and go back to class where you belong," but I was afraid that wouldn't fly with my boss, Mr. Lenzen, the assistant principal.

Besides, I could just hear the whine as the little caboose went out the door, "But what am I gonna DO, Mr. White?" The fact is, for some of these kids, no matter what advice I give them, or what coping skills I try to teach them, they just don't get it. For drama queens, drama is definitely king.

The other thing that kept distracting me was that I was still seeing that hand from Saturday night pop up out of the ground. The recurring mental replay hadn't exactly given me sweet dreams during the last twelve hours. Neither had the memory of tripping over a corpse. And, oh yeah, there was also the big hungry bear and Scary Stan in camo with loaded artillery in his hands.

But then, should all of that not be enough, I'd found a note attached to my bird feeder this morning. "*Stay out of the forest or you're next.*"

Don't get me wrong. I love threatening notes with my morning coffee just as much as the next guy. Adrenaline and caffeine. What a combination. Definitely jump starts a Monday morning after a long weekend.

And, believe me, it had been one long weekend.

By the time Mike and I had found a phone, led the police to the body, made statements and promised to buy tickets to the policemen's annual ice fishing fund raiser for the rest of our natural lives, it was Sunday morning. We took turns driving back home to the Twin Cities. I dropped Mike off at his place in the northern suburbs, then made it back to my town house on the south side just before noon. I filled the suet feeders hanging off my deck and passed out on my living room sofa. I woke up about six, showered, zapped a tray of frozen breaded shrimp in the microwave for dinner and listened to my phone messages.

The first was from the detective in Duluth—John Knott—who was in charge of the investigation about the body. He said there were no reports of missing grandfathers or uncles, so the Alzheimer's theory had gone into the circular file. There were, however, a few complaints about missing husbands, which, he said, wasn't that unusual on a Sunday morning; he said he'd be able to rule most of those out by early afternoon when the hangovers let up and the men meandered on home. He left several phone numbers and asked me to keep in touch.

The second was from my sister Lily. We don't get along very well, but can call a truce when it's mutually advantageous.

"Call me," she commanded. "I have a client who wants to landscape her backyard big-time for attracting birds. Help me out with this, and I'll keep you in birdseed for the next year."

Ah, Lily. Never let it be said that my sister doesn't know the power of a good bribe.

The third was from my girlfriend, Luce. Her last name is Nilsson, and though all the members of her family have been born on American soil for more than three generations, her dad still flies the Norwegian flag in his front yard and sings the Norwegian national anthem on holidays. But you don't need to hear Luce singing to know she has Norwegian genes. One look at her will tell you. She could be the poster child for the women of Norway. She's got long blonde hair, blue eyes, ruddy cheeks, toned muscles, and stands six-feet, two-inches tall.

"Bobby," her voice on the machine said.

Luce and Lily are the only ones who still call me Bobby, by the way. When I was little, I was Bobby to everyone. My mom says I was cute and round, with big chipmunk cheeks and a mop of dark-red hair. Now I'm tall and lean and broad-shouldered and most people have to look up at me, so I guess I don't come across as a Bobby anymore.

Except to my sister and Luce. Lily's excuse is that I'll always be her little brother just because she's older than I am, but not by much. Luce, being gorgeous and sexy (did I forget to mention that part?), doesn't need an excuse, as far as I'm concerned. She can call me anything she wants as long as she keeps calling me.

Of course, Luce has a habit of calling people anything she wants to anyway because, besides being tall, she's a little intimidating until you get to know her. She's the executive chef at a very classy conference center in Chaska, the old river town west of the Twin Cities, and she's—how do you say?—arrogant.

Not only that, but when she wears her poufy chef's hat, she's got to be about seven feet tall—a veritable giant. Put a boning knife in her capable hand, and it makes people nervous to be in the same room with her.

"If you're eating that microwave crap for dinner again tonight, I'm totally disgusted," Luce's message went. "Did you get the Boreal? And did you try that new little bistro on the North Shore I told you about? What did you eat? How were the desserts? Call me. You know where I am."

Yeah, I knew where she was, all right. In the kitchen. The problem we had was getting her out of the kitchen: executive chefs work afternoons and evenings. I work days. If it weren't for Saturday and Sunday mornings, we'd hardly ever see each other

Luckily, Luce is a birder too. That's how we met. We were both on an MOU—that's Minnesota Ornithologists' Union—trip to the northwest tip of the state, looking for a Northern Hawk Owl. There were about twelve of us in three cars, and she and I were crammed together in a miniscule backseat for two days, so we had lots of time to get acquainted with each other's knees and elbows. I typically don't meet many (make that any) beautiful thirty-something single women who even know what birding is, let alone are interested to the point of going on a birding weekend with a bunch of people who think standing in a mosquito-infested bog to see one particular bird is a peak experience, so I wasn't about to let the opportunity slide by.

Long story short—we got the Northern Hawk Owl, and I got the woman of my dreams. She's smart, she can cook, and she loves birds. That's three for three, as far as I'm concerned. We bird together whenever we can, which usually means weekend mornings during the school year. If I want to go for a birding weekend, I have to find other birders, like Mike, to go with me, since it's hard for Luce to get away overnight because of her job.

I returned her message (she was at work, of course) and said I was saving her some microwaved shrimp.

So here I was on Monday morning, my counselor game face on, giving the required sympathetic ear to today's drama queen. I did not, however, hear a word she said.

I was too busy thinking about that corpse.

And the note.

Because obviously, they had something frightening in common: me.

Sorry, Kim. Nothing personal.

The note, though—now that was personal. Not only was it clear that the note writer knew I had found the body in the forest, but it was equally clear that the note writer knew where I lived. Neither of those things made me feel especially comfortable, but it was the message itself that made me feel the worst.

Someone was threatening my life.

Because I had found a body?

God knew, I hadn't gone looking for one. Even though I'd read the note a hundred times already, I still felt like a bottom-dweller on the information chain: I didn't know what was going on here. Was I being threatened because I'd found a body or because I'd been in the forest? Or was it both? If my anonymous letter writer was trying to tell me something, I was going to need some help figuring it out. Exactly what was it that I had done that had earned this very special attention? And how in the world did the letter writer, whoever it was, find out so quickly that (1) it was, in fact, me who found a dead man, and (2) my backyard address? Which could only mean that unless there was a service provider for writing and delivering personal threats speedily across the state, my note writer was right here in town.

A very scary thought.

Which, of course, made me think of Stan.

Stan lived in Mendota Heights, not even twenty minutes away from Savage. No one else in town knew about my weekend. Besides Mike and Luce, I mean. Oh, and I guess the entire Duluth Police Department—they all knew about it. But they were in Duluth. It was kind of a stretch to think that one of Duluth's finest may have beaten a path to my backyard very early this morning to pin a threat to my feeder.

Which left me, again, with Stan.

Which meant he was taking our birding rivalry a couple shades too far. Although, if the rumors about him were true, clearing the field of opponents probably wouldn't be such a stretch for him to consider.

And then it hit me: could the dead man have been a birder as well?

Come to think of it, why would anyone else be up in those woods in mid-March? Detective Knott had already ruled out the Alzheimer's possibility, and certainly there were lots of more easily accessed remote places for a killer who needed a spot to dump a body, so it stood to reason that the deceased had chosen to be up there.

Before he was deceased, I mean.

At the same time, I knew that nobody actually lived there because it was federal preserve land. The woods were too thick for cross-country skiing and snowmobiles, and there were much better trails in other areas. Snow camping was possible, I supposed, but I didn't think you typically left behind a dead person with the candy wrappers, or if you did, that you would relieve them of their outerwear first. Deer hunting season was over months ago, so hunters should be guzzling their beer at home, not in the woods north of Duluth.

That left who?

Fugitives from justice?

Jail would be a warmer choice.

Illegal immigrants from . . . Canada?

Perish the thought.

Space aliens?

That was New Mexico's gig.

Birders?

Bingo.

Chasing Boreals was the only conceivable reason I could come up with for taking the plunge into that mind-numbing cold, let alone having to make the dough-boy fashion statement. Remember, you can only hear Boreals for a few short weeks during their mating season. If any other birders were hoping to add the species to their birding lists, they had to know that was the only window of opportunity for the year. Obviously, Stan had mined the old reports and come up with the same locations I had, but I couldn't say that really surprised me. Stan was almost as obsessive as I was when it came to chasing birds.

But neither Stan nor I was the frozen corpse presently thawing in the Duluth morgue. So who else would have known the location of that particular site?

A sinking feeling started rolling in my stomach.

Who else but the man who tipped me off, albeit most unintentionally?

Dr. Andrew Rahr, Boreal researcher.

"So, then, like, I said to Lindsay, 'You think I'm jealous? You're the one who's jealous. If I tried to poach on your territory, you'd kill me . . .'"

"Kim," I interrupted.

She stopped talking. I waited for her to make direct eye contact with me. It took a minute or two.

"I think this is one of those things you have to be mature enough to let go," I told her.

Drama queens love to be referred to as "mature," I've found. They respond much better to that than to "you sniveling twit."

Kim looked at me, shook her multi-colored hair extension things off her face and sighed. "Yeah, I guess I can do that, Mr. White. But so help me God, if she ever . . ."

"Bye, Kim," I said, handing her a pass back to class. "I'll see you later."

As soon as she was gone, I picked up the phone and dialed the detective's number in Duluth. It rang six times, then clicked.

"Knott here."

I started to leave a message. "Detective . . ."

"No, I'm here," Knott said. "It's my name. You know. Knott. K-n-o-t-t here. Okay, so maybe I should reword that."

And I thought I had name problems.

Chapter Four

This is Bob White."

"Oh, yeah, our birding corpse-finder. What can I do for you?"

I took a deep breath. "Do you know who the dead guy is yet?" As I said it, I thought it probably sounded pretty insensitive—"the dead guy"—but Kim had already sucked up my sensitivity quota for the day.

"Do you?" Knott asked me back.

We'd already been through this drill a couple times very early Sunday morning. Every time, I'd said, "No," because I didn't know the guy. At the time, I hadn't thought to make any *guesses* about his identity. Why on earth would I recognize a fellow found frozen in the woods north of Duluth?

Now, though, I had a growing, ugly, suspicion that I did know the man—not personally, exactly, but by reputation . . . and his work with the Boreals. If the body was that of Andrew Rahr, his death would send shock waves throughout the Minnesota birding community, not just because he was a respected researcher and ornithologist, but simply because he was a birder in Minnesota. Birders in Minnesota are almost like a big, extended family. Connected by a passion for birding, as well as a continuous flow of email information, Minnesota birders know each others' names, if not faces. If Rahr had died, that whole family would feel the loss.

Including me.

Hopefully, that would be all I felt.

Loss.

Not guilt.

I mean, the man had sounded pretty disturbed that one time on the phone, but certainly he hadn't been in danger, or feeling suicidal, had he? I was a counselor, for crying out loud. I could recognize when someone was making a plea for help, and help was the last thing Rahr had wanted from me when we had talked.

So, maybe now he was dead. And I'd found a death threat hanging on my bird feeder.

I realized that Knott was still waiting for my answer.

"I'd never met the man before I stepped on him Saturday night, Detective," I assured him one more time. "But now I have this bad feeling I might know who he is . . . or was."

"Try me."

"Dr. Andrew Rahr."

There was a moment of silence. "Okay. You win a cigar. Now you tell me how you knew the right answer."

The sick feeling I'd noticed earlier in my stomach was gone, but now my heart was slowly edging down inside my chest.

It *was* Rahr.

"I got to thinking about who would be up there this time of year," I explained to Knott. "I realized that Dr. Rahr was one of the few people who would know that particular location and have a reason to be there."

An image of the frozen body I'd stumbled over popped into my head. Knowing now that it was Rahr somehow didn't make sense in that picture, though. Rahr was a seasoned professional researcher. He'd been in the Minnesota woods in March for years. He couldn't possibly have misjudged the weather that badly.

Could he?

Or did he? Deliberately?

If that were the case—if Rahr had committed suicide—then Stan was simply taking advantage of a tragic death to jerk my chain with a threatening note, to try to scare me off from finding the Boreal before he did. And if that was the real story behind the note, then Scary Stan was even lower than the rumor mill supposed.

"White, are you still there?" Knott's voice floated out of the phone's receiver.

"Yeah," I said, realizing I'd zoned him out while I had zeroed in on other thoughts. "Just thinking."

"Me, too. The initial exam at the scene said cause of death was exposure, but I'm thinking that's pretty odd, seeing as the man had been working up there for years in the cold. I'm thinking there's something else going on here."

I was thinking that, too. But, unfortunately, suicidal people don't always leave good-bye letters. And if it wasn't suicide . . . I really didn't want to think about that at all.

I tried, instead, to focus on Knott. Though I'd just met the man the day before, I could clearly picture him, his lanky frame sprawled in his squeaky office chair. He'd be tilted back right now, staring at the ceiling thoughtfully. Mike and I had spent a couple of hours with him, most of it repeating our movements on Saturday night from the time we left our hotel after dinner to the time the police arrived at the gas station phone booth from which we'd called for help. The fluorescent overhead lights in his little office had shone constantly on his shock of jet-black hair which seemed to stick out at all angles from his head.

And I thought I had bad hair days.

"Rahr was obviously well-acquainted with conditions up there, seeing as he'd been doing field research for years," Knott was saying, echoing my own thoughts. "It's not like he was some neophyte in the woods. So why would he have been so inadequately dressed? Suicide? I don't think so. Granted, we all go a little crazy in the winter around here, but I can think of a lot quicker ways to kill myself than freezing to death on purpose," Knott speculated.

Instantly, I felt some of the pressure building in my chest ease up. If Knott had discarded the suicide option, that was good enough for me.

Of course, that left an alternative that was even less appealing.

If it wasn't an accident or suicide, then there was someone else involved in Rahr's death.

Someone who was up in the woods last weekend.

"How well do you know that forest, White?"

It took me another split-second to catch Knott's train of thought. In the same instant, I realized I didn't want to go there. In fact, I realized I'd really rather not be talking about this at all.

I'd rather be watching for those space aliens in New Mexico.

I'd rather have Kim back in my office, spitting drama.

I'd even rather be in the lunchroom on duty assignment.

Well, maybe not that.

Knott, however, was well on his way to this particular conversational destination. In fact, he was already pulling into the station and climbing out of the engine.

"I'm thinking murder, White. You're not a suspect, if that's what you're wondering."

I was wondering. Maybe he could hear my heart pounding against my ribcage. A murder suspect! That was something else we never covered in graduate school.

Knott paused, and I could sense that he was trying to decide if he should say anything more. He decided to go for it.

"We can tell that Rahr had been dead for about thirty-six hours by the time you found him. We know you and your friend Mike Smith were both at work. We checked. As for your fellow birder Mr. Stan Miller, he seems to be a little slippery so far to verify his whereabouts at the time of Rahr's death. We're having some trouble tracking him down, actually. It appears he must be self-employed. But beyond that, I don't have any leads. Nor do I have any experience with, or links to, this owl stuff, so whatever you can tell me would be helpful. Might give me a head start on some places to look. What do you say?"

At the moment, I was saying nothing. I was still thinking about what great fodder it would be for Mr. Lenzen at the next faculty meeting if he found out I'd been a murder suspect—even a very short-lived one.

On second thought, could I rephrase that?

I did, after all, have a death threat hanging over my head. One which, at this point, I couldn't be completely sure was entirely fake.

So, Stan was self-employed. Doing what? Or did I really want to know the answer to that?

What I did know was that I needed things to slow down. Maybe this was a lot more than a humble school counselor like me wanted to be involved with. God knew I had enough drama in my life every day thanks to Kim, Lindsay, and my other needy charges. For some reason, the idea of getting deep into a murder investigation was just not falling into place in my mind with dress code violations and catching kids sneaking a smoke.

Then again, I couldn't ignore the birding family connection I felt to Rahr. I'd spent months pouring over his reports, making me feel like I almost knew him personally. Certainly, I could give Knott some insight into birding and general information about it—if I knew anything he wanted. It wasn't like I was volunteering to track down a killer and go in with guns drawn.

Right?

And as for my rivalry with Scary Stan and his low-rent attempt to intimidate me with a melodramatic threat, well, I figured that was one less thing Knott needed to hear about right now. The detective had a murder case to solve. The least I could do was answer his questions about birding.

"Okay," I said. "What can I tell you?"

Twenty minutes later, I hung up the phone. I'd told Knott what I knew about Rahr's research and about how difficult it was to find the owls. I told him about birders and how we all kept lists: lists of birds we saw in the state, in individual counties, all over the country and even the world. I knew birders who kept lists of birds they sighted while doing other things: "birds I saw while brushing my teeth," or "while I was riding a tractor," or "while hiding from my in-laws." I'd even heard one birder say she kept a list of birds she saw while having sex. I didn't ask who was having the sex—she or the birds; I figured I'd already gotten way more information than I wanted. Some of this stuff I had told Knott in the woods on Sunday morning, explaining why Mike and I were there. Now, knowing who the dead man was, we'd gone over it again, trying to find leads for Knott to investigate.

Then, out of the blue, something Kim had said earlier flashed into my head—something about jealousy.

I remembered that Rahr had said something about sabotage in our short phone conversation back when I was plotting my Boreal strategy. I'd chalked it up to his having a bad day, but maybe there was more to it than that. Maybe he really was paranoid, and for good reason. He obviously thought someone was messing with his research, but he also obviously didn't know who that someone was, if he was reduced to making wild accusations on the phone to a total stranger.

Who might be jealous—professionally—of Rahr? Thanks to his work with the Boreals, Rahr had an international reputation. Had he stepped on someone else's toes along the way?

Rahr was, after all, dead. Maybe I was being naïve about academic politics, but I thought death was a rather extreme form of retribution for toe-stepping.

Or, if not professional jealousy, could Rahr have been dispatched by a crazed birder who'd seen one too many cuckoos?

The truth is, anyone who has birded for any amount of time knows how competitive some birders can be, especially when it comes to adding elusive birds to their lists . . . and then not letting anyone else know where the sighting took place. But could any birder be so jealous of a bird sighting to murder someone?

Stan's face popped into my head for about the hundredth time that morning. I wished it would quit doing that. But if the shoe fits . . .

Besides, even though the owls were a challenge, all the birders in the state already knew basically where they were. It wasn't like it was a never-before-revealed secret. Rahr had been publishing his findings for years in the MOU newsletters, since the state organization was his primary financial supporter for the research. True, the reports were a pain in the ass to decipher, but they were unquestionably available to the public.

And even to consider that a birder would commit murder to bolster his or her own list . . . now, that was unthinkable.

Wasn't it?

"Hey, Mr. White."

I looked up from my desk. It was Jason Bennett, a Savage senior, who, thankfully, didn't know the meaning of the word "drama."

For that matter, he didn't know the meaning of the word "style," either.

He was standing in my office doorway, dressed in his usual attire: fatigue pants, a striped polo shirt, and a down vest. Definitely not GQ material.

"Hey, Jason. What's up?"

"Dude, I'm bummed. I brought these excellent deer hooves to school to show-and-tell my friends, but Mr. Lenzen just nabbed me in the hall and said I should go directly to my counselor, do not pass go, do not collect $200. He said I was violating the school weapons policy. With deer hooves? Anyay, here I am."

I looked at the two deer hooves Jason was holding. I'd seen enough deer in my days with the DNR to know that the cuticles in question were indeed the real McCoy. "Very cool, Jason."

"Way cool, but weapons? No way, dude. These are natural artifacts. I got them at a garage sale. How cool is that?"

"Well, Jason," I said. "Maybe they're not weapons to you and me, but Mr. Lenzen, he's . . ." Anal. I wanted to say anal, but I didn't think that was a good thing to call a colleague, let alone my boss, in front of a student.

"Anal," Jason said. "Definitely anal."

I cleared my throat. "Well, let's just say he's trying to stick to the letter of the law here," I said. "Tell you what. I'll just keep the hooves in here for the rest of the day, and you can take them home after classes. That way you're disarmed, the rest of the students are safe from hoof violence, and Mr. Lenzen can be happy knowing he's upheld the law of the land."

"Cool," Jason said. He put the hooves on my desk and left.

Odd mementos of a hunting trip, I'd say. Antlers I understood, but hooves? It reminded me of an article I read once about poachers in Africa and how they managed to sell every part of the animals they killed. I didn't think poaching was a problem in Minnesota, though. We have more than enough deer to go around.

Heck, if you want a deer, just drive a country road after dark. Cars are deer magnets. They practically throw themselves at them. I'd gotten one myself last November. I was coming home in the dark after attending a Sunday matinee of the high school's fall musical, and suddenly, out of nowhere, a deer was standing in the beams of my headlights. I started to hit the brakes, remembered you're not supposed to do that because that makes the deer slide up your front hood and shatter your windshield, so instead, I swerved off to the right shoulder of the road. I heard a thunk, felt the impact of the deer hitting my left front fender and coasted to a stop. I got out and looked across the road. I expected to see a deer carcass, or at least a deer hobbling off into the forest on the other side, but there was nothing. Bambi had disappeared.

When I got home, I checked the front of the car. Bambi may have vanished, but he'd left a wad of fur behind on the hood, and he'd taken my left headlight with him. Not a fair trade as I saw it. When I dropped the car off at the auto repair shop the next morning, I noticed that the car I happened to park next to was likewise adorned with fur and missing its right headlight.

Which meant that somewhere, two deer had a pair of headlights between them. Maybe they were pretending to be a car. Maybe they were plotting.

"Mr. White?"

The voice was quavery, just barely holding together. It was Lindsay, the other half of today's drama queen duo.

"Lindsay," I said. "Come on in."

I put thoughts of poaching and headlights aside and put on my "I'm in your corner" listening face and leaned back in my chair for the duration of what I was sure was going to be a rather lengthy, painful recitation.

Man, do I love Mondays.

Chapter Five

"How big a yard are we talking here?"

I popped open the can of soda that Lily had handed me as we walked through the front display room of her landscaping shop and headed for her little office in the back. Since her place—Lily's Landscaping—wasn't too far from school, I'd stopped in on my way home.

"That stuff will trash your stomach lining," she said, nodding to the can as I took my first sip.

"You gave it to me," I said, feigning indignation.

Her expression was filled with contempt and older-sister superiority. "Yeah, because I know you drink it. That doesn't mean I think you *should*."

"You must really love me," I said. "You're worried about my diet."

When we were kids, my mom always worried about what we were eating, or not eating.

"Did you have any fruit today?" she'd ask. "You need to drink milk at every meal, remember."

When we complained about her nagging, she just patted us on the head and said, "I love you, too." It always reminded me of watching a mother bird feed her babies, sticking food down their little gullets with all the finesse of a pile driver.

It occurred to me that Luce had remarked on my eating habits recently, too. I smiled. This was obviously a female-of-the-species thing—love meant worrying about what the other person ate. Guys didn't equate eating habits with love. We equated eating with . . . eating. Love had nothing to do with the dinner menu. Maybe Smokey and I had more in common than I had realized.

"Mrs. Anderson has just under an acre," Lily said, spreading a sheet of drawing paper across her worktable. On it, she had marked the yard dimensions, sited the house and sketched in a creek flowing through a small pond at one end of the property. A couple stands of trees and shrubs were already noted on the paper.

"You need three things to attract birds," I told her. "A food source would be good, a place for cover and shelter that also provides nesting materials, and water."

I pointed to the pond. "She's got the water, so that's taken care of, although the yard is big enough, she might want to put in a couple stone birdbaths in other places in the yard to attract some smaller birds, like finches or wrens. She'll get ducks, geese, and maybe some herons or egrets with the pond. She might want to enlarge it a bit."

Lily jotted some notes on the paper.

"What kind of trees are these?" I tapped the paper where she'd marked the already existing stands.

"Mostly old growth stuff. A few dead trees, oak, some nice maples."

Lily swept aside a short wave of hair that fell across her cheek. She's only thirteen months older than I am, and people used to think we were twins when we were teenagers, which we hated. We have the same auburn hair, the same grey eyes, and for a while, we were even the same height. But then I shot up. Since she topped out at only five-foot-four (if you can call that "topping out"), she has to look up to her "little" brother. I figure it's a form of psychological payback for all the times she lorded it over me when we were kids. Just to be sure, though, I call her shrimp every once in a while to rub it in. She usually kicks me if I'm within range.

"Dead trees are good," I said. "They provide nesting spots, so you'll want to leave them. Maples work too. What about some evergreens or berry-bearing bushes?"

I took the pencil from Lily's hand and drew in two big circles for some pines and cranberry shrubs. "That would provide both nesting shelter and food sources, as well as some nice color. Actually, white jack pine would be really nice. Have you got a supplier for that?"

Lily chewed on her lower lip. "Yeah," she said after a moment. "I could try that new outfit where I got the Christmas trees from. The stock was excellent, and the prices even better. I think they're up in Two Harbors, just north of Duluth on Lake Superior. Let's see—their name was . . . kind of a funny name, I remember. Oh yeah! Very Nice Trees, I think."

I met her eyes. "Very Nice Trees? You've got to be kidding," I said.

"Maybe it's not the most imaginative company name I've ever heard, but they really were very nice trees," Lily pointed out. "Actually, they were the most perfectly shaped Christmas trees I've ever seen. I sold them out in days and made a good profit. Truth in advertising is nothing to be sneezed at, you know." She rifled through the filing cabinet behind her and pulled out an invoice.

"Yup. Very Nice Trees. Mailing address P.O. Box 487, Two Harbors, Minnesota. Say, weren't you just up there over the weekend?"

Was it really only yesterday? It felt like days at least.

"Yeah. Mike and I were birding. We found a body."

Lily gave me a quizzical look. "A . . . bird body?"

"Nope. Human."

Lily's rusty eyebrows shot up almost into her hairline. "Say what?"

I told her the birding-goes-bad story of the weekend.

"The good news, though, is that I'm not a suspect," I assured her. "The bad news is that we didn't get the Boreal, so I'm thinking I'll be back up there this next weekend."

"Give it a rest, Bobby," Lily said. "I don't like the idea of you up there with something like this going on. There are some real whackos tucked away in some of those remote spots, you know. I don't know if they're like the militia or survivalist cults you read about in the news once in a while, but I wouldn't go looking for them. Even some of those conservation people up there get a little weird."

"I'm not looking for anyone," I reminded her. "I'm looking for an owl. But thanks for the concern. I love you, too, even if you are a shrimp."

Her foot drew back for a kick, but I'd already jumped away.

I zipped up my jacket and headed for the front door of the shop. "Hey," I called back. "If I do go this weekend, do you want me to check out Very Nice Trees for you? I could see if they've got very nice white jack pines."

"That'd be great," Lily replied, sticking her head out of her office. "If I do this yard like this, I'm going to need a lot of them, too." She looked at me suspiciously. "Is this going to cost me extra?"

"No charge," I said. "Just keep that birdseed coming."

Still half facing backwards, I stepped outside and almost walked right into Stan Miller.

"You're going back this weekend?" he asked.

Startled, and my head flooded with events of the weekend, the possibility that he was maybe Rahr's killer, that he had already threatened me with the note on my bird feeder, and that he was there right now to do me harm, I didn't exactly answer him.

"What the hell are you doing here?" Okay, maybe that wasn't the friendliest greeting I could have offered, but considering everything, it was the best I could manage spur-of-the-moment. Besides, I was ticked that he'd been listening in on my private conversation with Lily. Well, I considered it private, even though I'd just been shouting across the shop to her. I didn't know anyone else was around. He could have announced himself or something, but instead, he'd just sneaked up on me, and I sure didn't like the idea that now he knew my birding plans, too. Especially if he was my note writer.

"Stan! You're early," Lily said, coming out of her office.

I watched her walk over to Scary Stan, a smile on her face. I think my mouth was hanging open.

"You know him?" I asked her.

"Yes, I know him," she replied. "Is there a reason I shouldn't?"

I grabbed her arm and dragged her back into her office, shutting the door behind us.

"That's the man who almost shot me this weekend!" I said in a harsh whisper. "He's Scary Stan, the birder. Everyone thinks he's either a former government agent or a mob hitman or . . . or . . . just certifiably crazy."

Lily crossed her arms over her chest. She'd shifted her weight to one hip and was tapped her toe. "You're the one who's crazy here, Bobby. Stan Miller's an accountant. We met two months ago at a Wild hockey game. Since then, we've gone out a few times. He's also been helping me with my bookkeeping. If he's a birder, I didn't know it. And if he's the man who shot at the bear for you, I'd think you'd like to offer him your thanks, along with an apology for acting like such an idiot." She opened the door and stalked out of the office back to Stan. I followed her.

"Sorry about that, Stan," she said, casting me a rueful look. "My brother is having a mental breakdown or something. He says you're a mob hitman or a former government agent. Are you?"

Thank you, Mistress of Humiliation.

"No," Stan said, his voice as flat as his eyes. "I'm not."

"Did you take a shot at Bobby this weekend?"

Stan's eyebrows lifted a fraction of an inch as his eyes made a quick slide in my direction. I swear I could read his mind. *Bobby?*

"No," he said again, slowly and carefully. "I scared off a bear that was considering lunching on him, though."

Lily turned to me. "Satisfied? I'll admit I didn't know you two were acquainted, but out of fairness to Stan, I'm not going to hold that against him." She went back to lock up her office. "I'll be with you in a minute, Stan," she called over her shoulder. "Just ignore my brother."

I stepped closer to the man. "An accountant, huh? What kind of accountant wears face paint in the forest and carries a crossbow when it isn't deer hunting season? Tell me, Stan, do you have any sidelines to that accounting business of yours?"

Not a single fleeting expression crossed his face. For all the movement he wasn't making, the man might as well have been one of the stone sculptures in Lily's showroom. I wondered if he was even breathing.

"I do some contract work."

It's alive! I wanted to shout.

"What kind of contracts?"

His lip twitched. I think he was smiling.

"None of your business."

I took another step in his direction and nodded back towards Lily's office.

"This seems awfully coincidental to me," I said, keeping my voice too low for Lily to hear. "You're dating my sister, and you showed up right where I was birding this weekend. Of all the square miles in Superior National Forest, we ended up only feet apart. What are the odds of that happening, Stan? Even if you researched the same reports I did to find a Boreal, the odds against us being in the same place at the same time are astronomical. Do the math. You're an accountant. On the other hand, I always let Lily know where I'm staying overnight when I go birding. As a precaution."

I leaned towards him, my voice going even lower.

"Are you using Lily to keep track of my Boreal chase? Because if you are—"

"Let's go!" Lily said, practically hurtling out of her office to take Stan's arm and pull him out the front door. "Lock up for me, will you, Bobby?"

I stood on the front step and watched them climb into Stan's top-of-the-line Lexus. The accounting business must be good, I thought. Or maybe it was his "contract work." Then it dawned on me. Stan had denied he was a hit man for the mob or a former government agent.

That didn't mean he wasn't *currently* a government agent.

Or a sniper. Or crazy.

Lily had neglected to include those options.

I thought again about Stan's spooky ability to show up without making a sound. For an accountant who supposedly spent the majority of his time at a desk in front of a computer, he'd sure looked fit in his bomber jacket and jeans when he'd left just now with Lily. I'd also gotten the impression on Saturday night that he'd been comfortable handling a rifle, which, I knew from very personal experience, he could shoot very accurately. At the same time, he wasn't exactly a conversational wizard, if you know what I mean. I had yet to hear him utter a sentence with more than five words in it.

Stay out of the forest or you're next.

Okay, eight words.

Stan must have worked all night on that one.

"No, Lily, I am not satisfied," I announced to the empty parking lot. "Stan Miller is hiding something, and I think that makes him even scarier than he already was."

I walked to my car, avoiding the puddles of melting snow that covered the path to the parking area. A light breeze touched the back of my neck, and I decided to make one more stop before I headed home. Hopefully, it would help me forget about Stan Miller for a while and the fact that my sister was having dinner with a man more fluent when he wrote a threatening note than he was when making polite conversation.

Five minutes later, I parked my scarlet tanager-red SUV next to the sewage ponds outside the old water treatment plant near the Minnesota River. I grabbed my binos from the glove compartment and scanned the water. I wanted to see if the thaw and breeze had drawn any new migrants in.

Folks new to birding don't realize that some of the best places to find rare birds, especially migratory ones, might not be out in the countryside, but right in towns. Sewage ponds are good examples: water that stays open year-round attracts birds. Over the years, I've found more than thirty occasional species (occasional meaning they are here in the state only sporadically) and even two lifers (birds people might see once in their life) right here at the sewage ponds, not even ten minutes from my town house.

Sure enough, I spotted two migrants making an early haul back to their summer homes further north: a Greater White-fronted Goose and a Canvasback Duck. White-fronted Goose is almost a misnomer—this goose is actually gray, although it has a distinctive white area around the base of its bill. The "Greater" part is correct, however, since there really is a Lesser White-fronted Goose.

Maybe Lily's truth in advertising applies to geese, too.

The Canvasback, on the other hand, has a perfect name: its back is the color of white canvas. Combined with its ruddy chestnut head (which Luce says reminds her of my hair color), it's a real standout on the water. And if that weren't enough to identify it, the Canvasback has an unmistakable profile: its head and bill form a long ski-jump that no other diving duck has.

Now that I thought about it, Lily used to tease me about my nose, along with everything else she could think of. She said it was long and turned up just at the end, like a little ski-jump. Yup, me and the Canvasback; ski-jumps unite.

Okay. When you start comparing yourself to a duck, it's time to go home.

The day had obviously been a lot longer than I had realized.

I got back in the car. Chances were that by tomorrow, the goose and the ducks would be long gone, but I'd still post it on the MOU email list serve tonight when I got home in case someone else wanted to try to see them before they took off. Keeping up with the email was the way I'd managed to see so many birds over the years, so I wanted to return the favor to other birders. Of course, it was also the way I'd managed to not see a lot of birds, too. I couldn't begin to count the times I'd seen a posting of a sighting, taken off to see it, and after driving for hours to get there, the bird was nowhere around.

Oh, well. That's part of the deal when you bird. Part of the appeal of birding is the hunt, and while I still get a thrill from actually finding the bird (either by sight or sound), I have to admit the most satisfying finds are the ones that take the most work, the ones that really challenge me.

That's why I wanted the Boreal this season so badly I could almost taste it. I knew I could find it. I knew I'd gotten close.

Just not close enough.

By the time I got home, it was almost six o'clock. A little gray-and-white Junco was hopping around on my deck, snatching up sunflower seeds that had fallen from the feeder. There weren't any new death threats attached to it, nor were there any visible explosive devices (my imagination was having a field day with what kind of "contract work" Stan might perform), so I figured I was home free for at least another evening. My phone message light, however, was blinking. I punched it and listened while I hung up my jacket in the front hall closet.

"White. Knott here. What do you know about a group called Save Our Boreals? S.O.B. And I thought I had name problems. Call me at my home phone, will you?"

The second call was from Luce. "I've got good news and bad news. The good news is I'm Channel 5's "Chic Chef" of the week. The bad news is I have to film the segment on Saturday, so I can't go up north this weekend like we had planned. Can I have a rain check for the following weekend? I'd really like to get that Boreal with you. Let me know. I'll be home after ten."

I dialed Knott's number. It rang once.

"Knott here."

I tried to resist, but couldn't.

"Are so," I said. I heard a groan over the line. "It's Bob White. You asked me about that S.O.B."

"I'm listening."

"This is what I know. Early last year, there was some talk by the Department of Natural Resources about having a lumber company come into parts of the Superior Forest and clean up areas that had too much old growth to make room for younger trees. One of the areas they were targeting was right near where the Boreal Owls nest. Practically overnight, this S.O.B. group popped up and raised such a stink about it that the DNR dropped the plan. All the information S.O.B. used in its literature came right out of Rahr's reports, so I assume they were in bed together. Why?"

"I think the honeymoon had ended," Knott said. "Mrs. Rahr was in my office this afternoon. She showed me a letter her husband received in February. It was a threat. Said he'd better quit giving the owl tours and bringing in all those tourists because it was, and I quote, 'compromising the work we do to maintain the integrity of the Boreals' habitat.'"

Rahr had gotten a threat. Gee, we could have formed a club. But his letter obviously wasn't from Stan. Its sentences were too long.

But, holy shit! The owl tours! I'd completely forgotten about the owl tours.

Last year in early April, Rahr took small groups of birders up to his research sites to listen for the owls. His reason was to solicit more funding for his work, but I remembered reading complaints from other birders in the MOU monthly newsletter, accusing him of encroaching on the subjects of his own study. I'd never gotten up there for a tour myself because it was during softball season, and I coach the tenth grade girls' team at school. Once the season starts, I'm pretty limited to local birding only. By the time the next newsletter was published, Rahr and the owls were old news, and the concerns of readers had moved on to other birding topics.

"One more thing," Knott added. "We got the coroner's report back. There were indications of head trauma. Unless Rahr deliberately banged his head repeatedly against a tree, someone else did it for him."

I dragged my hand through my hair. This was not what I wanted to hear.

"Oh—and something else. Your buddy Stan Miller? The one who lives in Mendota Heights, according to your MOU membership roster? He doesn't exist. At least, not in any kind of data bank we can access. I thought we had a line on him the last time I talked to you, but it vanished. Into thin air. You know, Bob, I really do need to talk to him—you've placed him at the scene of a murder, and he just might have some good answers to the questions we've got hanging. Are you sure you got his name right?"

Oh, yeah, I was sure. Scary Stan Miller. Accountant and "contract worker." Lily White's dinner date. Accomplished birder. Possible lunatic.

Ghost.

Chapter Six

It was Tuesday, and I had been sentenced to a slow death in the media center. It was my turn to monitor the last of the sophomores taking their language skills standards tests.

The majority of the students had completed the tests in their regular classrooms long before noon. The stragglers—a few dozen or so of them—were assigned to finish the work in the media center, supervised by me. Whereas I would have liked to kick them out of there and get them back into class, these kids had this scoped out. By stretching out their test-taking, they got a reprieve—an excused reprieve—from the classes they were supposed to be attending. Had I offered this same group of students the incentive of an early dismissal as soon as they were done with the tests, I had no doubt they'd be done in record time. Instead, they had all gone into sloth mode to while away the rest of the day in the media center.

Supervising still let me get some work done, though. In front of me on the desk, the pile of senior graduation credit reviews I needed to plow through was slowly shrinking. I finished the one I was working on and glanced up to do a quick head count of the students around me who were still testing.

"Mr. Whi-i-ite, can I go to the bathroom?"

A girl dressed in a shiny low-cut sweater and ripped jeans glued to her hipbones had her elbow propped on the table next to her test. She was slowly waving her hand back and forth, back and forth, rolling her eyes at the ceiling.

For a split second, I didn't see the girl's arm.

I saw Rahr's hand popping up in front of me.

I shook my head to clear it.

"I *can't* go to the bathroom?" the girl drawled, leaving her mouth hanging open at the end of her request.

I looked at the girl. It was like seeing evolution in real time. Except . . . backward.

She'd taken my head shake for a "no."

"Yes," I told her. "Go. Please. But you have to come right back here."

Unfortunately.

She slid off her chair and wandered out to the hall. On the way, she passed a table of three boys who kept insisting they weren't finished yet. No surprise there. They were too busy napping between each question or waiting for new pathways of neurons to spontaneously form in their brains.

Funny thing, though—they all seemed plenty alert when the girl walked by. Some neurons just work better than others, I guessed. Or was it a case of primal instincts edging out higher level thinking skills?

Too bad the state didn't set high school graduation standards for hormone levels. These kids could blow it away.

By the end of the school day, I was left with just two students watching the clock and timing down to the minute when they would hand in their tests.

Actually, the day's assignment wasn't that bad. It gave me a whole day to catch up on paperwork, something I never managed in my office where accessibility was critical, but completely time-consuming. That aspect of my job was also one of the reasons I took real pleasure in birding on the weekends—in contrast to constant distraction, birding was time I could spend in single-minded pursuit.

As opposed to the multiple-minded pursuit my head had been spinning its mental wheels on since talking with Knott last night.

The dismissal bell rang just after the last tests were laid on the table in front of me. I stacked them in a box and piled my papers together.

"Hey, good-looking. Pretty please can you tell the nice man I'm not here to burn down the school?"

I turned around to find Luce standing just behind me with a security guard, who looked disgruntled. She gave me a little peck on the cheek and pulled up a chair from a neighboring table. I smiled and nodded to the guard who turned and left.

"I'm on my way to work, but these scones jumped out of my oven and cried, 'Take us to Bobby, take us to Bobby,' so here I am."

She handed me a brown lunch bag that warmed my fingers and released a scent that was already making me salivate.

"What's new at school?" she asked.

I peeked in the bag and groaned in delight. Luce had made my favorite: white chocolate raspberry. "I am your slave forever," I said.

"Yeah, yeah, that's what they all say," Luce laughed, removing her coat. Today, her long blonde hair was neatly braided and wound in a coil on the crown of her head; the pale pink t-shirt she was wearing put a rosy glow in her cheeks.

"Put a couple candles on your head and you could pass for Santa Lucia," I told her.

"Who?"

"Santa Lucia. Come on, you're Scandinavian. You know Santa Lucia—she brings baked goodies to good little boys on her feast day in December, wearing a wreath of candles in her hair."

"Sounds like a fire waiting to happen," Luce sniffed. "Santa Lucia is Swedish, Bobby. I'm Norwegian. And Santa Lucia does not bring goodies to good little boys. She brings saffron buns and coffee to wake up the family."

"So, where's the coffee?"

She made a grab to take back the scones, but I was faster and held them out of her reach.

"What's new? Let's see—aside from watching thoughts struggling against all odds to be born in the heads of reluctant sophomores, not a whole lot," I said, telling her about my day in the media center. "I did, however, get caught up on credit reviews for seniors, and I'm happy to say we will, indeed, be graduating quite a few of them in June."

I filled her in on the latest news from Knott about the investigation into Rahr's death that had now turned into a murder investigation.

"His head had been bashed?" she asked. "Yikes. That sounds pretty vicious, Bobby. It sounds like something that would happen in a big crowded city teeming with psychopaths, not in the peaceful pine forests of northern Minnesota. Who would attack Dr. Rahr? He was an owl researcher, for heaven's sake."

"Yeah, I know. I don't have a clue. But then again, why would I? It's not like I'm the detective, here. I'm just the poor schmuck who found the body."

"Come on, Bobby, let's play detective," Luce said, leaning back in her chair.

I waggled my eyebrows at her. "I'd rather play doctor."

Luce rolled her eyes. "Pay attention. Money is supposed to be the biggest motivation for murder. At least, that's what all the mystery novels I read say. Then it's revenge and love, I think. Or is it revenge and jealousy? Either way, we'd better check out Rahr's love life. Maybe he wronged some woman. Maybe he left her for the sake of his research."

I opened the bag of scones again and inhaled.

Luce gave me a funny look.

"Therapy," I said and closed the bag. "I had a rough day."

And night. But I didn't tell her that. I deliberately hadn't mentioned to Luce about the part of my discussion with Knott about Stan Miller. The non-existent Scary Stan Miller who was dating my sister. Luce and I had had arguments before about my over-protective attitude towards Lily, and I just didn't have the energy to get into it with her right now. After I'd hung up with Knott, I'd thought about leaving a phone message for Lily about Stan's non-entity status, but figured she'd just delete it and refuse to speak to me. I did, however, give Lily's telephone number to the detective, hoping he could get through to her. Hoping she wouldn't hang up on him, too, thinking it was a friend of mine I'd put up to a prank. Nothing like trust between siblings, right? Anyway, my worrying about Lily's poor judgment when it came to men, let alone her physical safety, had kept me awake much of the night. She might be the Mistress of Humiliation, but she is my sister.

"Focus, Bobby."

I put the bag of scones on the desk.

"According to Knott," I explained, "Rahr and his wife were happily married for thirty-seven years. Three kids and five grandchildren. The only time he spent away from her was the weekends he spent in the woods researching the Boreals. That's why she didn't suspect anything when he didn't come home last Friday night. He usually camped on-site. He knew what the weather was like and was prepared for it. That's why the lack of adequate clothing on his body was so weird. He knew better. Knott thinks that maybe the killer knocked Rahr out against a tree, then wasn't sure he was dead, so he stripped him down to make sure he'd freeze to death before he could hike out for help."

I closed my eyes, remembering a frozen corpse.

I didn't think hiking out had been much of an option for him.

"It was below zero there last Friday, Luce—I know, I was there," I reminded her.

Mike and I hadn't wasted any time finding our birding spots that night, it was so bitter. We had had a nasty wind chill, too. With that kind of cold, a person could be in serious trouble within thirty minutes. Rahr couldn't have made it out in a flannel shirt even if he had recovered consciousness after getting his head bashed. I shook my head slowly. "Whoever it was," I concluded, "made sure Rahr wasn't going to be talking to anybody."

Luce frowned. "Okay, maybe not a woman scorned. What about plain revenge? By the time the dust settled last year after the DNR and S.O.B. arm-wrestled over clearing the forest, there were lay-offs in the logging companies up there. That had to hurt quite a few workers. Maybe a terminated employee decided to pin the blame on Rahr for his job loss."

I had considered that angle, too, but thought it was a stretch that some laid-off logger would have taken the time to track down Rahr, follow him up to the owl sites, bang his head on a tree, then strip him down to make sure he would die because he hadn't done a better job of killing him in the first place.

Besides, Rahr was just a researcher. He hadn't taken a really visible role in the controversy—nothing like the media attention S.O.B. had commanded. I thought that if a laid-off logger was looking for someone to pay back for his loss of employment, it would be someone from S.O.B., not Rahr.

"Although," I said, remembering the demonstration I'd seen earlier, thanks to the testing students, of the superior strength of primal instincts compared to higher-level-thinking skills, "I suppose a crime of passion is possible. In the heat of the moment, momentary insanity could rule someone's actions."

But Luce's mention of jealousy as a motive had reminded me of something else. After my counseling sessions yesterday with Kim and Lindsay, I had tried to think of who might be jealous of Rahr, and why. Late last night, a possible answer to that question occurred to me.

Jealousy isn't always about relationships.

In the academic world of research, the world in which Rahr moved, jealousy could be about reputation.

Or the lack thereof.

As a graduate student, I had observed both subtle and outright competition between professors. Research grants were hot commodities. Those who got them, got ahead in publications and positions. Those who didn't, didn't. In some cases, losing out on a grant was a bump in the road of academia. Professors got over it, put their egos aside and continued to work together. In other cases, it led to major career highway reconstruction, causing some professors to leave departments because they couldn't abide their colleagues' crowing.

Grants weren't the end of the competition, either. Say a junior professor did land some funding. Even though he or she might be the team leader, a senior professor with more credentials might be assigned as overseer of the project. Then, when results were finally published, guess what? The researcher who initiated the work had to share the credit—and the glory—with the senior staffer, who may have done little more than sign off on the text.

Finally, to add insult to injury, tenure—job security—was typically awarded to faculty members with the most publications and research credits. Promising young teachers who were already spread thin between meeting the demands of their students and the requirements of research had a tough time making the cut. As a result, you get the "publish or perish" mentality that seems to plague the world of academia.

So, I had to wonder. Could Rahr have had a professional opponent who had taken the "perish" part of the formula to a new high, or rather, low? Was there a researcher somewhere who was so desperate for an opportunity that he decided to create one by removing Rahr?

"That," Luce said, "sends chills up my spine."

"Mine, too," I agreed.

Luce checked her watch and grabbed her coat. "Got to go. Soup base waits for no woman." She leaned toward me and kissed the corner of my mouth.

Another chill chased up my spine.

This chill I liked.

A lot.

I gathered up my papers and walked Luce out of the media center.

"Looks like I'm on my own, then, for this weekend for chasing Boreals. While you're sweating under the studio lights, I'll be slogging through snow." I held Luce's coat for her while she shrugged into it. "The wages of birdwatching, I guess."

Luce patted my cheek. "Poor baby. Guess I'll just have to make it up to you later." She trailed her fingers slowly over my lips, her blue eyes wide and laughing.

"Promises, promises," I said. I gave her a quick kiss on the cheek and whispered, "Get out of here before I drag you into the old choir room and have my way with you."

Luce laughed. "The choir room?"

I nodded. "It's the secret love-nest of choice this year. I surprised two couples there last week. They all had passes to see their counselors but never showed up, so I went exploring.

Something to do with the risers in the room, I understand. Want to find out?"

Luce punched me in the shoulder and left.

I walked back to my office, filed the credit reviews and checked my daily calendar. I had two hours before I was expected in downtown Minneapolis for an MOU board meeting.

"Mr. White."

It was Mr. Lenzen, the assistant principal.

"I see you have deer hooves on your desk. I assume they are the ones you confiscated from Jason Bennett?"

As always, Mr. Lenzen was impeccably dressed in his trademark three-piece suit, trousers creased and shoes shined. He stood just outside my door, as if he couldn't bring himself to cross the threshold into my little domain.

I almost expected him to whip out a can of spray antiseptic.

"Yes, they're Jason's," I answered. "But he knows he can't have them in class, so I'm keeping them quarantined here until he takes them home."

"They need to be removed from the building," Mr. Lenzen corrected me. "Otherwise, they're an incident just waiting to happen."

Give me a break, I thought.

"What kind of incident?" I wanted to ask, but didn't. "Will they rise up on their little cuticles and imbed themselves in someone's . . ." But I didn't say that either. Instead, I nodded and said I'd take care of it.

"There's something else I need to discuss with you." He took a deep breath, like a swimmer about to dive into infested waters, and stepped into my office. "May I?" he asked, indicating my visitor's chair.

"Of course," I replied, sitting back in my own desk chair. "What's up?"

He took out his handkerchief and lightly dusted the seat. It's not like the chair is ever unoccupied long enough to attract dust, but I didn't think, at the moment, he'd appreciate a list of its recent occupants. He sat, crossed his legs and folded his hands in his lap.

"Well, apparently, *you* are, Mr. White. I had a call from a Detective Knott yesterday, asking me to confirm your whereabouts last Friday noon. Needless to say, I was quite unprepared for his revelations that you had discovered a corpse over the weekend and were, of necessity, considered an initial suspect."

He hesitated, waiting for me to comment.

I hesitated, waiting for him to go away.

"I think you're aware of how important I deem Savage High School's public image to be," he finally forged ahead. "We are the educational standard bearers of our community, and I expect only the highest professionalism and integrity from each and every one of our staff."

Yada, yada, yada. Been there, done that. I'd only heard this speech a few dozen times in the last five years—usually when a school bond issue was about to go before the voters. Since there wasn't anything currently on the block, I had to wonder: where was he going with this?

"As a result, I've decided it would be in everyone's best interests if you took a leave of absence until this—investigation—is resolved."

It took a minute for what he said to sink in.

He wanted to suspend me.

He wanted me out of here.

Whatever happened to innocent until proven guilty?

The jerk.

"Mr. Lenzen, I'm not a suspect in a murder case," I reminded him. "You yourself confirmed to the detective that I was here at school."

"Yes, I did." He neatly recrossed his legs. "But I feel your presence here at this point will only fuel speculation and distraction for both our students and our staff until the case is closed."

Until the case was closed. That left things pretty wide open, I'd say. What if the case was never solved? My leave of absence might turn terminal—or more accurately, it might turn into a termination. I'd lose my job.

Gee, thanks, but even despite lunchroom duty, I'd rather not.

On the other hand, maybe there was another way to think about this, I realized, and I shouldn't be looking a gift horse in the mouth. Even though, at the moment, that horse was appearing more like an ass.

"I'm prepared to make some financial concessions," Mr. Lenzen said, which was his way of saying I'd get some kind of pay during the absence, but not full salary. Knowing how he operated, I had no doubt he'd already checked the legalities and was maneuvering to get what he wanted—without leaving himself open to an even bigger public relations nightmare of employee litigation.

"I need to think this over," I hedged. "Give me a moment here."

I tipped my chair back and gazed at the water stain on my ceiling.

Did I mention my luxury office accommodations?

I mulled over the possibilities. If I took the leave, I'd have extra time to hunt the Boreal and an extended partly paid vacation. Not bad.

Of course, if I took the leave, I would be leaving my students adrift. What would Kim and Lindsay *DO*?

Finally, if I took the leave, I would, in effect, be giving Mr. Lenzen the last word.

Not if I could help it.

"Here's what I'll do," I told him. "I'll tie up some things tomorrow, then take a personal day on Thursday and Friday. No leave of absence. At least, not yet."

What I didn't add was that I'd head for Duluth and ask Knott to put the pressure on Mr. Lenzen to take me back by Monday in exchange for whatever assistance I could give him in his investigation. If I drove up on Thursday, I could pick up an extra night of owl hunting, too. Since I needed to use up the personal days anyway, using them to search for the Boreal sounded like a good idea.

And—big plus, here—Scary Stan wouldn't even know I'd left town, because if he asked Lily, she'd tell him I'd said that I was leaving for Duluth on Friday after school. Which meant that on Thursday night, I'd have the forest all to myself.

Except for a Boreal Owl or two.

I hope.

Chapter Seven

I put my visit with Mr. Lenzen behind me—literally—as I headed for my board meeting in Minneapolis by way of the Bloomington Ferry Bridge, which spans the Minnesota River.

After being informed of my possible suspension, it was a much-needed shot in the arm to be out in the brilliant March afternoon—the kind of afternoon that promises spring will eventually return, even to frozen Minnesota. The sky was clear, and there were some stretches of open water in the river, just the kind of liquid streaks that attracted fishing birds.

I glanced up through the windshield. High above, soaring on thermals, two Bald Eagles gracefully scribed broad circles. One was mature, his head and tail blazing white against the bright blue sky. The other was immature, still showing brown feathers, but gliding just as majestically as its elder. Together, the birds spiraled in the sky above the river, their wings barely moving as they rode the currents bringing warmer air back to the valley.

As always, whenever I see Bald Eagles, I was transported back to the first time I saw one at Lake Pepin, on the border of Wisconsin and Minnesota. Remembering how awe-struck I had been, I could feel a smile tugging at the corners of my mouth.

I'd been about five years old, as I recall. It was a sub-zero day in January, and my mom had a bad case of cabin fever. She told my dad if we didn't get out of the house for a while, she was going to lock herself in the closet and eat a hundred bags of Oreo cookies. I thought that sounded like fun, but I guess in her mind, it was a threat. She'd read some newspaper article about how Bald Eagles congregated around Lake Pepin in January because there was open water for them to fish and feed, and she thought it would be something interesting to see, as well as a preferable activity to gorging herself on Oreos.

Back then, Bald Eagles were still considered an endangered species. To further convince my dad to make the four-hour round-trip drive, she said she wanted us to see them in the wild before it was too late—something about her patriotic duty and American heritage and a legacy for her children. (At the time, I thought she said a *leg* for her children, and I couldn't figure out what eagles had to do with my legs.) I think she said something about Dodo birds and Passenger Pigeons, too, but I couldn't make any sense of that part either.

So she and my dad bundled up Lily and me in our little snowsuits (some things never change), and we drove for almost two hours to Lake Pepin. The sky was bright blue, and there wasn't a cloud in sight. The snow was piled so high on the shoulders of the highway that it looked like we were driving through tunnels of ice, and the reflected glare of the sun off the snow made it hard to look out for very long. Lily and I played car bingo in the back seat, calling out trucks, horses, stop signs and trailers until we got into a fight about who saw a red barn first.

Looking back, I can't imagine how a long car drive with two little kids fighting in the back seat was better than cabin fever for my mom, but I guess anything was a welcome change at that point.

Anyway, as we got closer to the lake and the road started rising up into the bluffs, my mom told everyone to start looking for eagles. Having only seen a picture of an eagle in my mom's little bird guide, I wasn't expecting much—just some long-winged birds circling over the water. Then, just before we got to the turn-off above the lake that my mom said was the best place for watching the eagles, my dad started seeing them.

"Oh, my gosh!" he yelled, startling everyone in the car, because my dad never raised his voice. "Look at all those eagles!"

He started pointing through the windshield, and I pushed my face against the car window, trying to see what all the excitement was about. What I got was a really cold cheek, thanks to the freezing glass.

But then my dad parked at the observation lookout, and we got out of the car, and there they were—scores of huge Bald Eagles soaring on thermals, diving to the water and plucking out fish. More were sitting in treetops along the lake. Their snow-white heads and tails caught the sun in a stunning contrast to their dark-brown bodies, and their massive wings beat slowly, powerfully, as they passed just yards above us. I held my breath in what I thought was awe (though it was probably because the air was so bitter cold it literally hurt to breathe, but I didn't know that then), and I stood absolutely transfixed. I had never before seen anything like these eagles in my life—big, beautiful, flying wonders.

To a young boy, they were pure magic. I took one look at these wild, fantastic creatures, and it was all over for me.

Love at first flight, I guess you could say. Now, after all these years, and all the miles I've logged looking for every species in the state, birding was as natural to me as breathing.

And that reminded me of Luce bringing me scones, her breath on my cheek when she kissed me in the media center.

I loved Luce, too.

And not just because of her scones.

I drove over the bridge, and the eagles were gone, but I picked out a Red-tailed Hawk sitting on a utility cable near the highway. Below it, long yellow grasses lay matted with melting snow. The hawk dove down in predator mode, picked up a mouse for its dinner and flew off.

Talk about fast food.

Luckily, I had brought two of Luce's scones to snack on while I drove downtown, so I wasn't tempted to detour through any drive-through for an early dinner. I wanted to make good time and beat the worst of the traffic into town to give myself a chance to review the agenda before tonight's meeting. As the newest member of the MOU board, I wasn't sure yet what to expect of the evening, but I wanted to at least refresh my memory of the items that were on the table.

I was also hoping I could do a little research about Rahr, so I'd have something to offer Knott when I saw him again. If

Rahr had had any enemies, I figured there was a good chance one of the longtime MOU board members would know about it, since Rahr had a long association with the group and had even received funding for his research from us for several years. Just because the state birding community was tight didn't mean it didn't have its share of squabbles.

As luck would have it, Jim Petersen was the first to arrive—after me, I mean—for the meeting. He pulled up a chair next to mine in the little downstairs conference room at the Bell Museum of Natural History on the University of Minnesota campus where the MOU is headquartered.

"Bob," he said, clapping me on the shoulder. "Good to see you. Beautiful day, isn't it? Did you see anything on the way in to the city? I understand the Minnesota River's got some open water."

I told him about the eagles and the hawk and the Canvasback and the White-fronted Goose I'd seen yesterday. As a lifelong birder and one of the founding fathers of the Minnesota birding organization, Jim was rarely unaware of what birds were in town or passing through; at somewhere around seventy-eight years old, he'd seen species in the state that I'd give almost anything to get on my Minnesota list. We talked a little more about the weather and what migrants the southerly winds might bring. Then I asked him what he knew about Dr. Rahr.

"A tragedy," he said, shaking his head. "What is this world coming to when a man can't even be safe birding?"

Caught by the room's overhead lights, the rim of white hair that ringed his balding head gleamed white; it suddenly struck me that Jim resembled the eagle I'd seen on my way to the meeting—not only did he have the white head, but he had golden eyes, a sharp nose and imposing height. If he fully extended his long thin arms, they'd make a wide, though perhaps spindly, wingspan.

I wondered if he ate a lot of fish.

"I met Andrew maybe ten years ago," Jim explained. "I was working on putting together a birding guide for the Arrowhead region of Minnesota, and he was just starting to study the Boreal Owls. It was a passion for him, you know. He was teaching at the university and spending time in the woods on his own nickel, mapping out the owls' range and breeding habits. Back then, MOU wasn't funding any research, so this was really his labor of love."

"Did he ever have any assistants with him that you know of?" I asked.

That was probably expecting a lot, but I figured it couldn't hurt. Jim had a good memory. He could tell you about birders he knew fifty years ago. Whether or not he could remember the names of researchers—whether or not he even knew the names of any researchers—I had no idea.

"Or did Rahr ever complain about someone doing similar research with the owls or talk about colleagues trying to horn in on his work?"

Jim shut his eyes and rubbed his hand over his forehead, almost as if he were trying to massage a thought into the front of his consciousness. Would it work? If it did, I was going to patent the process and sell it to the parents of sophomore sloths everywhere. I'd make a million bucks. At least.

After a moment, his eyes popped open and focused sharply on me.

"I do remember something like that, Bob. It was probably after the first year we funded Andrew. Maybe four years ago, now. He had a grad student from the university working with him, and I remember he didn't like the boy. I asked if he wanted us to include a stipend for the boy to work with him the next year, and he said no, he didn't trust him to do the work. I got the impression the boy had a big head, like he thought he knew better than Andrew how to conduct the study. Kind of a prima donna, I guess."

"Rahr was a prima donna?"

"Not Rahr, Bob. The boy."

"Jim, how've you been?"

Dr. Phil Hovde walked into the room and reached out to shake Jim's hand and then mine. "Bob, good to see you. Beautiful day, isn't it? Saw on the list-serve that you got a White-fronted Goose and Canvasback yesterday."

"Yup, I did," I said. "Welcome back, Dr. Phil. You're back a little early this spring, aren't you?"

Dr. Phil, a retired orthopedic surgeon, and his wife, Myrna, are snowbirds. That means they migrate south every January and February to a condo in Florida, where they can soak up sunshine instead of taking turns shoveling snow. Tanned and fit, they both look younger than their seventy-odd years, and if it weren't for the time I saw his silver toupee fly off on a windy afternoon we shared birding, I'd think that mop of hair on his head was his own. He was, however, a dedicated birder and enthusiastic board member, so I forgave him his annual winter abandonment, along with the hairpiece. He was also rolling in dough thanks to his former medical practice and a slew of lucrative private investments. When MOU finances had run especially low at the end of last year, he'd picked up the slack out of his own generous pockets.

"Just by a week or two," he assured me. "Myrna was missing the grandkids pretty badly, and I needed to check on some business, so here we are."

"We were talking about Andrew Rahr," Jim told Dr. Phil. "Do you remember when he had that grad student working with him?"

"Sure do," Dr. Phil said. "I offered to help fund another year for that assistant, but Andrew said no way. He thought the kid was undisciplined. Had a problem with authority. Like he didn't want to put in the hard tedious work of the actual research, but just wanted to get to the finished product instead. No guts, all glory. I think Andrew was afraid the kid would jeopardize the study."

Dr. Phil's face suddenly blanched under his tan. "Oh, my gosh," he said. "You don't think that kid was involved in Andrew's death, do you?"

I wondered why Dr. Phil made the same connection I'd considered. "Why do you say that?" I asked.

"Because," Dr. Phil said, "when Andrew turned down my offer for funding the kid to come back, I remember what he said because he was so vehement about it."

"What did he say?"

Dr. Phil looked at me, then at Jim and back again at me.

"He said, 'Over my dead body.'"

None of us said anything for a moment or two.

"That was four years ago," Jim reminded us.

He was right. Four years was a long time.

Then again, I'd been chasing the Boreal for almost twenty.

Maybe four years wasn't so long, after all.

"Do you remember the grad student's name?" I asked.

Dr. Phil shook his head. I looked at Jim. He shook his head, too.

"Jim! Phil! Bob!"

Bill Washburn walked into the room accompanied by Anna Grieg. "Beautiful day, isn't it?"

Everyone shook hands. After a minute or two of weather talk, we all took seats at one end of the long conference table. Bill works for a utilities company, and Anna is a police officer out in one of the suburbs on the east side of St. Paul. Like me, they were relatively new to the MOU board. I guessed Bill was in his late fifties and Anna about ten years younger.

When I first started birding as a kid, most of the birders I met were between fifty and seventy years old. I was the odd duck who wasn't even in his teens. Back then, birdwatching had the reputation of being a hobby mostly for senior citizens.

In the last few decades, however, that image has really been changing as more and more people have become interested in outdoor activities, environmental issues, and observing wildlife.

These days, birders come in all ages, shapes, and sizes. The increase in birdwatchers has, in turn, fueled all kinds of related businesses, including the bird stores springing up all over the place now, special interest magazines, birding equipment catalog sales, novelty underwear, you name it. (All right, I confess—the only bird-themed underwear I've seen was on the sale rack at a local discounter. They were boxers, and the birds were flamingos. Glow-in-the-dark flamingos. I wonder if that would qualify for that one birder's list of birds that woman saw while having . . . never mind. Where was I? Oh, yeah . . . the growth of a fabulous hobby.) As a result, birdwatching has gone mainstream—it isn't just retirees hitting the birdseed anymore. In fact, it's been the fastest growing outdoor activity in America for the last ten years.

And, until I found Dr. Rahr's body last weekend, I thought it was probably the safest outdoor activity.

Now, I wasn't so sure.

Dr. Phil got the meeting underway. We ran through the minutes from the last meeting, approved them and moved on to tonight's agenda. Anna presented suggestions for alternate ways to collect members' dues, since our current method seemed to lack urgency, as well as effectiveness.

"The problem isn't that people don't have the money," she pointed out, "it's just that no one realizes that the date stamped on their address label is their dues date. I think if we just sent emails out as reminders, that would work better."

"But does everyone look at email?" Bill asked.

"Everyone in MOU does," Jim said. "Whenever I post a bird sighting, I get calls and responses for the next two days. If I miss a day of MOU email, I feel out of the loop."

I knew just how he felt. I checked it first thing in the morning before leaving for work and again when I got home at night. In the summer, I checked it several times a day. Of course, there were always some birders who refused to share information on the Web. Rahr had been one of them. In all the years he'd worked with the owls, he had never posted any Boreal sightings. His refusal to do so was one of the reasons I finally tried speaking with him on the phone. But like I already said, that got me nowhere. At least the email system was successful in keeping other, more cooperative birders connected.

Even Stan had posted sightings via email.

"How current is our email list?" I asked Anna. I'd given Knott the residence address for Stan, but not his email address. If the detective had that, maybe he could track down Stan—make him exist again—to question him about his activities in the forest.

"Well, we have to rely on members keeping us updated," Anna replied. "Not very reliable, but it's all we've got."

In this case, it could be enough, though. Stan used his email. I made a mental note to check through my deleted email file when I got home. I'd find one of Stan's postings and forward his address to Knott.

An odd thought crossed my mind. Who was stalking whom, now, Stan?

"I move we use email reminders to collect dues," Bill said, and the motion passed unanimously. "Now that we have secured our dues income, do we want to continue using some of that money to fund the Boreal Owl study?" He looked at the rest of us, his bushy eyebrows raised in question. "Does anyone know if there is going to be any more Boreal Owl study, in light of—ah—recent events?"

"Actually, we were talking about that before you got here, Bill," Dr. Phil said, tapping his pen against the table.

"There doesn't seem to be anyone working with Dr. Rahr this year, so I'm guessing the study is suspended."

Gee, me too, almost! I thought. *Suspended, that is. My professional career down the drain. Glug, glug, glug! How was I going to support all the birds depending on my feeders? How was I going to support me?*

Funny, isn't it, how sometimes the real weight of a conversation escapes you at the time, then comes roaring back at an inopportune moment to bite you in the ass? Well, sitting there in that MOU meeting was both my inopportune moment and my ass. My livelihood was on the line! That meant I was going to have to do a lot more to save my career than just hightail it up to Duluth and sic Knott on the big bad Mr. Lenzen. For the first time, it occurred to me that I was going to have to take some real initiative in not only helping Knott solve the crime, but in helping him to actually find a killer because until he found him, it was my future that was up for grabs.

Or down the drain.

Either way, not where I wanted it. Location, location, location.

I tuned back in just as Anna unfolded a sheet of paper that she had retrieved from her purse.

"Maybe not," she said. "I got this email last night from a man who says he worked with Dr. Rahr some years ago on the owl project, and he's very interested in picking up the study."

"You're kidding," Dr. Phil said, laying his pen down. It rolled, and I noticed it had some letters printed on it. Probably some promotional item he'd picked up somewhere. Heck, half the pens on my desk at work are advertising either an insurance company or a bank; with my salary, free pens are a perk I don't turn down.

"Who is it?" Jim asked.

"He's an adjunct professor at the university in Duluth, his email says. Bradley Ellis is his name."

Jim turned to me. "I think that's the kid," he said, a trace of excitement in his voice. "I could never get his name straight. It sounded like two last names. Bradley Ellis, Ellis Bradley. He's the one Dr. Rahr couldn't wait to get rid of."

"You said he's an adjunct professor?" I asked Anna.

"Yes, he says he got his doctorate at Cornell last year and started teaching in Duluth just this January." She scanned his letter. "He says he was stunned to hear of the death of his former mentor, Dr. Rahr, but feels it would be 'an honor and fitting memorial to continue his work without interruption.' What do you think?"

I thought I would call Knott as soon as I got home. Had he heard about this guy? Bradley Ellis? Or was it Ellis Bradley? Whichever it was, he was right there in Duluth, for crying out loud. And he knew all about the owl research. He even knew Rahr. I had to believe Knott was checking him out. But I was still going to call.

"I think someone should talk to this fellow first," Dr. Phil said. "We want to get an idea about his background, his expertise. That's our usual procedure for making grants, and that shouldn't change." Then he shook his head. "But that takes time, and the Boreals aren't going to be available for more than another few weeks. I don't see funding happening this year, I'm sorry to say."

"I'm going to Duluth on Thursday," I said, the words practically popping out of my mouth. "I could talk to him."

I could. And while we were chatting about his credentials for continuing the research, I could also ask him more about his history with Rahr. Maybe he'd even say something important that I could pass along to Knott, something that Ellis might be too careful to say to the detective, but not so careful about saying to a fellow birder. Maybe he'd incriminate himself. Maybe I could make a citizen's arrest.

Then again, if Ellis was the killer, and I confronted him about it, maybe he'd just pound my head into an office wall and leave me for dead. "It happens a lot up here," he'd tell the police. "People pounding their heads against things until they kill themselves. Cabin fever, I guess."

Jim and Dr. Phil both narrowed their eyes at me. I shrugged.

"I'm going to be up there looking for the owls," I told them. "I—uh—got a couple personal days to use, so I'm going up. I'll see if I can talk with Ellis, and I'll let you know what I think."

If I lived through it, that was.

"Gee, Bob, that would be great," Anna said.

Dr. Phil caught my eye, his eyebrows raised in question. "In light of what we were discussing before the meeting, Bob, are you certain you want to be up there birding right now? It sounds like there might be some—ah—concerns about personal safety in the forest. I don't want you to put yourself in any kind of potentially volatile situation."

Jim agreed. "Phil has a point. Maybe this isn't the right time to pursue this. The Boreals will still be there next year. And we'd have more time to evaluate this Ellis fellow."

Bill, however, wasn't convinced. "I think we're overreacting to Rahr's death," he told the two men. "It was an isolated incident. One of those odd, awful things that just happens. A random act of violence—isn't that what they call it? I can't imagine it had anything to do personally with Dr. Rahr or his research. He was, tragically, simply in the wrong place at the wrong time. I, for one, hate to see us miss even one season of monitoring the owls. We all know how quickly habitat can change. And remember how close we came to losing ground when the DNR was talking about allowing some logging. If it weren't for that S.O.B. group, we'd already be looking at a reduced territory for the study. I say we stay on top of this. Let's have Bob talk with Ellis, and if he approves, I say we give Ellis the funding."

"I want to do this," I assured Jim and Dr. Phil. "I'll be fine."

I hoped.

I asked Anna for Ellis's letter, and she handed it to me. I figured I'd be passing it along to Knott within the hour via email.

Was I a great junior detective or what?

Probably the "what."

We moved on to the last topic for discussion, which was the MOU booth for the state fair in August. For the first time in five years, we had the option for relocating from the spot next to the Pig-on-a-Stick fried pork chop stand to a spot beside the Amazing Cheese Curd Palace.

"That's a tough call," Dr. Phil said, absolutely serious.

"Those Pig-on-a-Sticks get a lot of traffic," Bill said.

"But everyone eats cheese curds," Jim said.

"Who ran the booth last year?" Anna asked.

Everyone looked at me.

I held up my hands in surrender. "I confess. I ate enough pork chops to put me off pork for at least six months. But I never touched a cheese curd."

"You're joking," Anna said, shocked.

"Okay, maybe not six months, but definitely two."

"No, I mean about the cheese curds. How can you go to the fair and not eat cheese curds?"

I didn't have an answer to that, other than cheese coated in crispy fat had just never appealed to me. True, I've eaten a lot of junk food in my time, but a guy has to draw the line somewhere.

"I don't know," I told Anna. "Cheese curds just aren't high on my food radar, I guess."

"Believe me, if our booth is next to the Curd Palace, they will be. Take it from me, Bob," Dr. Phil said, patting his round belly. "I know what I'm talking about here. I have yet to miss a state fair."

By the time I left the meeting, traffic was moving smoothly. I got home in about forty minutes. On the way, I thought about Rahr and Ellis.

What exactly had Ellis done to anger Rahr? Jim had suggested that the younger man might have taken shortcuts with the research, and I had no doubt that would have really ticked off Rahr, who seemed to be compulsive about protocol, judging from his annual reports. If Ellis had been guilty of that, Rahr certainly wouldn't have given him good recommendations, though, and I couldn't imagine that Ellis would have been able to get into

Cornell's doctorate program without them. Cornell was hot stuff in ornithology.

And now Ellis was back in Duluth, teaching. Rahr must have known about that because the university wasn't that big. Had they talked? Argued? Locked horns?

Ellis returning to Duluth was something else that didn't quite make sense. Sure, Duluth had an excellent university, but with a Ph.D. from Cornell? I would have thought Ellis would have landed somewhere more prestigious. A Big Ten school. Or Top Five. Or Top Twenty Places to Spend Lots of Tuition Money That Will Hopefully Get You a Really Good Job When You Graduate Schools, or whatever they called the big-gun universities. With that kind of degree in his pocket, Ellis certainly would have found more than an adjunct position. Adjuncts were academic limbo—contracts were up for grab every year. So why would a newly-minted Ph.D. stoop to an adjunct position?

To check out the academic climate before making a commitment to a particular college? To test the waters for a full professorship?

Or how about to create a job opening by edging out another professor—one who had rejected him rather nastily in the past? Exactly how deep—or deadly—did professional jealousy—or vengeance—run?

When I got home, I dug out the copies of Rahr's research I had pored over prior to making my trip north last weekend. I had to sift back three years, but there it was—a report coauthored by Rahr and Bradley Ellis. There wasn't anything that stood out in it, just more of the same range reporting and population analysis covered in the other reports. Ellis's name was on it, which meant he could claim it as a publishing credit, an important credential in the academic world. If there had been discord between the two, it didn't show in their work.

I picked up the phone and called Knott.

"Knott here."

"Yes, you are," I replied. I couldn't help it.

"White? Is that you?"

"Yup. Sorry to bother you at home, Detective, but I thought I should give you a call. I've got a name—Bradley Ellis. Do you know him?"

"No, I don't," Knott said. He paused. "But I tried to talk with him today. He wasn't in. According to Rahr's secretary at the university, Ellis had been trying to see Rahr for most of last week. He'd practically been beating Rahr's door down, the secretary said. Unfortunately—or coincidentally, depending on how you see it—Ellis is now out of town for the week. How do you know him?"

"I don't, but his name came up at our MOU board meeting tonight. Apparently, he wants to take up where Rahr left off studying the owls. They worked together four years ago." Which meant that there was a better than good chance that Ellis knew the exact spot where Rahr's body was found. "He sent one of the board members an email last night."

"Last night?"

"That's what she said. He'd heard about Rahr's death and wanted to jump right in with the Boreals."

Then it registered in my head what Knott had just said. "He's out of town?"

"Yeah. He had a lab class last Friday morning, but didn't

show. The secretary said he called in Monday afternoon and said he'd had to leave town suddenly because his father had had a heart attack, and he didn't know when he'd be getting back."

Leaving Ellis unaccounted for on Friday, the day Rahr had been killed. Now he was out of town with a seriously ill father, yet he had taken the time to contact Anna. Not to mention how quickly he had found out about Rahr's death.

I repeated to Knott what I had heard from Jim and Dr. Phil and confirmed that Ellis and Rahr had worked and published together.

"Anything else?" Knott asked.

"Yeah," I said. "I've got Stan Miller's email address for you." I read it off to him. "He uses it all the time, so you've got to be able to locate him that way, don't you?"

"I hope so. Right now, we need a lead badly in this case, and I'm fresh out. Is that it?"

"Well, there was one more piece of critical business at the meeting," I told him. "We have to decide if we want the MOU booth to stay next to the Pig-on-a-Stick spot or move next to the Amazing Cheese Curd Palace."

"Tough call," Knott agreed. "Those Pigs are good, but everyone loves cheese curds."

Chapter Eight

I lined up the shot and tossed the ball. It arced up, then swooped soundlessly—just like a Boreal Owl—through the basketball hoop.

"Sweet, White-man."

Alan Thunderhawk took the ball back out to the top of the key and made a jump shot. It bounced off the rim. I went up for the rebound and landed with Alan at my back. I pivoted and got a shot off around him.

Swish.

"You can't be this sharp at six in the morning," Alan complained, retrieving the ball. "It's unnatural. What do you do, mainline coffee?"

"Nope," I said. "I'm the early bird, remember?"

Alan and I go way back. We roomed together as undergraduates at a small college in southwestern Minnesota. Then after various detours on both of our parts, we ended up working together at Savage. He's Lakota and teaches American history. Before he got his teaching license, Alan went to the west coast and spent a few years as a community organizer and then worked for an environmentalist group. After that, he got his doctorate in political science. But he missed Minnesota and didn't want to work in higher education, so he came home to Savage to teach.

Of course, the local school board jumped for joy to hire Alan. We've got quite a few students at Savage who come from the nearby Sioux community; having a Native American on the faculty was Mr. Lenzen's public relations/equal opportunity dream-come-true. As far as our illustrious assistant principal is concerned, Alan can do no wrong.

Man, I'd like to tell him a couple stories. But Alan is my best friend, and I refuse to blow his cover.

Every Wednesday morning, Alan and I meet in the school gym for a before-work game of basketball, which almost kills him because while I am, indeed, an early riser, he's the original night owl.

That's not to say he's a doormat on the basketball court at six in the morning, however. On the contrary. Alan has this competitive streak a mile wide and years of experience playing on high school and college basketball teams. I may get the jump on him in the first ten minutes when we play, but by the time we're done, he's wide-awake and lethal. A regular predator.

We finished the game and hit the showers in the locker room. I told him about my possibly looming suspension and outlined my plan to avoid it. He agreed that Mr. Lenzen was an anal ass and offered to jerk his chain on a regular basis while I was out.

"I'll get the rumor mill running," he said. "Do you want me to spread stories that he's a closet axe murderer or a weekend cross-dresser?"

"Gee, thanks, Alan. I'm sure that'll really help."

"Hey, no problem," he said. "What are friends for?"

Twenty minutes later, we were sitting in my office, drinking lousy but hot coffee and eating the rest of the scones Luce had left.

"I don't know, Bob," Alan said, licking the last crumbs from his fingers. "You may have to bite the bullet and marry this woman. She can cook and she likes birds."

"She worries about what I'm eating, too," I said, reaching for another scone.

"She worries about what you're eating?" he echoed. "White-man, this is serious stuff. What more do you want?"

Nothing, I thought. I was happy. Luce was happy. That worked for me. Did I have to want something more?

Besides steady employment.

"I'm telling you, she is one good woman," Alan continued, pulling his still wet, shoulder-length black hair back into the ponytail he wore for class. He smiled. "If you're not interested, I could be."

"She likes tall men, Alan," I said, a hint of faked condescension in my voice.

"Hey, I'm tall!" he bristled. "I'm six foot!"

"Sorry, Professor. She's got you beat by two inches. Besides, Luce doesn't stand in line for anyone, and when it comes to women, you've got a waiting list a mile long."

Alan shrugged. "Yeah, but so far, no one's made the cut."

"Got a question for you, Alan," I said, smoothly changing the subject. (That's one of those things they teach you in counseling programs—how to direct the conversation where you want it to go. Right now, I knew I didn't want it to go into Alan's love life. Or lack thereof.) "When you were doing your environmental activist thing, did you ever meet people who were—well—extreme? I mean, like off the wall? Psycho? Bonafide crazies?"

Alan took another sip of his coffee. "All the time. It's one of the reasons I decided to get into teaching and get off the firing line. I figured I had a much better chance surviving a class of sugar-overloaded kids every day than I had of living through a bomb planted under my car by some loony. Of course, some days, I question the wisdom of that decision."

"Are you kidding me?" I asked. Car bombs sure weren't on my list of must-have adventures.

"No way, White-man," he replied. "When was the last time you were alone in a room with twenty-nine high school students?"

I balled up my napkin and threw it at him.

"Okay. Real story. When I went to work in Seattle after we graduated from college, I was doing grassroots organization. Not quite the same thing as being an environmental activist. I wasn't out on a little boat on the open sea trying to stop whaling ships or chaining myself to the fences around nuclear plants. My job was much less dramatic or camera-worthy. I worked at teaching citizens to form groups to address specific issues. Sometimes they were neighborhood groups, sometimes they were bigger. I helped them define priorities, develop strategies for reaching goals. Anyway, it was just after the 'war in the woods', and some people were still a mite testy."

"War in the woods?"

Alan smiled. "Do the words 'Northern Spotted Owl' mean anything to you?"

Of course, they did. In the late 1980s, conservationists became alarmed at the decreasing population of the Northern Spotted Owl in the Pacific Northwest. Since the owls only breed and raise their young in extensive areas of old-growth forest, the blame for the decrease naturally fell on the logging industry for clearing large tracts of woods. The resulting controversy over habitat had not only touched off a firestorm of debate and confrontation between environmentalists, the timber industry, and the government, but it had also launched the media on a feeding frenzy of all things ecological.

In June 1990, after about four years of negotiation, litigation, and prime-time exposure, the United States Fish and Wildlife Service declared the Northern Spotted Owl an endangered subspecies. The Pacific Northwest logging industry was ordered to keep their hands (and saws) off at least forty percent of the old-growth forest within a 1.3-mile radius of any spotted owl nest or owl activity.

The loggers weren't happy. The industry suffered loss of revenue and loss of jobs. Whole towns slipped into poverty. Some of the interactions between timber companies and environmental activists got really ugly; ecoterrorism made the owl its poster child. It was another four years after that before the Northwest Forest Plan was formulated and, supposedly, ended the owl battles. In reality, the war in the woods had just gone underground. Today, years later, the main players were still tap-dancing around the status of the Northern Spotted Owl.

"I met all kinds of people as an organizer," Alan went on. "Most of them were good folks, reasonable people, who wanted to make real improvements in their communities. But invariably, you ran into someone who was . . . passionate . . . about a cause."

"Passionate," I repeated. "Or . . . unpredictable?"

"That, too," Alan agreed. "One night after a meeting—we were organizing for a river clean-up, I think it was—this guy comes up to me and starts talking about his experience as an activist. I think he wanted me to know that he wasn't some novice who would shy away from hard work and refuse to take any risks. He told me he'd been involved with some high-profile campaigns, including protests and actions at paper mills to eliminate discharges that were poisonous to the environment. Apparently, though he didn't come right out and say it, he had also helped spike trees during the war in the woods."

"Spike trees?"

"Very nasty business."

Alan picked up Jason's deer hooves that had apparently taken up residence on my desk, since Jason hadn't returned for them. "Are you using antlers in all of your decorating these days?"

"Just hooves," I said. "What about the spikes?"

"To keep loggers from cutting trees near the owls, certain individuals pounded big metal spikes into the trees at random locations. They'd pound them in so deep you could hardly see them. Then when the loggers tried to cut the tree, their chainsaws hit the embedded spikes, which snapped the saws." He put the hooves back on my desk. "When the saw snapped, it could whip back and hit the logger. People got hurt. One guy got killed that way."

For a minute or so, neither of us said anything. I thought about good intentions gone awry and how only a few bad apples can, unfortunately, appear to spoil the whole bushel.

"Mr. White?"

I looked up to see Lindsay standing in my doorway. Her eyes were filled with tears.

"My cue to leave," Alan said, grabbing his gym bag and coffee cup. "Don't want to keep my first hour waiting. Far be it for me to deny them their beauty sleep. If I don't see you before you leave," he said from the doorway, "be careful."

His eyes focused sharply on mine. "I mean that, Bob. Be careful."

And I hadn't even told him about my personal death threat yet.

Alan left, and I waved Lindsay into the room.

"Lindsay," I said. "You want to tell me about it?"

"Oh, Mr. White," she sobbed. "It's not at all what Kim thinks. She thinks she knows what's going on, but she's wrong. I'm not flirting with Brad. It's like that's what's in her head, and so that's what she sees. But it's not that way."

"Lindsay," I said again. "Could you put that in plain English for me?"

She grabbed a handful of tissues from the box on my desk and blew her nose.

Waiting for her to get control of herself, I handed her some more while she continued to cry.

Finally, I just handed her the whole box.

"I'm not after Brad," she blubbered. "Kim has already made up her mind about what's going on, and so everything that happens she makes fit with what she thinks, but it's not the truth!"

Sometimes, in the midst of all their teenage angst and drama, high schoolers actually do see things clearly.

I looked at Lindsay and smiled. "You know, Lindsay, that's a very common human failing. We all do it at times. We see what we want to see, or what we expect to see. It's a rare person who can look at the world and see what's really there, instead of making the world fit what she's already decided should be there."

Lindsay looked at me like I had just landed from another planet and spoke an unintelligible language. Nice try, I told myself, but no cigar.

"Okay, Lindsay," I sighed. "Want to tell me about it?"

She sure did.

After about forty minutes and half a box of tissues, she went to class, and I thanked God I wasn't a high school kid. I checked my voice mail, since I'd put everything through while I talked with Lindsay. There was one call. It was from Knott.

"Weirdest thing," his message ran. "We did a more exhaustive search around the area where you discovered Rahr's body, and you'll never guess what we found. Trees with spikes in them. What do you make of that?"

Tree spikes. I'll be damned.

"As for Stan Miller, he continues to not exist. Not a trace. That's making me real nervous because it means he's using a false identity, and that means trouble. And, while I've got you on the phone, Bob, why the hell didn't you tell me you talked with Rahr the night before he was murdered?"

Make that double-damned.

I'd been afraid that little detail might come up.

I replaced the receiver in its cradle and stared at it. I had a feeling that the next time I talked with Knott, it wasn't going to be pretty. The phone rang.

I was afraid to pick it up. It might be Knott.

It rang again.

For crying out loud, I couldn't be afraid to answer my own phone, could I?

"Bob White," I answered it.

Fortunately, it wasn't Knott.

Unfortunately, it was someone else. A someone else with a deep voice I didn't recognize who said, "Stay home. We're not kidding."

But before I could thank the caller for that succinct clarification, the line went dead.

It hadn't been Stan. After speaking with him—sort of—on Saturday night and Monday afternoon, I was familiar enough with his voice to know it hadn't been him. So that was a good thing. At least Lily's new beau wasn't into making threatening phone calls in addition to writing threatening notes and not existing. Great! Now I could have something positive to say about him when my folks asked me about him. "Yup, he's really scary and he hates my guts, but he does not make threatening phone calls. What a gem, huh?"

Of course, that also meant one of two things: one—either my bird feeder note wasn't from Stan at all, but instead was from the anonymous caller, or two—Stan and the caller were working together. The caller did say "we." But if Stan hadn't penned the note, then someone else had, and if that were the case, then I had to conclude that the note and the phone call were connected, which meant that at least two people—the "we" in question—I couldn't identify were trying to keep me away from the owls.

Bottom line: regardless of whether or not Stan was involved, I was now the subject of a group project.

And that begged the question: *What's the assignment?*

Chapter Nine

By Wednesday afternoon, I was beginning to think I might have made a mistake by bargaining with Mr. Lenzen to use my personal days. Maybe I should have taken the suspension, after all. And thanked him, too.

Kim had followed Lindsay in my office, and by the end of the day, I'd seen them both three times—twice individually and the third time, together. Talk about drama. I had a headache that wouldn't quit, and my semester's supply of tissue boxes was decimated. I thought if I had to be a sympathetic listener for one more minute, I would probably rip my counseling license from the wall and gleefully feed it to the paper shredder tucked under my desk.

Which wouldn't work, anyway.

The shredder, I mean. It had been broken for months. But even if it did work, shredding my license wouldn't stop me from being a counselor. Because even when the students made me crazy, there really wasn't anywhere else I'd rather be working. Despite the drama, I love the job. And when I love something, I can't give it up.

Like birding. Even when I've gotten anonymous letters and phone calls telling me to quit.

In between the soggy acts of the Kim and Lindsay show, I'd been playing telephone tag with Knott, and it was almost three-thirty in the afternoon before we finally connected. I told him what Alan had told me about the war in the woods and spiked trees. He said they'd also found a rather large hammer in a melting puddle of snow at the base of one of the trees and were hoping to get some fingerprints, though he thought the possibility of being that lucky was pretty slim. I apologized for not telling him about my phone conversation with Rahr and promised to answer all his questions when I got to Duluth the next day.

"They better be good answers," he warned me. "You held back on me, Bob. That doesn't make me real happy." I could hear his chair squeaking. "You got a day off?"

"Yeah. It's in lieu of an official suspension by my assistant principal. I guess I'm a public relations liability at the moment."

"Why is that?"

"Because a certain detective called to verify my whereabouts last Friday and apparently used the words 'murder' and 'suspect' in the same sentence, which gave my boss a minor stroke, which he took out on me in the form of a suspension, which I managed to reduce to a 'pending' suspension."

"Oh. Sorry." He paused. "Do you get paid during a suspension?"

"Some, I think."

"But you'd rather not have to find out, I'm guessing?"

"That's right. So I'm taking tomorrow and Friday as personal days off to come up to Duluth to redeem myself with both you and my boss, except he doesn't know that, yet. I'm counting on the influence of that same detective to make sure I'm back at my desk on Monday."

"You scratch my back, and I'll scratch yours." Knott must have been tilting back in his chair, because I could hear more squeaking over the phone line. "It's a deal. Can you make it here by lunch tomorrow?"

We made plans to meet at Grandma's down by the harbor at noon. I figured I'd get an early start and swing by the university mid-morning to see if Ellis was back. If he was, I could talk with him and kill two birds with one stone (not one of my favorite metaphors, I have to admit, but effective, nonetheless): interview him for the MOU owl study and pick up whatever information I could pass along to Knott. I told the detective my agenda, and for a moment, just as I was about to hang up, I considered telling Knott about the note and the phone call, but decided to wait for tomorrow's lunch. Instead, I asked him for a favor.

"Don't tell anyone I'm coming to town, okay?" I said. I guessed by the silence over the line that he was wondering about the reason behind my request, so I offered him a half-truth as explanation. "I want to outmaneuver a birding rival. He thinks I'm not heading north till Friday, and I don't want to take a chance that somehow he might find out otherwise."

"Oh, I get it," he answered. "One of those friendly birding competition things you told me about, right? My lips are sealed, Bob." He paused. "As long as it really is a friendly little competition. Because the more I'm learning about Rahr's world—the politics of academia, the S.O.B. people, even the DNR—the more I'm beginning to question if all these bird-loving people are tucked into one big happy nest, if you know what I mean."

I had to admit, I had my doubts sometimes, too. Why did something as simple as protecting the natural world seem to end up so often as a major production with a whole cast of heroes and villains, not to mention a thousand supporting players?

"I think you ought to watch your back, Bob," Knott added. "That's all I'm saying. Friendly competition or not. I already have one birding-related crime to solve. I really don't want another one."

Neither did I. But until I knew for sure what Stan was—or wasn't—involved with, I also couldn't gauge the seriousness of my anonymous note and call. If Scary Stan was just playing a mind game with me, I wasn't going to call in the police. On the other hand, if I found out that Stan was guilty of anything other than dating my sister, then I would definitely cry "wolf!" loud and clear and welcome the police into my life. The last thing I needed was to be hunting for owls while someone else was hunting for me.

I packed up my briefcase, straightened my desk and turned off the lights.

"I'll be back," I told my chair, then locked the door and left.

Minutes later, I pulled into Lily's parking lot, in hopes she'd be around so I could get a phone number for Very Nice

Trees, since I'd told her I'd check out the supplier on my next trip north. I also needed to pick up some suet. But, it remained to be seen if she would even speak to me after the little scene with Stan the other afternoon. I spotted her behind some statuary in the showroom and walked over, but I made sure I stayed out of her kick range.

"I need the number for Very Nice Trees," I said. "I'm going to be in Two Harbors this weekend, so I thought I'd do that look-see thing for you we talked about."

As I expected, she didn't smother me with any sisterly affection. She gave me a "Die, you scum" look that I remembered well from our childhood, then turned her back on me to go to her office. A moment later, she was holding out an invoice to me. "It's on here."

"Look, Lily," I said, taking the sheet of paper. "About the other day, I'm sorry about my overreacting to Stan. I—"

"Was an idiot," she finished for me. "I don't know why you have to go ballistic every time I date a guy. Stan is a very nice man. Not the greatest conversationalist, I'll admit, but he certainly knows his stuff when it comes to accounting. He's been helping me with my taxes for this year, and so far, he's saving me a ton of money, Bobby. Although he does seem a little concerned about the profitability margin I posted from those Christmas trees."

She pointed at the invoice in my hand.

"I called them yesterday to get directions for you, but I got their answering machine instead. But there was a message on the machine."

Her pupils dilated and her breathing accelerated. A red flush began to creep up her neck.

"They've got an absolutely unbelievable deal on ladyslippers for next month. You won't believe this."

Now, we may have our differences, but I know my sister. There are only two things that consistently turn Lily White pink: 1) the prospect of big profit, and 2) tickets to Minnesota Wild hockey games.

But the Wild wasn't playing tonight, which meant only one thing.

Lily was seeing big dollar signs.

"Ladyslippers are pricey little flowers," she said, excitement rising in her voice. "They usually sell for $150 to $200 retail, so I don't include them in too many landscape plans. Plus, they're hard to get. But Mrs. Anderson would really like a big garden of them in that landscape I'm working on. I told her it might not happen. But now, Very Nice Trees is offering them wholesale at $100 a plant, which means I can make a big chunk of profit."

"Wait a minute," I said. "Did you say 'per plant'?"

Lily was grinning. "Yup."

"And just how many plants go in a big garden for Mrs. Anderson?"

Lily was practically choking on her grin. "One hundred!" she finally managed to spit out. "I can make $5,000 on ladyslippers for one yard alone—and that's selling at the low retail price. If I charge her $200 per plant, I can make—"

"Ten thousand." I did the math again just to be sure I had it right. Both Lily and her supplier, Very Nice Trees, stood to make ten thousand bucks each from this one transaction alone. And if Very Nice Trees had lots more ladyslippers to sell, they were going to make a bundle. I wondered just how many ladyslippers they had in stock. I couldn't imagine their costs were that much—you just needed the right growing conditions. Like the conditions up north. Find the right spot, grow the flowers and bring home the money. In this case, a *lot* of money.

Maybe, I thought, I should consider growing flowers—expensive flowers. Like ladyslippers. I could tell Mr. Lenzen to take my job and . . .

I folded the invoice into my wallet. Lily was almost bouncing off the walls. But then I remembered she'd said ladyslippers were usually hard to get.

"So, how come these people are swimming in ladyslippers?" I asked her. "You just said quantities of them weren't exactly easy to dig up."

Lily rolled her eyes. "Ha ha," she said.

"What?" I said. "What did I say?"

"'Dig up,'" she replied. "Not easy to 'dig up.' Cheap landscaping humor, Bobby."

She stopped the bouncing thing and started chewing on her lip. "I know. Usually growers have very limited supplies. The availability of so many plants—expensive plants—bothers me a little. A lot, actually."

She leaned against the statuary.

"I tried calling Very Nice Trees a couple more times yesterday, but never got anything but the answering machine. When I did business with them at Christmas, I didn't have any problems. The trees were beautiful, fresh and priced great. It was a small lot like any small supplier might provide. Nothing odd, there. The trees were perfect. I even called the Better

Business Bureau just to be sure there haven't been any complaints about them."

"And?" I asked.

"Nothing. No complaints."

She turned in her chair, looked out her window and sighed.

"But then when Stan noted my profit from the trees, it got me thinking about it, again. I keep imagining those pickup trucks you see every spring cruising new neighborhoods with a load full of trees for sale at low, low prices. I always think they're stolen merchandise because reputable growers don't sell out of the back of a truck like that." She chewed her lip again. "One hundred ladyslippers? Nobody has that many."

Lily turned her grey eyes up to mine. "I'd love that big chunk of change, Bobby, you know that. But I'm an honest businesswoman, and I'm not naïve. And I'm . . ." she winced, hesitant to say it, ". . . feeling . . . not quite right about Very Nice Trees."

"Feeling?" I placed my hand over my heart in shock. "You? Feeling? You, the Mistress of Humiliation?"

I held up my hand to stop her as she started to open her mouth. "I'll see what I can find out, shrimp. If something's not nice at Very Nice Trees, you'll be the first to know." I paid her for my suet and headed for the sewage ponds.

Another blast of winter was rolling in when I parked the SUV. The water chopped on the ponds. I pulled my parka hood up over my head, hunching my shoulders against a growing wind chill. The goose and Canvasback were gone, as I expected. I hoped they were hitting nicer weather than I was getting.

When I got home, I put the new blocks of suet in the feeders on the deck. Almost as soon as I shut the sliding glass doors, a male Pileated Woodpecker flew in and perched on the suet, chipping away bits for his dinner. I watched for a minute as he hammered and stopped, hammered and stopped.

Was that what it had been like for Rahr? Someone hammering his head against a tree until he lost consciousness?

This was really getting to be lousy, I thought. I couldn't even watch birds at my feeder without thinking of a murder. I turned around and headed for the kitchen.

Something hot and filling sounded good for dinner, so I browned a pound of hamburger, tossed in a can of corn and a can of tomato soup. Mulligan stew, my mom always called it. True, it couldn't hold a candle to what Luce could do in the kitchen, but without Luce in the kitchen, it was a reasonable alternative. I wasn't completely without cooking skills, after all.

I was, however, without Luce.

For a couple minutes, I thought about how nice it would be to have her here tonight. A cold wind outside, a fire in the fireplace, snuggled up together planning a weekend of birding.

Which reminded me—I needed to check the weather to make sure I'd be driving to Duluth tomorrow. If a blizzard was on the radar, I wouldn't be going anywhere. I turned on the television and stretched out on the sofa.

Imagine my surprise when John Knott appeared on the screen, talking with reporters.

"We have no suspects at this time," Knott was saying as the snowflakes fell between him and the microphone held in front of his face. "But we are actively pursuing leads."

The blonde woman holding the mike moved closer to him. "Is it true you suspect involvement on the part of the activist group Save Our Boreals?"

"No comment at this time."

Knott's face was immediately replaced with the face of the station anchorman.

"Earlier today, we spoke exclusively with Margaret Montgomery, Director of Save Our Boreals, the environmental activist organization headquartered in Duluth," the anchorman reported.

The face on the screen changed again. I almost shot off the sofa.

It was my mom.

I looked again.

No, it wasn't.

It was, however, someone who could have passed for her twin. There was the same wavy chestnut-colored hair cut in the same style as my mom. There were my mom's big blue eyes and high cheekbones. The woman on the screen even had my mom's red reading glasses in her hand.

But this was not my mom.

This was Margaret Montgomery, director of S.O.B.

"We were shocked to learn of the sudden death of Dr. Rahr," Montgomery told the reporter. "He was a dedicated researcher and good friend of our organization. Our prayers and sympathy go to his wife and family."

"Are you aware that Save Our Boreals has been mentioned as possibly suspect in Dr. Rahr's death?" the reporter asked.

"Yes, I am aware of that," Montgomery said, cool and relaxed in front of the cameras. She obviously had had plenty of experience with the media. She looked directly at the interviewer, and her body language shouted confident, concerned and respectful. I know all about body language. Another skill courtesy of graduate school.

"Unfortunately, environmental activist organizations are often scrutinized more intensely than other groups in a situation like this for two reasons." Montgomery held up two slender fingers to count off. "One: people are suspicious of us because of the negative publicity environmentalists have often unjustly—or not—received in the past, and two: finding a scapegoat is always a temptation. I can tell you without reservation that the membership of Save Our Boreals is made up of very fine individuals who care deeply about our natural world and those who work so hard to preserve it. I can't imagine any hard feelings between anyone in our organization and Dr. Rahr."

Pretty speech. Although she obviously hadn't read the letter that Rahr's wife had passed along to Knott—threatening someone wasn't what I'd call characteristic of a warm, fuzzy relationship. Of course, if she had a leash on some loonies up in the woods, I don't expect she'd be sharing that with a television reporter and the rest of the viewing audience, either.

"When you say 'negative publicity,'" the reporter pressed, "are you referring to the confrontation last spring between S.O.B. and the DNR over the Boreal Owls' breeding grounds?"

Montgomery smiled. Damn! It was even my mom's smile. Did my mom have an identical twin from whom she was separated at birth, and we never knew about it?

What else was my mom hiding from us?

I bet it was about Lily. Finally. Confirmation.

Lily wasn't really my sister.

Okay, so maybe we looked like twins for a while there, and we both have the same cleft in our chins like our dad, and the same hair, and the same eyes, and the same irrational fear of falling up—rather than down—stairs, but other than that, we don't resemble each other at all.

Besides, she was always mean to me when we were growing up.

Heck, she was still mean to me. Today I had had to pay for my own suet, even after I apologized for what I had said about Stan.

Montgomery was still talking, and I caught the last thing she said.

". . . As my years of experience as both a lobbyist and organizer in this arena have taught me, it's that the best solutions—and resolutions—only come about when all the parties involved make honest disclosures and seek consensus for the good of the human and natural communities alike."

Well, duh. That was a real eye-opener. Montgomery sure had the publicity-release fluff stuff down pat. But that was her job. She was an experienced lobbyist. It certainly explained her professional presence on-camera. I wondered what other environmental groups she had worked with.

The weather was next. No blizzards on the way. A warm front moving in. Nice weekend for northern Minnesota.

I picked up the phone to call Mike. I hadn't talked with him since I dropped him off on Sunday morning.

"Do you want to try for the Boreal again this weekend?" I asked. "I know it's short notice, but I'm going up tomorrow, and you could meet me in Two Harbors on Saturday."

"I can't. I'd like to, but if I'm gone another weekend this month, Maryann is going to kill me. It's Colleen's eleventh birthday, and we've got ten giggling girls coming over Friday night for a sleepover party."

"Take them owling," I suggested.

Mike started laughing.

"I'm serious," I said. "They get to be out at night, in the dark, sneaking around. Little girls would love it."

"Bob," Mike said, "Little girls love giggling. They make way too much noise for owls. Believe me, owls aren't going to hang around a bunch of giggling girls."

Just for a moment, I felt something catch, then slip away in my mind.

Something about noise and owls.

I shook my head, but couldn't get it back.

"Bob? You there?"

"Yeah," I said. "Just spacing out. Sorry." I remembered the other reason I had called Mike. "I need a favor."

I explained to him how I wanted to check out Very Nice Trees for Lily when I went up to Two Harbors. "But all I've got is a box number. Could you call someone at the post office up there and get me a street address?"

"Bob, Bob, Bob," Mike said. "People have box numbers for a reason. One reason is privacy. You're asking me to call another post office to get information for you that isn't public?"

"Yeah."

"Don't you think that's presuming on our friendship?"

"No."

"Good. I don't either. I'll get back to you as soon as I get it. But it might take a couple days."

"Whatever you can do, Mike. I'll be at the same hotel where we always stay in Duluth. Just leave a message if I'm not in. You're the best, buddy."

He laughed. "Tell Maryann that. I'm making points being here this weekend, but I want to run up the score big-time, so I can do that long birding weekend with the MOU out in Blue Mounds in May."

That was one of my favorite trips, too. The prairie in the southwestern part of the state would be blooming then and the Dicksissels and Blue Grosbeaks easy to find. Mike wished me luck on hunting the Boreal, and I hung up the phone.

I got off the sofa and walked over to the sliding doors to my deck and looked out. A very bright full moon illuminated the woods and pond that stretched beyond my yard. Even through the glass, I could hear the clear hoots of the Great Horned Owl that lived behind me.

Whoo-whoo-whoo. Whoo-whoo.

In my head, I listened again to the rising flute-like notes of the Boreal Owl's call: *who, who, who who-who-who-who.*

Would I find him this weekend?

I sure hoped so, since the mating season was half over, and my window of opportunity for this year was shrinking by the day. Make that by the night. If I didn't get him this weekend, I only had two more weekends—four nights—left. And next year, there wouldn't be a new report from Rahr to help me scout locations.

Unless Ellis stepped in.

Was it just bad timing that Ellis showed up in Duluth shortly before Rahr's murder?

Or was it perfect timing?

I closed the drapes across the glass doors.

Whack!

Something had hit my sliding door. Hard. I pulled the drapes open again and looked out at the deck.

A bloody Great Horn Owl was laying about a foot from the door.

My phone rang. I picked it up.

"Stay home," a voice hissed into my ear.

Chapter Ten

Snow was lightly falling as I left the cities behind me and headed north on I-35 to Duluth. I'd set the alarm for five o'clock, thinking I'd beat the morning traffic rush that could gridlock commuters for hours. As a result, I made great time and cleared the northernmost suburbs within an hour of leaving my house. Granted, I'd checked my rear-view mirrors more frequently than I usually do, but since I hadn't once spotted a car or truck that was marked with a "We're tailing you" billboard, I was feeling pretty confident that my escape from Savage was unobserved. As long as the snow continued to melt as soon as it hit the pavement, my plan to make it to the university by mid-morning would hold. If the temperatures fell, however, and the highway iced, I could be in for a long, and very slow, drive to the North Shore.

As it was, the snow stopped south of Pine City, and the traffic was surprisingly light. Usually when I headed north in the winter, the road was filled with skiers and snowmobilers going up for a weekend of playing in the snow. In the summer, it was packed bumper-to-bumper with campers, boaters, tourists, and vacationers.

This morning, though, it was too early for weekend drivers, and most of the cars I passed seemed to be business travelers making the Twin Cities-Duluth trek. Before I realized it, my lead foot had gotten heavier, and I was cruising at eighty-five miles an hour.

Someone else, however, did realize it and wanted to share that little bit of information with me.

Lights flashing, the highway patrol cruiser pulled me over.

"Morning. You in a rush, sir?"

The state trooper at my window was a woman I didn't know. That surprised me—not that the trooper was a woman, but that I didn't know this particular trooper. Over the years, I've had the pleasure of making the acquaintance of quite a few members of the highway patrol since I spend so much time behind the wheel chasing birds. In fact, I'm probably one of the few people in Minnesota to have been issued speeding tickets in every single county of the state.

Another dubious honor, I know.

"No, Officer," I responded. "My mistake. I wasn't paying attention to my speed."

I didn't tell her the reason was because I was thinking about a dead owl on my deck and the fact that I was now sure Scary Stan was not behind the threats because if I knew nothing else about Stan, I knew for a fact he wouldn't kill a bird. Which, of course, had led me back to the conclusion that I had not wanted to reach yesterday: that someone else was making a new hobby of threatening me. Remembering both Alan's remarks about ecoterrorists and Montgomery's interview on the television, I'd decided the most likely suspects were some fringe S.O.B. sympathizers. That also seemed to fit with what Knott had said about Dr. Rahr's threatening letter. So all I had to do was add personal vigilance and an impenetrable forcefield to my strategy for finding the Boreals and I should be just fine.

Or at the very least, alive.

Since when did birding become a survival sport?

"I drive this road a lot," I told the trooper, "and I just went on automatic, I guess."

"Automatic speeding?"

I smiled.

She didn't.

She checked my license and insurance card, went back to her car to write the ticket, then came back and handed it to me. Before I could get back on the road, though, she showed up at my window again.

"Are you that bird guy they told me about? I saw your plates, but it didn't click till I got back to my car."

She was referring to my vanity license plates. They read BRRDMAN. When I got them, I hadn't planned on becoming a state-wide highway celebrity. Nowadays, I secretly hoped that my plate recognition was keeping my ticket tally lower, not higher. Although that didn't seem to be the case this morning.

I nodded. "That would probably be me."

She held her hand out to shake mine. "Then I expect I'll be seeing you on a regular basis, Mr. White."

I shook her hand and smiled. "In that case, make it Bob."

This time she did smile back.

"I'm Chris. Chris Maas." Before I could comment, she added, "What can I say? My parents thought it was a hoot. My brother's name is Pete."

She walked back to her cruiser. I watched her in the mirror for a second or two and then carefully pulled out onto the freeway. I set my cruise control at a sedate sixty-five. I was bummed about the ticket. My New Year's resolution was to not get any tickets this year, and I'd only made it to late March.

Notice I didn't say the resolution was to not speed.

Just not get any tickets.

The rest of the drive to Duluth was uneventful. No troopers, no tickets, no tails (as far as I could tell). I downed two apple fritters at a gas station in town and mentally apologized to Luce for my poor eating habits. I turned up the hill, away from the harbor, and drove to the university campus. After a minute or two of circling through the visitors' parking lot, I found a space outside the Biological Sciences Building, or BSB, as it's known by the locals.

Originally located in the downtown area, UMD now sits on the hill above Lake Superior, giving students both a bird's-eye view of the water and a biting taste of the cold winds that can whip over it in the winter. In their great wisdom, the campus planners connected all the buildings with tunnels and enclosed walkways, providing tender-skinned students with protection from the frigid elements. I'd heard some of our Savage alumni who attended the school say they felt like moles for part of the year, hidden away in underground warrens, while others took advantage of the indoor environment to wear pajamas to class.

Located at the edge of campus, the BSB was the most recent addition to the university's facilities, housing labs, classrooms, departmental libraries, and offices. As an adjunct professor of environmental studies, Ellis would have his office here.

So would the repositories of all information: the department secretaries.

If you want to know who's in and who's out in any college department, ask a secretary. And I don't mean just the physical location of in and out. Secretaries know all the dynamics of office relationships. They know who's ticked at whom, who's doing the heavy lifting in the office, and who's got other irons in the fire. Besides juggling a hundred clerical and administrative tasks, good secretaries learn to identify the moods of the people they work with and often notice details others overlook.

And that was why the first person I was looking for this morning was a secretary, preferably one who knew both Rahr and Ellis. Since both men were based in the BSB, I was hoping I might pick up some helpful insights into their working relationship from the department secretaries. Okay, maybe even a little dirt. I had, after all, promised my fellow MOU board members that I would check on Ellis's credentials—just because he personally wasn't available didn't preclude my obtaining some information.

I mean, it's not like I was snooping, exactly.

Close, but not exactly.

And if a secretary told me something I thought Knott might like to know, there was nothing wrong with passing it along, right?

Especially if it got me back in Knott's good graces. I knew I was skating on thin ice since I'd neglected to tell him about my phone call with Rahr. At the time, I just hadn't thought it would help. Now, I realized it was a major error in judgment.

I locked the car and walked to the building. The air was brisk and felt great after a morning of driving. The weather had turned. Unlike the previous weekend I'd spent freezing in the woods, the air was spring-like—instead of closing my throat against the cold, I wanted to drink it in. Without a doubt, Old Man Winter was starting to lose his grip on Minnesota's North Shore.

The down side was that it meant time was running out on the Boreals' mating season and any chances I had to find them. Though I hated to admit it, my pending suspension from work was a birding blessing in disguise if it produced my owl. If it didn't, and Knott couldn't convince Mr. Lenzen to take me back on Monday, then it would be only the beginning of a very long weekend—a weekend that might possibly extend into weeks, or even months.

With only partial pay.

If I was lucky.

Not this camper, I decided. I was going to set my sights on something good coming out of this weekend, even if I had to make it happen myself.

Problem was, at least two other someones apparently had their sights set on me. And to make matters worse, I really didn't know why.

It definitely looked like lunch with Knott wasn't exactly going to be happy hour.

I walked into the BSB lobby and looked around for a directory but couldn't find one. Then I looked up. Suspended high above my head were large department symbols, pointing visitors down different corridors to the various departments. The symbols were hewn out of native rock. Big pieces of native rock. I couldn't decide which was scarier: the thought that I could be squashed like a bug if one of those rocks came tumbling down, or the possibility that my tax dollars had helped pay for them.

I picked out a symbol that looked like a primitive drawing of a wave curling around the earth and hoped it meant environmental science. After following it down a wide corridor that made several turns, sure enough, I ended up . . . in front of a water fountain.

I retraced my steps, mentally cursing the architect who sold the university on the symbol sign posts. This time, I chose a rock that was etched with what looked like a mass of tangled worms. Or maybe it was spaghetti. If it led me to a food court, I was giving up.

Thankfully, it didn't. A couple turns of another corridor and I found the environmental sciences department.

I had chosen wisely.

I pushed through the glass office doors. Across the room, behind a reception desk, there was an attractive, dark-haired woman. She smiled as I approached.

"Can I help you?"

"Yes," I said. "I was hoping you could tell me a little about Bradley Ellis. I understand he's an adjunct professor here this term."

She dropped the pen she was holding. She leaned back in her chair.

The ground shook.

The room darkened.

Lightning cracked.

Just kidding.

But something happened because Ms. Smiling Secretary disappeared.

Ms. Furious took her place.

"Are you from the police department?" Ms. Furious shouted at me.

I took a step back from the desk.

"Because if you are, I don't know anything more than I've already told you people! Dr. Ellis is out of town. His father is ill. I don't know when he'll return. That's all you're going to get. Now get out!"

I figured if I didn't move, she wouldn't see me. Maybe I could back up very slowly and follow the worms back out of the building. I could enter the warrens under the campus and lose myself in the pajama-clad throngs. I could drive down to the harbor. I could hide in my hotel room.

"I'm sorry," I said. "I certainly didn't mean to upset you. I'm not a detective."

That seemed to help a little. Not much, but a little. Ms. Furious downgraded to Ms. Seething.

"I'm here on behalf of the Minnesota Ornithologists' Union," I told her. "Dr. Ellis sent an email saying he'd like to do some research for us."

"Oh."

The dark abyss closed up as suddenly as it had opened.

Ms. Smiling Secretary was back.

"I'm sorry," she apologized to me. "It's just been so terrible around here this week with the police asking questions, over and over, and poor Bradley—Dr. Ellis—gone to be with his father. It's just been overwhelming, really. It reminds me of last year, when we had all those logging people in here arguing with Dr. Rahr. And all those S.O.B people, too. I wouldn't have been surprised if someone had started throwing punches. It was awful. Honestly, it was a three-ring circus in here by the time the DNR put an end to it."

Now she was Suzy Talks a Lot.

I nodded in understanding. Actually, I was afraid to open my mouth.

Suzy picked a pen out of a glass jar on her desk, pulled a notepad in front of her, and began to write. She smiled up at me. "Now, what was your name?"

"Bob White," I told her. "I'm a member of the MOU board. I wanted to talk with Dr. Ellis about the Boreal Owl study."

I noticed that the pen she used had *Save Our Boreals* stamped on it. For some reason, the pen looked familiar to me, but I couldn't place it. I wondered if she was a member of the group, or if someone had left it behind last year during the three-ring circus.

"He's already had experience, you know."

My gaze shifted from the pen in her hand to her face. Now she was beaming, almost like I've seen parents do on Back to School Night when they're proud of their children. Except she certainly wasn't old enough to be Ellis's mother.

Considering her multiple personality routine, I couldn't imagine her as anyone's mother. She alone probably had enough issues to keep a whole class of counselors-in-training busy for at least a year or two. Maybe three. I didn't even want to consider how kids of hers might turn out.

"He spent a season working with Dr. Rahr a few years ago," she offered. "That's when I first met him, actually. I was Dr. Rahr's secretary at the time."

Bingo.

Ms. Multiple knew both Rahr and Ellis. I'd hit pay dirt on the first shovel dig. I bit the inside of my mouth to keep myself from grinning. "And you are?"

"Alice. Alice Wylie."

Then it happened again. The woman—Alice—morphed again. This time into Ms. Press Release.

"I can't tell you how upsetting Dr. Rahr's death has been for all of us," she said, her voice totally flat. "It's just unthinkable. I haven't seen Dr. Ellis this week, but I'm sure he'll just be sick about it. Since he started here in January, he's often remarked that he owes Dr. Rahr a great deal."

Then, for the blink of an eye, Ms. Furious was back. "In fact, if it weren't for Dr. Rahr, Dr. Ellis wouldn't be where he is today in his academic career."

Gee, do you think I could go out and come in again and we could start this thing over? I wanted to ask. Because this whole multiple-personality thing was really starting to creep me out. Without a doubt, I was definitely getting a bad feeling here. But what?

Something weird was going on with Alice Wylie.

Not only was she doing a good imitation of a really serious clinical psychological disorder, but her tone of voice was confusing me. I couldn't tell if she was defending Rahr or damning him, or if it was Ellis that she was defending/damning. Whichever it was, it also didn't jibe with the press release she'd just recited, a comment that seemed to suggest that a mutual admiration society existed between the two men.

But I knew that mutual admiration wasn't the case. Or at least, it hadn't been the case when Rahr refused to keep "the kid" on, as Dr. Phil had reported.

Which made me wonder what Ellis had really meant in his email when he said he owed Rahr.

Depending on how I took Alice's statement, I could come up with a variety of spins.

If I took it as an indictment against Rahr on Ellis's behalf, that could mean that Ellis had made his remark out of resentment, rather than gratitude—that he might be further along in academia if Rahr hadn't shut him down with the Boreals. True, he'd earned his doctorate from Cornell, which was no mean feat, but was it possible that Rahr had somehow slowed him down professionally?

On the other hand, if I took Alice's words as praise for Rahr, then maybe Ellis's email remark was likewise complimentary.

Unless he was being sarcastic.

Or vindictive.

Get a grip, I told myself. Just listen. Stop looking for innuendo. Collect the information and let Knott do the detective thing. That's what he got paid for. Not me.

"You know," Alice was saying, lowering her voice, "some of these professors can be pretty petty about their colleagues. I've even seen them deliberately sabotage each other's chances for promotion and funding grants. Not here, of course," she added quickly. "I've worked at other colleges in the state and seen it all. But it's different here."

She sniffed, grabbed a tissue and dabbed at her eyes. My guess was that Ms. Vulnerable had just arrived.

"Everyone is so supportive of each other's work that it's like working with your own family," she said, her voice quivering. "That's why Dr. Rahr's death was so disturbing. Nothing like that ever happens here."

I waited to see if she'd say anything more, but she—all of her—seemed to be finished. Believe me, I wasn't complaining. I thanked her for her time, and she promised to get the message to Ellis when he returned. As I wound my way out, following the worm back to the building's lobby, I passed an office door that was slightly ajar. Thinking it was worth a try to speak with another department member, I knocked. When no one answered, I pushed it open.

Papers were scattered across a wide oak desk. On the wall behind it, photographs and diplomas hung in the space between filled bookshelves. One photo in particular caught my eye: it showed a man on skis shooting a rifle. Next to it was a diploma from Cornell University. I leaned in a little to read it. It belonged to Bradley Ellis.

"Can I help you?"

I jumped at the man's voice right behind my shoulder. I hadn't even heard him walk in. I turned around and found myself looking at a big muscular guy about my height, maybe my age, with salt-and-pepper hair cut close to his scalp.

"Yes," I said, pointing at the photo. "Who's the biathlete?"

"I am." He stuck his hand out in introduction. "Bradley Ellis."

I shook his hand. "I'm Bob White."

"Do you compete?" he asked, nodding towards the photo.

"No," I replied. "I ski, but I don't shoot. Do you compete?"

"Not any more. When I was younger, I had the time to get to races and train, but full-time employment put an end to that." He folded his arms over his broad chest and looked me squarely in the eye. "Not much demand for armed cross-country skiers, you know."

I shifted a little uncomfortably on my feet. "No, I'd guess not."

"So . . . is there anything else I can help you with?"

Gee, now that you mention it—confess to murder, maybe?

But since I figured the odds of that happening were zero to nil, I tried to talk my way out of my embarrassment at being found loitering in someone's private office.

Okay, maybe not loitering exactly.

More like . . . spying.

"Your secretary said you were out of town, and I happened to see your door open, so I thought I'd check," I explained. It sounded lame even to me, but it was the best I could come up with spur-of-the-moment.

Obviously, people who were detectives were highly skilled in their profession: they knew how to handle getting caught while snooping, while I felt like a bumbling idiot.

Maybe because I was a bumbling idiot?

It wasn't my fault that we never covered the finer points of spying in my counseling classes.

"Actually, I just got back about an hour ago," Ellis said.

He moved away from me and leaned his hip against his desk. With one hand, he straightened the papers on it into a neat pile. I noticed his hands looked strong and weathered, definitely more the hands of an outdoor enthusiast than a classroom pedagogue. I could easily imagine him hiking in the woods or paddling a canoe, dressed as he was in a worn flannel shirt and heavyweight jeans. As for proof that he could ski and shoot, I'd just seen it on the wall.

"I don't always check in with the receptionist," he said, smiling a little. "I have a bit of a reputation around here as a maverick, I suppose. An aversion to authority, some people might say."

The "kid"—as Jim had called him—was definitely a six-footer like me, but he was carrying probably thirty more pounds, all of it muscle. Teaching environmental science was obviously a better workout than being a high school counselor, even with the coaching I did.

Maybe I should start lifting weights with Alan, after all. He was always telling me I should.

"I'm on the MOU board," I told Ellis. "I'm up here for the weekend to look for the Boreals, and I thought I'd stop in to say hello and talk with you about taking on the study."

"So you got my email," he said. "I know the timing seems lousy and probably disrespectful, but I know how much the research meant to Andrew, and I think it would mean a lot to him if it weren't interrupted."

"You two worked together before, didn't you?"

"Yes, we did." Ellis shuffled some more papers. "After the one season I spent with him, I decided I wanted to pursue my doctorate in environmental studies instead of biological field research, so I took off for the East Coast. I'm afraid he wasn't very happy with me." He smiled briefly at me. "Sometimes, it's hard for mentors to let their mentees go."

"And now you're back," I said.

Brilliant observation, Bob! I gave myself a mental headslap.

"Yes. I am."

He didn't elaborate. After a moment of silence, I asked him how his father was doing.

"Not great," Ellis said. "I left on Saturday . . . no . . . Friday to fly home to Michigan. I'm sorry—after being away, my days are all mixed up right now."

"Bradley!"

We both turned to see Alice in the doorway.

"Hello, Alice."

"I didn't know you were back," she gushed, beaming. Ms. Proud Parent in action.

"Alice, are these yours?" He pulled a pair of red reading glasses from his chest pocket. "I found them on my desk."

"Oops!" She blushed and took them from his hand. "I was in here the other day—I hope you don't mind—to see if you had any plants that needed watering, and I must have left them here. I'm always losing these little guys, you know. I'm missing another pair, too, so if you happen to find them," she smiled again, "you know where I am."

I gave myself another mental headslap.

She wasn't Ms. Proud Parent.

She was Ms. Lovestruck.

In fact, Alice was so focused on Ellis, I wasn't sure she realized I was standing there in the room, too.

Ellis, on the other hand, was sending out cold waves that were almost palpable. I decided it was time for me to make an exit.

"I won't keep you," I told Ellis, edging toward the door, giving Alice a nod as I slipped past her in the doorway. "I expect you have a lot of catching up to do after being out of town. I'll be in touch. The board wants to make a quick decision about funding you."

Ellis turned his attention away from Alice and back to me. "That would be great," he said. "Maybe we could talk more this afternoon? I've got a couple appointments, but I'll be free after three."

"Actually, I thought I'd take another look at that Boreal site in the daylight," I told him. "The one where . . . uh . . . Dr. Rahr . . ."

Ellis nodded. "Unbelievable, isn't it? I just can't get my mind around it. I keep thinking Andrew's going to walk in the office any time now and say it wasn't him they found up there. He'd hate to have his work left undone."

He threw a quick glance at Alice, who was still standing in the doorway.

"Alice, could you find me a cup of coffee, please?"

"Certainly!" Alice made a quick about-face and headed off down the hall.

"Good help is hard to find," I commented.

Ellis sighed. "You can say that again."

I got the clear impression he wasn't including Alice in the "good help" category.

"Maybe we could have a drink later this evening and talk about the study," I suggested. "I understand there's a new spot on the North Shore. I promised a friend I'd check it out."

"The Splashing Rock," Ellis said. "It's excellent. What time do you think?"

We settled on eight o'clock.

"I'd really love to have that study in my lap, Bob," Ellis told me as we shook hands again. His eyes were intense. "I've been thinking about it . . . for years."

Oh, really? Exactly what had he been thinking about it? How he would do the study differently if he were in charge? How it had affected his academic and professional career, for good . . . or ill?

Because it had definitely affected it.

That much was clear from what Ellis had just told me about the reasons behind his change of field and his departure for the East Coast. Given what Dr. Phil and Jim had said about Rahr's opinion of Ellis after their season together, it didn't sound like it was an amicable separation, however. At least, not on Rahr's part, unless "over my dead body" was a secret code in field research language that meant you really liked your coworker. Somehow, I doubted that. If I believed Ellis's version, though, Rahr's anger was the result of a mentor's possessiveness—not the result of protocol discrepancies.

Having dealt in a very limited way with Rahr, myself, I had to admit that the possessive quality didn't surprise me. Rahr had been jealously protective of the work he was doing with the Boreals. He hadn't wanted to share any details with me. And it's not like I was another researcher trying to steal his thunder, or his study. I was just a local birder. He couldn't possibly have felt threatened by me, yet his words had suggested a definite wariness, if not downright paranoia.

Still, the question nagged at me as I walked out to my car. Had Ellis left the study of field biology willingly, or was he forced to abandon it because of his experience with Rahr?

I thought again about what Alice had said, that Ellis told her he wouldn't be where he was today if it weren't for Rahr. Was that a good or a bad place, according to Ellis? Call me a half-empty-glass kind of guy, but I didn't think that landing an adjunct professorship was anything to brag about when you were in your mid-thirties, like Ellis was. A full professorship, preferably a tenured one, was the plum most academics wanted in hand by that point.

So what did Ellis owe Rahr? Gratitude for good advice, or payback for blocking a career move?

Man, this suspicion thing was insidious. For the second time in less than an hour, I told myself to quit playing at detective and let Knott do his job.

Knowing from experience that the best way to get my mind off other matters was to take it birding, I drove down the hill to the harbor and over to Park Point, a swath of shoreline that fronts the south edge of Lake Superior. Yesterday, on the list serve, someone had spotted a Scaup and two Buffleheads there. The fact that they were usually the first of the waterfowl to return to Lake Superior in the spring could only mean that early migrants were already on the move. I pulled my binoculars out of the glove compartment and looped them over my neck, got out of the car and walked down to the shore.

For the next forty-five minutes, the only things I wanted to find were birds, not murder suspects. I lifted the binos to my eyes and tried to identify a duck out on the glassy water.

"Hey, Bob."

I slowly lowered my glasses to my chest and turned around.

It was Scary Stan.

Why was I not surprised?

Chapter Eleven

He nodded toward the lake. "Bufflehead?"

I noted that he had binos slung around his neck, too. "Yeah. What are you doing here, Stan?"

"Birding."

"No. I mean, yeah, obviously, I can see that. But what are you doing right here, right now, while I'm here, right now?"

He looked at me with flat eyes like I was babbling. Which I kind of was doing, because I had convinced myself that Stan was not stalking me, and here he was, at Park Point, three hours north of where we both lived, alone with me on an empty shore in the middle of a Thursday morning. Not to mention that he had once again appeared soundlessly behind me, which was really starting to unnerve me. Knott couldn't get a bead on this guy to save his soul, but all I had to do was turn around and there he was.

"Who are you?" I finally spit out.

"Stan Miller."

"No! Stan!" I was almost shouting at him. "Who are you? I mean, really? You show up right after I find a body, you scare off a bear—maybe saving my life—you don't exist according to the police who want to talk to you about the scene of a crime, you move like a ghost, and everyone in the MOU thinks you're either in the witness protection program or some kind of hired gun. Plus, I have the distinct impression you are inordinately interested in my own movements, to the point of using my sister to keep tabs on me. So, what is going on here, Stan?" I got right in his face. "Who are you?"

"You're upset."

"Damn right! I got a death threat on my bird feeder, an anonymous phone threat at work, a dead owl on my deck, and I thought you were behind it." I paused to catch my breath. "At least, I did until the dead owl showed up. Then I figured—I hoped—it wasn't you."

"It's not me."

"I know! So that means it's someone else, right?" I rubbed my hand over my eyes.

"Have you told the police?"

I looked at him between my fingers. This from a man who himself refused to cooperate with the law? Who, according to those same police, didn't even exist?

Apparently, Stan's guessed-at talents included mind-reading, because he looked me in the eye then and said, "It's a cover."

Duh.

"Well, yeah," I said, "and a darn good one, too, since all of one or two MOU members might actually believe it. Come on, Stan! Anyone who's gone birding with you can tell you're not just an accountant. So which is it? Are you a former hitman or CIA in rehab?"

Stan let out a sigh. "I'm a hired gun. But it's not what you think."

Great. Just great. My sister was dating a mercenary. Was he going to have to kill me now?

"That's why Knott can't find me," he added. "Until the job I'm currently working is finished, I can't talk with him. It might jeopardize the contract."

"What about me? Am I jeopardizing your contract?" A sudden rush of cold hit my spine. No one knew where I was—alone on a deserted beach with a self-confessed assassin.

Did I know how to have a good time or what?

"As long as you don't know my target, you're not a problem, Bob."

Gee, why didn't that make me feel a whole lot better?

"About those threats," Stan added, "it sounds like you're a problem for somebody else. Could be a serious problem, too."

For a minute or two, neither of us spoke. Stan put his binos to his eyes and gazed out at the water. "Lesser Scaup."

I looked through my glasses and saw the duck, identifying it by its distinctive "nail" at the tip of its short, flat bill. Under other circumstances, I would have been happy to be standing here with a birder of Stan's caliber; as it was, I was having a hard time keeping his birding skills foremost in my mind while I was, at the same time, wondering about his "other" abilities.

Were those particular abilities behind his reason for being in the woods last weekend with a rifle and a crossbow? What kind of target required that kind of armament?

Don't ask, I told myself. *Remember, you don't want to be Stan's problem.*

"About Lily."

Stan's voice broke the silence.

"I am using her. At least, I was. In the beginning. But not to follow you."

I lowered my binos and turned to look at Stan. For a split-second, I thought I saw a flicker of fear in his eyes.

"When she finds out, she's going to kill me, isn't she?"

I couldn't keep a smile from spreading across my face. "You got that right." For a second, I almost felt sorry for him; when it came to the art of payback, Lily had it down to a science. No matter who he really was, or what he was doing, Stan was going to suffer. Guaranteed.

"So, you're saying that your showing up at the Boreal site last weekend was a total coincidence?" I asked, hoping for a little more revelation. "You know, for some reason, I have trouble believing that."

"Didn't say it was coincidence," he corrected me. "As a matter of fact, it wasn't coincidental at all for me. I planned it." He shot me a penetrating look. "I knew there were Boreals there."

"The annual reports," I said. "You researched them like I did."

"Actually, no." He looked out at the lake again.

"Then how?"

"Inside source."

I realized that Stan's sentences were getting noticeably shorter again. His conversational battery was probably getting ready to self-destruct.

"What source?"

"My sister," he said. "Alice Wylie."

I blinked.

He was gone.

Chapter Twelve

"Tell me again why you didn't tell me about your phone call with Rahr."

Knott and I were working our way through a basket of hot, thick-cut, deep-fried onion rings, waiting for our burgers to arrive from the grill at Grandma's Saloon. An institution in downtown Duluth since before I was born, Grandma's had wood-plank floors and stained-glass windows that screened the busy street outside from the noon mob inside. Despite (or maybe because of) its high-fat menu, Grandma's was always packed; even my haute cuisine queen, Luce, loved lunch at Grandma's whenever we hit the North Shore.

After my unplanned rendezvous with Scary Stan at Park Point, I'd joined Knott at the little table he was holding for us at Grandma's. Being the observant man that I've trained myself to be, I could tell he was still steaming that I had neglected to share with him my first and last, one-and-only, phone conversation with Rahr. When I tried to pick up the laminated sheet listing the day's specials, he flattened his hand on the sheet, pinning it to the table.

"Tell me about the phone call, Bob. Now would be nice."

So I did. I explained how I'd given up trying to contact Rahr through email, since he never responded. I told Knott that after repeated attempts, I finally caught Rahr at his office the night before Mike and I headed to Duluth to hunt the Boreals.

"He didn't want to talk with me," I said. "He accused me of giving out the locations of his study sites to other people, which was nuts, because that's why I was trying to talk to him—to *confirm* the sites."

When I'd denied it, Rahr had practically shouted at me over the phone, saying he was sick of being sabotaged by people who were supposedly on his team. Then he had hung up. The reason I hadn't told Knott about it as soon as I realized that Rahr was the freezing victim was that I didn't think it was important. Then, when Knott said Rahr had been murdered, I figured he didn't need me telling him about Rahr's long-distance temper tantrum with me, since I'd already been removed from the suspect list. It just didn't occur to me that there might have been a lead buried in my conversation with Rahr—that something he'd tossed at me in his anger might be an important clue later in a murder investigation. *His* murder investigation.

Of course, now that I was sitting in Grandma's with a peeved detective on the other side of the table, repeating my reason for omitting to tell him about a phone call with a man who was murdered less than twenty-four hours later, I was becoming increasingly convinced that not only had I been blindingly stupid, but also that I might be facing some kind of criminal charges because of it.

"Stupid," Knott said, shaking his head. "That was stupid, Bob. Never not tell the police something that might relate to their investigation. Eventually they'll find it out anyway, and that makes you look bad."

"Yeah, I got that now," I assured him. "Really. I do. I will never make that mistake again. Trust me." Since he hadn't slapped handcuffs on me yet, I was beginning to hope I still might walk out of Grandma's a free man. "Just out of curiosity, how did you know I had talked with Rahr?"

He took another onion ring from the basket.

"I'm psychic, Bob. But no one can know. In fact, now that I've told you, I'll have to kill you."

"Give me a break."

"I already have. You'll notice the cuffs are in my pocket and not on your wrists." He finished the onion ring and wiped his hand on his napkin. "Your emails and phone messages, Bob. We got Rahr's computer and phone records, and you were all over them the last two weeks. Didn't take a rocket scientist to track that down."

Our burgers arrived, and he waited till the waitress was gone to lean towards me. "Plus, there's a certain secretary at the BSB who apparently listens in on phone calls and was happy to tell me about Rahr getting in your face."

"Let me guess. Alice Wylie."

"One and the same. You know her?"

I told him about my visit to the university. "But I'm not too sure about the one and the same part," I said. "She can switch personas faster than any drama queen I've ever worked with at a high school. In counselor-speak, I'd say she's got issues."

"I don't know about that," Knott said, "but she's just odd enough to set off some alarms for me." He took a big bite of his burger, chewed and swallowed. "I checked with Human Resources at the university and—get this—I found out that Rahr wanted Alice gone. She'd been his secretary for the past eight years, but three weeks ago, he told HR to transfer her because she was—and I quote—'manipulative, intrusive and unreliable.' Pretty strange, coming from a man she'd worked with for eight years already. Anyway, much to HR's relief, Alice jumped at the move to the environmental sciences department and started there on Monday."

No surprise there. After seeing her with Ellis, I had no doubt why she had jumped. I polished off my burger and washed it down with ice water. "Settled right in, didn't she?"

"Yup." Knott reached for his coffee. "I guess that day off on Friday was just what she needed to make the transition."

"Friday?"

"Friday," Knott repeated. "It seems that weird Alice wasn't at work. So far, I don't know where she was."

A piece of my conversation with Ellis popped into my head.

"When Ellis told me he left town to see his father, he started to say he left on Saturday, then he corrected himself to say Friday." I looked directly at Knott. "He said he was confused about dates. Was it a slip of memory . . . or a slip of the tongue?"

"Good ear, Bob," the detective replied. "If Ellis said he left Friday, he was feeding you a line. We checked flight lists. Ellis didn't leave on Friday. He left on Saturday. I don't know where *he* was on Friday, either."

He caught the waitress's attention and ordered us both a slice of apple pie.

"But I intend to find out. I've got an appointment with Dr. Ellis at two o'clock." He took another sip of coffee. "And since we're sharing secrets now, I'll even tell you about the fingerprints on the hammer."

"You're kidding me," I said. "You *got* fingerprints off a hammer in the snow?" Then I realized he hadn't sounded exactly ecstatic. "Whose are they?"

"You're right, I am kidding. Unfortunately. We didn't get fingerprints off a hammer in the snow. But Mrs. Rahr identified it. The hammer belonged to her husband."

For a minute, I didn't say anything. The hammer was Rahr's? Rahr was spiking trees? Alan had said that was a tactic of environmental terrorists to stop tree cutting, but Rahr's sites were protected. That battle had already been fought. So, why was Rahr spiking trees now?

"We've got nothing at this point," Knott finally sighed, frustration evident in the tone of his voice. "We've talked to all his associates, his friends, his wife, and all we've got are more questions, missing alibis, spiked trees, a hammer, and a trail that's getting colder by the minute. And I'm not talking about the weather. Even S.O.B is taking us nowhere. We've run a check on all their members and we can't trace that letter to anybody."

To emphasize his point, he mashed the last bit of piecrust flat on his plate.

"Now I'm thinking that letter might just have been from some wacko who wanted attention and gets off on making anonymous threats to frighten people," he said. "I talked with a detective in Minneapolis yesterday, and she said it's not that uncommon for people involved in environmental controversies like Rahr was last spring to get letters like that from people who aren't even connected to any of the principal players. Mrs. Rahr did say her husband seemed upset about something for the last few weeks, but he wouldn't tell her what it was. She said every time he went up to check out his Boreal Owl sites, he came back agitated. So I keep having this gut feeling that there's a key in the location, but I just can't find it. If you hadn't found him, who else would have? Who goes up there to that particular spot?"

"Well, actually, I can think of two people who might," I said.

"Two?"

"Yeah."

Knott held up his hand and ticked off his fingers. "Ellis."

"Yeah."

"Alice?"

"I just said Ellis."

"No. Alice. Not Ellis."

"The secretary?"

"She was Rahr's secretary for eight years. She typed the reports. She had to know the sites, didn't she?"

Of course she knew the sites. On paper. That's what she had passed along to Stan, enabling him to find the sites for locating the Boreals. Stan was the second person I had been thinking of who knew the sites. But Alice herself in the forest? I hadn't considered that. A scary thought, to be sure. No telling who she'd turn out to be in the middle of the night in the deep, dark woods. I seriously doubted it would be Little Red Riding Hood.

Knowing now about Alice's tipping off Stan about the Boreal sites, I could begin to see where Rahr's angry comments to me on the phone might have come from. He'd said that someone was sabotaging him. Someone who was supposed to be on his side. After the MOU meeting, I had assumed Rahr was referring to Ellis, but now I had to wonder if, instead, he had caught Alice passing information along to Stan. I guess that could qualify as "manipulative, intrusive and unreliable." Although I questioned if it was enough to warrant terminating an eight-year working relationship. No wonder Knott had been so interested in what Rahr had said to me on the phone—and angry that I hadn't told him sooner.

But, as it turned out, that bit of anger was a drop in the bucket compared to how he felt after I told him about the letter on my bird feeder.

And the phone call.

And the dead owl.

And my conversation with Stan.

I thought he was going to have a stroke.

Or lock me up.

Or both.

Chapter Thirteen

"What the hell do you think you are doing?" he exploded. All the heads in Grandma's turned in our direction.

"Please," I smiled at all the restaurant patrons, "excuse my friend. He's having a bad day."

"I sure as hell am *now*," Knott spit out, though at a lower decibel than his previous remark. "And when were you going to let me in on these little tidbits of trivia, Bob? At your funeral?"

Okay. When he put it like that, I had to admit everything did look a lot grimmer than I had wanted to believe. If we were talking about my funeral, then getting suspended from work really wasn't such a big deal after all.

"I'm telling you now," I pointed out to him. "See, this is why I wasn't thinking it was so urgent. I'm okay. I'm in one piece. I'm breathing."

"Only because I'm not choking you to death."

I took a long drink of water to give myself a minute to think. "I didn't see how this could help you with your case," I finally said. "I thought it was Stan jerking my chain, and then, by the time I realized it wasn't him, it was late last night, and I was going to be seeing you today anyway."

Knott dragged both of his hands through his already unkempt hair. I hoped he found it a soothing gesture because it didn't do squat for his personal appearance. After a moment or two, he propped his elbows on the table and buried his right fist in his left hand. His eyes locked on mine.

"This is what we are going to do. First of all, we are going to have every person in the department who knew your name on Sunday make a list of every person they talked to in order to try to track down who sent you the note. The fact that it happened so fast after recovering Rahr's body has to mean there's an important connection between the two, and we need to find it. At this point, I'm leaning towards it being an S.O.B. member, so I'll have Ms. Montgomery take another run through the membership roles and see if she can remember anything unusual about anyone."

That made sense. I nodded in agreement.

"The second thing we're going to do is get Alice in for a thorough questioning. Ms. Multiple has things she's not telling us, I'd bet money on it. As for Ellis, I'll decide what to do with him after our little chat this afternoon. As for Stan, I'm guessing from what you said that he's some kind of federal agent on a case, and that's why we're getting nowhere trying to track him down. Assuming, of course, that he was telling you the truth, and wasn't just laying more smoke screen."

"Yeah," I said. "I'm wondering about that, too. Especially since Alice is his sister. I wouldn't exactly call that a great character reference. For all I know, he could be her evil twin."

Knott shrugged.

Good. More anxiety. Just what I was hoping for.

"And the last thing we're going to do," Knott said, "is keep you out of the woods."

No!

"No! John, I've only got a tiny window to get this owl. You can't be serious. Look!" I spread out my arms to include everyone in the diner. "No one's stalking me today. No one even knows I'm in Duluth except for you and Stan."

Knott rolled his eyes.

All right, maybe the fact that Stan knew I was here wasn't the most comforting thought, especially since I'd just conceded I didn't know how far I could trust him.

And then I had a brilliant idea.

"John, what if I had Stan go birding with me? Then I wouldn't be alone, and even if he wanted to, he'd be crazy to kill me because I'll tell him that you know he's with me."

I stopped to mentally review what I had just said: "he'd be crazy to kill me." Well, that would be one way to put that rumor to rest, wouldn't it? For once and for all, everyone in the MOU would finally know if Scary Stan really was looney tunes. Of course, if he was, then I'd also be very dead. I barreled on.

"And that's making the worst case assumption that he wants to kill me, which I really don't think is the case. Yeah, he wants the owl, but he told me that I'm not the 'contract' he's working on. Let's face it—he's had plenty of opportunities already if that was his intention. Besides, my gut is telling me to trust him on this one. Come on, John. He's a birder. We speak the same language. Sort of. Give me a break here."

Knott studied my face and sighed. "All right, Bob. Bird with Stan. But keep in touch. And I better not hear any crying from you if you end up dead." He tossed his napkin on his plate. "It's the location, Bob. I'm sure of it. Whoever is behind your threats wants you to stay out of the forest. That's clear. So there must be something up there that they don't want you—us—to find."

"Boreals, John. There are Boreals there."

He shook his head. "And I'm saying that still doesn't work for me, Bob. Why would someone who wanted to protect the owls kill Rahr, the one person who's been their biggest champion? And why are you the only birder being warned to stay away from those same owls?"

I hadn't thought of that. If other birders were getting threats, it would have been all over the MOU email. As it was, no one had made a peep about anonymous warnings.

"I'll tell you why," Knott offered. "Because you've got the reputation of being one of the best birders in the state. Persistent. Rahr's killer knows you'll be back, and that's a problem for him, because he doesn't want anyone in the area. I'm convinced that if we can figure out why that is, then we'll be able to figure out who the killer is." He placed some bills on the table with the check and stood up. "It's the location, Bob. I'd bet money on it."

We pulled on our coats and headed for the door. His reasoning made sense, but I had the feeling that we were still missing something. Exactly what, I didn't know.

Besides the name, address and motive of Rahr's killer, I mean.

"One last thing," Knott said. "I know this is a long shot, but do you happen to know if Rahr used eyeglasses?"

"I have no idea," I answered. "Why?"

"We found some under his body. At first, we assumed they were his, but his wife told me he rarely used glasses at home, and she didn't recognize this particular pair. Just grasping at straws, Bob, but right now, it's the only tangible thing I've got."

He held the diner door open for me. A brisk wind was coming off the lake.

"By the way," he said, "I'm curious. After talking to Ellis, have you decided what you're going to tell the MOU board members?"

I pulled my collar against my neck. "I'm going to say that I've made up my mind." I paused for extra drama. "I've decided to go with the cheese curds."

Knott laughed. "Smart ass."

Not nearly smart enough, I thought. Knott was way ahead of me—he already knew that Ellis and Alice both had no alibis, but possible motive. He was as good at what he did as I was at birding, and I was one of the best in the state, if I do say so. Being around Knott on the trail of a killer almost reminded me of myself chasing down elusive birds—there's this intense focus that, at the same time, sucks in data from all kinds of physical and sensory sources. Some of my birding friends even joke with me that once I set my sights on chasing down a bird, the bird doesn't have a chance. As I watched Knott walk away from the diner, I had the feeling that the same could be said of him.

Then again, I had yet to score a Boreal. I silently wished Knott better luck with his hunt than I'd had so far with mine.

Since it was only early afternoon and I had hours before I could try to owl—assuming I could track down Stan—I drove over to the airport, where someone had spotted a Snowy Owl earlier in the week. Although I'd already seen one this winter, I have a soft spot for the big guys—the Snowy was my original nemesis bird, and it took me nine years to get my first one.

I was in high school when I started that particular chase. Every winter, as soon as I got home from school, I checked the list serve to see if anyone was seeing a Snowy Owl close enough to the cities for me to get out and see it before it got dark. Of course, in the winter, in Minnesota, it's dark by four in the afternoon, so that left me a window of barely an hour to get out and look. I think I must have chased after one about six times each winter and never got it.

Then, one winter—I was out of college and doing a stint with the DNR—it was like people were seeing Snowy Owls everywhere. I went after one that had been seen about forty minutes from where I lived, but two blocks down the road from my place, I was at a stoplight, and lo and behold, a Snowy Owl flies in and perches on the power lines right next to the road. I couldn't believe it. Nine years of driving all over the state, and I finally find the owl within walking distance of my apartment.

When I'd told Luce that story, she had laughed and noted that the Snowy Owl was a generous bird. I replied that after nine years, it could afford to be.

Since then, I've seen a Snowy almost every winter. It was like once I got it, the game was over. But I still liked to see them, big and white, gliding noiselessly, gracefully, over open fields looking for rodents. That's why the airport in Duluth was a good place to find them. Unlike the Boreals who hide out in thick forests, Snowy Owls take up residence near open spaces; the flat grassy areas around airport runways provide a veritable buffet of small prey for the owls.

I drove the road that bordered the airport's property and looked for the bird. Sure enough, I spotted the owl on the top of a large ridge of snow piled beyond a runway. His big white body almost blended in with the snow on which he was perched, though the snow was looking dingy, probably a result of jet exhaust. After a minute or two, he swept down to nab his afternoon entrée, a rodent who had brashly broken cover to cross the field, unaware of the owl's hungry surveillance.

For some reason, I thought of Knott and his meeting with Ellis, but while I could easily picture Knott swooping down on Ellis, I just couldn't imagine Ellis as either a helpless rodent or unaware. If Ellis was Rahr's murderer, I was afraid that Knott would be in for a long, tough chase and an elusive solution to a murder case.

Which could only mean bad news for me and an unlikely return to work by Monday . . . if at all.

Suddenly, I felt like the Snowy's snack, exposed and helpless in the face of what was happening around me. I didn't like Knott telling me I couldn't bird alone. I didn't like my job hanging in the balance. I especially didn't like getting threats and finding dead birds on my deck. In fact, I wasn't going to take it. Not any more. I turned the car around and headed back to the university.

My gut agreed with Knott's—an important key to Rahr's murder was in the location. So that's where I was going. But this time, I was keeping the detective firmly in the loop. No more secrets. I was going to take him along with me.

Chapter Fourteen

When Knott walked out of the BSB shortly after two o'clock, I was waiting for him at the curb. I hopped out of the car, told him I was going up to the scene of the crime and wanted him to tag along. He cocked his head, apparently considering my offer, then said to give him five minutes. I watched him jog to his car, slide into the driver's seat and make a couple of phone calls. Then he jogged back and climbed into my passenger's seat.

"So what's the plan, Sherlock?" he asked.

I groaned silently when I saw that he was grinning. "Let me guess. Alice complained to you that I was there this morning, asking a lot of questions and upsetting her."

"Actually, she said you were upsetting Dr. Ellis. And she asked me to keep curiosity-seekers and nut cases away from the Environmental Sciences Department. If you hadn't already told me at lunch about your visit here, I might have been concerned that you were doing a little investigating of your own on the side. But seeing as I was forewarned, I handled Alice very diplomatically." He made an obvious display of checking my speedometer reading. "I thanked her for her sharp attention and told her I'd run a thorough background check on you, and that you wouldn't be bothering her or Dr. Ellis again. That made her happy."

"Is my speed a problem for you?"

"Not for me. I'm not the one with the reputation for attracting traffic citations."

Great. Why was I not surprised that he knew?

"When I told the dispatcher I was going into the woods with you, she laughed and said I should make sure my seat belt was fastened. You're a famous man, Bob. Not only are you a hot shot birder in the state, but you've got the whole Minnesota highway patrol looking out for you."

Unfortunately.

"So, I repeat, what's the plan?"

I told him how his insistence at lunch about the importance of location had stuck with me and that I was tired of waiting for some breaks in the case when my job was riding on the line.

"I'd thought I'd convince you to call Mr. Lenzen and threaten him to reinstate me," I said, "but then I realized it wouldn't do any good. He may be a stubborn ass . . . assistant principal, but I can't fault him for doing his job as he sees fit."

Whether or not I agreed with it.

"Besides, no matter how I resist it, it seems like I'm attached to this murder," I told Knott, "or it's attached to me. Either way, I want the whole thing to go away, so I can go back to work and not worry about anonymous phone calls or someone delivering dead birds to my doorstep. But the only way that's going to happen is for you to solve the case, and I figure—I'm hoping—that our two brains together can do it faster than just yours alone."

I took a curve a little on the fast side, and Knott braced his arm against his door.

"Why would someone kill an owl researcher?" I asked, my eyes back on the road. "Yeah, Rahr could be difficult, but murder? The man studied birds. I mean, birding is a great hobby. It's safe, fun, always in season, and you get to be outside. What's not to love? For cripe's sake! I spend the end of every summer out at the state fair, promoting birding as the perfect way to enjoy and appreciate the rich natural diversity of the great state of Minnesota. And now, one of the country's most distinguished ornithologists gets whacked while he's out birding. It isn't exactly a ringing endorsement of the hobby, John. Just the opposite—who wants a hobby that can get you killed?"

"NASCAR drivers?"

I couldn't stop a smile. "Besides them. Sorry. I guess the stress is getting to me."

"No apology needed."

I glanced over at him. He wasn't looking too happy himself.

"I take it the meeting with Ellis wasn't productive."

"Nada. Zip. He says he spent Friday at home, getting ready to leave on Saturday. His dad was hospitalized early that morning, and he got the call shortly afterward. The hospital and phone records concur. We only talked half an hour. He had some meeting to go to."

Neither of us said anything for a couple of minutes.

"I know the feeling, Bob. I feel like time's running out on me, too. Almost a week after the fact and no arrest. Doesn't look good for the detective in charge."

"That's why I figured we needed another approach here," I said. "You're right. We've got to be missing something else—besides the murderer."

"Yeah, I know," Knott agreed. "But you've got to admit, Ellis and Alice make some good suspects. They've got opportunity, motive—maybe—and means. I'd bet either one of them could have taken on Dr. Rahr. Ellis is a brick house, and Alice looks pretty strong."

"Ellis's motive would be?"

"Revenge for past slights—real or imagined—and the desire for professional advancement and recognition by taking on the owl study. Publish or perish, isn't that how it goes? Cutthroat academia."

Exactly what Luce and I had speculated when we were playing amateur sleuths earlier in the week. Except now, it didn't seem like playing at all. Now, the stakes were a lot higher. Knott and I were looking for a killer.

In hopes I wouldn't be his—or her—next victim.

"And Alice?"

Knott considered, then shook his head. "Not sure, there. Like you said, she's an odd duck. Could be anger at Rahr that he booted her out after eight years, or her infatuation with Ellis. After Ellis took off for his meeting, I went back to HR and tried to get more details about Rahr's complaint against Alice. You were right, Bob. He'd caught her passing along his most recent research data to someone—Stan, obviously—without his consent. Or maybe she wanted to do a big favor for Ellis, thinking she could advance his career and win his affection by getting rid of Rahr. Who knows? Maybe they were even in it together."

If that were the case, I didn't expect their association to last very long. When I'd seen Ellis and Alice together that morning, he had seemed pretty annoyed with her. I know the last person I'd trust in a murder plot would be someone who seemed as unstable as Alice. And even after as brief an interaction as I'd had with Ellis, he did not impress me as someone who suffered fools gladly.

Which reminded me of Lily, and the showdown with Stan that was sure to come when she found out he'd been using her. He may have been some kind of professional agent, but I sure didn't see that making any kind of difference to Lily's way of thinking. When it came to picking a fight, Lily was an equal opportunity pugilist.

Which made another possibility pop into my head. I didn't like it at all, but I had to cover all the bases. I kept my eyes on the road and spelled it out for Knott.

"Or maybe Alice hired her brother Stan to kill Rahr. He did admit to being a hired gun who did contract work. And he knows the forest, John. Plus he didn't seem too surprised when he saw Rahr's body last Saturday night. You have to wonder, don't you? I know I'm taking a chance that he's being honest with me, that he's not setting me up as his next victim, but Rahr might be another matter altogether. "

I took a quick glance at Knott. He was frowning and staring straight ahead. "Yeah," he finally muttered. "You have to wonder about a lot of things."

We were out of the city and the road was dry. Traffic was practically non-existent into the forest during this time of year. I took a quick glance at my speedometer. I was driving just over the speed limit. Knott obviously noticed me checking my speed because he chuckled.

"You are a speed demon, aren't you?"

I shrugged noncommittally. "I don't mean to be. It's just that my car speed isn't important to me, I guess. When I'm chasing a bird, what's important is getting to the next birding location. Location, location, location, as my—"

"Real estate agent would say," Knott finished for me. "Yeah, I've heard that one, too. My mother bought a condo last month, and I thought the whole buying process was going to kill me before she finally closed on it. If her agent had said the word 'location' to me one more time, I was going to shoot her."

"But it's true for birding as well as real estate," I explained. "Location is key. If you know where the bird showed up before, chances are better than good that you'll find it there again."

An old green pick-up truck zipped up behind me, then flew past in the straightaway. I caught a fleeting glimpse of letters stenciled on the driver's right jacket sleeve: DNR. Department of Natural Resources. My old employer. Maybe my future employer if Knott didn't get this case solved. The truck must have been going eighty-five.

"Where's the highway patrol when you need them?" I muttered.

"So," Knott was saying, "you think that if we know exactly where Rahr was working, we'll find the reason he was

killed there, too?" He shook his head. "We've already looked, Bob. We didn't turn up anything, except spikes in the tree, a hammer, and a pair of reading glasses."

"But maybe I'll see it differently. You weren't looking at it the way a birder would. That's why I wanted to see the site in the daylight. It's not that much further. I hope you've got your hiking boots on."

We pulled into the same parking area where I'd parked last Saturday night. Forty minutes later, we were deep into the woods, slogging through muddy stretches on the trail where the warmer temperatures of the past few days had made inroads on the snow cover. The trail looked wider than I had remembered—probably the result of being tramped down by all the police personnel who must have passed this way as they secured and investigated the murder scene. In the daylight, the woods didn't seem nearly as dense as they had that night, but now I could see how hilly this particular area was. Little ravines riddled the hillsides, some plunging sharply just off the trail, while others were barely a crack in the earth. In another two or three weeks, the snow melt would produce all kinds of flowing streams down those ravines, making the ground even spongier than it was already beginning to feel underfoot. Later on, petite ladyslippers would sprout up amidst the rocks and earth. I suspected that the investigators were grateful they hadn't had to bring in any heavy equipment for their work, because if they had, it would probably be getting mired in mud by now.

"Are we there yet?" Knott called from behind me, about twenty yards down the slope I had just crested. Lost in thought, I had gone into my automatic hiking mode, making long strides that often left other birders behind. I stopped and turned around.

"Two more bends in the trail, I think," I shouted back.

Something whizzed past my head, and the white pine trunk next to the trail exploded. A loud crack echoed in the woods.

"Get down!" Knott yelled.

He didn't have to say it twice. I was already dropping into the mud and tasting dirt.

Damn! I thought. *Some idiot was shooting in the forest!*

And then I thought again. *Double-damn! The idiot was shooting at* me*!*

The next thing I knew, Knott was beside me, crouched, a gun in his hand.

"Are you all right? Did you get hit?"

I lifted my head and looked at him. I couldn't think of a single thing to say.

"Bob!"

I blinked. "Maybe I should rethink the part about birding being a safe hobby?"

Knott let out a soft whistle and helped me up. I swiped snow and mud off my parka and jeans. "This has never happened to me before. Swear to God."

"You've never fallen in the mud?"

I gave Knott the evil eye. He grinned.

"Being shot at," I clarified. "I've never been in someone's rifle sights before, let alone felt a bullet go by."

Although, I reminded myself, that wasn't entirely true. Just last weekend, Stan had fired a gun just yards from me to scare Smokey the Bear away. But that shot had been for the bear, not for me.

Hadn't it?

Knott scanned the forest in the direction the bullet had come. "Whoever it was, is gone now. I couldn't see anyone from where I was, down there. But up here . . ." He spread his arms to include the open area where we were standing. "You were a sitting duck, Bob."

I stared at Knott. "Gee, thanks for sharing. I feel so much better."

Actually, I wasn't feeling better at all. My legs were feeling weak, and I thought I might throw up. Knott grabbed my arm and put his other arm around my back, bending me forward at the waist. Then he pushed his hand against the back of my neck. "Push against my hand," he ordered.

I did, and the nausea went away. After a minute, my legs felt stronger, too. I straightened back up.

"Not fun," I said.

"No, not fun," he agreed. I thought he looked angry.

"You don't think it was a random shot, do you?"

"Do you?"

I shook my head slowly. "This is protected land. There shouldn't be anyone up here with a gun, let alone someone shooting it." I looked Knott in the eye. "It makes me think we've got to be on to something. Something about the location."

"I'm sure of it, now," Knott agreed. "But I'll be damned if I know what it is."

He looked around again. The last bit of the day's sun was lighting up the hillcrest where we stood. There must have been a fire here at some point, I guessed, to have cleared this space in the middle of the forest. It was getting dusky and I couldn't make out any blackened stumps, though. Had it been logged at some point? There were plenty of old logging trails in the area, so I supposed that might have been the case.

"Let's get out of here," Knott said. "I don't want to encourage another shot just in case the shooter's still around, and I sure don't want to be here after dark."

That made two of us. Earlier, I had considered sticking around for nightfall to listen for the Boreal, but after being somebody's target practice, I chucked that plan. There were other places to hunt the owl, and right now, they were looking real good to me. Places where I hadn't found a body or gotten shot at.

"By any chance, did you tell anyone you were going to be up here this afternoon?" Knott asked as he drove my SUV towards Duluth. He'd insisted I take the passenger seat for the ride back to town, in case I got a delayed shock reaction, but I figured it was just an excuse to keep me away from the gas pedal. "A long shot, I know, but I've got to ask."

I groaned at the metaphor, and he grinned brazenly.

I did. Knott was wondering, just as I was, if I'd inadvertently invited the shooter to follow me up to the Boreal trail. Since leaving home this morning, the only people I'd talked with were Ellis, Alice, Stan, and Knott. And Chris Maas, the highway trooper. Since I doubted the trooper had been tailing me all day, that left Ellis, Alice, and Stan. Both Ellis and Alice knew I was going to Rahr's site this afternoon, I realized. Ellis had asked to see me after three, which would have been after his meeting with Knott. I'd told him I was coming for a look up here in the daylight. And Alice had been in the doorway, hanging on Ellis's every word.

"Alice and Ellis," I told Knott. "They both heard me say I was planning to come here. I'm meeting Ellis for a drink after dinner tonight. We're supposed to talk about the study."

"Let me know if he doesn't show up," Knott said. "Or if he's surprised that you do."

Two hours later, I walked into the room I had reserved at the hotel where I always stay when I bird in Duluth—The South Pier Inn. But as I reached for the light switch, I could feel the hairs on the back of my neck stand up.

Someone besides me was in the darkened room.

I froze, my hand mid-air. Across the room, a figure was silhouetted against the big window that looked out on the lake.

My heart hit my throat so fast, I gasped. Scenarios flew across my brain like geese against the moon, and none of them were nice. I wanted to leap back out of the room, but my legs had somehow solidified, rooted themselves in the carpet.

I stared at the shadow, knowing my death was upon me.

There was so much more I wanted to do in life. I wasn't through yet.

I could almost see the headlines of the Duluth Herald: "THE SECOND BIRDER IN A WEEK KILLED."

And I was just going to stand there and let it happen.

The figure slowly spun around.

"Hey, gorgeous," Luce said.

Chapter Fifteen

And my world began to spin as usual again. Breath came to my lungs, and my spinning brain focused on one object. Luce. I walked across the room and wrapped my arms around her, holding her tightly against me. All the horrible thoughts and fears evaporated. She made me feel safe and secure. She slid her hands around my neck, and I kissed her long and hard.

"Gee, maybe I should surprise you more often," she whispered.

She had no idea.

"What are you doing here? I thought you were filming on Saturday."

"Change of plans. The station called first thing this morning and wanted to film at noon, so we got it done. I decided I deserved a long weekend—with you—so here I am."

I hugged her again. "You don't know how happy I am to see you." Close encounters with a bullet can do that, I guessed. Fearing imminent death sure could, too. I mean, I'm always happy to see Luce, but this was more than happy. This was more like ecstatic. So ecstatic, I practically had her in a death grip.

"I'm beginning to get the idea, Bobby," she wheezed. After a minute, she pushed me away. "Hey, your clothes are damp. What were you doing, wading in after the ducks on the lake?"

I kissed her one more time. "Sit down. Let me tell you how my day went."

I kicked off my boots, stripped off my parka and sat down next to her on the bed, then filled her in on the details, starting with the note on my bird feeder and ending with the dive into the mud and the *whiz* of the bullet. When I got to the part about being someone's clay pigeon, those Norwegian blue eyes of hers turned into ice.

"And Knott didn't do a thing?"

"Luce, he was at the bottom of a hill. He couldn't see anything but the slope ahead of him. The gunfire came from the other side. By the time he got to where I was, the shooter was long gone."

"You don't know that!" Beneath her protest, I could hear some anger creeping into her voice. "I can't believe you guys walked back. What if you'd gotten shot at again and this time, you'd gotten hit?"

She smacked my shoulder with her fist.

"Ow! What was that for?"

"For doing such a stupid thing! I should be smacking your head. What were you thinking?"

Maybe I should have skipped telling her the shooting part. I didn't know she'd get violent.

"And you got another ticket! I swear, I let you out of my sight for five minutes and you get in trouble."

And then she burst into tears.

"Hey, Luce, it's not that big of a deal," I told her. "I didn't lose my license."

She tried to sock my shoulder again, but I caught her hand and pulled her close. I put my arm around her shoulders and brushed a few blonde strands off her forehead. I tried the one thing I knew would distract her.

"Want to go eat?"

She sniffed and blinked a few times to clear the tears from her eyes. "Yes," she whispered. "Can we try that little bistro I told you about?"

Twenty minutes later, we were going north on the shore road to the Grand Superior Lodge's new restaurant. It was a cloudless night, and the stars filled the sky in a way they never do in the cities; the road was unlit except by my headlights, and we passed only one car on the short drive to the restaurant.

"Are you sure this is supposed to be a good place to eat?" I asked as I drove. "They're not exactly drawing in hordes, judging from how empty the road is."

"It's still pretty new," Luce said. "And it is a week night. I'm sure they're busier on weekends."

Ahead of us, a deer darted across the road. I remembered the *thunk* Bambi had made last fall when he hit my car. That got me thinking about the deer hooves sitting back in my office in Savage. Was there any possibility that I had stumbled into the rifle sights of an illegal deer hunter this afternoon? I had to admit, that was a much less disturbing—albeit still dangerous—

explanation for the bullet than that it had been specifically intended for me. Could it have been that Knott and I were so focused on Rahr that we had mistaken a simple poacher for a murderer?

I turned to Luce. "Do you know anything about deer hunting?"

Dumb question, I realized. Luce was a chef, not a hunter.

"Of course I do," she answered.

I shot her a quick look of surprise. I've never disguised my total aversion to guns and hunting, but then, I didn't recall her ever broaching the subject, either.

"My dad wasn't going to let the fact that I was a girl dissuade him from sharing hunting weekends with his only child." Out of the corner of my eye, I saw her smiling in the light from the car's instrument panel. "If I can shoot it, I can cook it."

Now there's a recommendation for a woman. Have gun, will get dinner.

"Why?" she asked.

"Just thinking. Maybe that's what happened this afternoon. You know—somebody hunting dinner and they almost got me instead."

"You don't look like a deer, Bobby. Or a stag. Trust me."

"It's the antlers, right? I don't have the antlers. I guess I just can't make that stag fashion statement, huh?"

Luce laughed, but I knew she was right. That, however, meant the shot was deliberate, which was what Knott and I had concluded. The idea that someone was watching me while I hiked in the woods was bad enough; the idea that a shooter was loose in the forest, putting innocent hikers in his rifle sights, was even worse.

And then there was the worst thought of all: that someone had tried to kill *me* in particular. Because in all that forest, there was no way that someone who wanted to shoot hikers in general had just happened to be in the same place with me and Knott. Someone was expecting me.

Stay out of the forest.

And only Ellis and Alice had known I was going to be there.

Ellis. A man who could aim and shoot in the winter woods well enough to compete in biathlon races.

As for Alice, I had no idea of the extent of her talents. Or, for that matter, of her personalities.

Could she somehow have been behind my threats? The idea rippled through me with a little frisson of recognition. If, as Knott had suggested, she had listened to my conversation with Rahr, she would have known I was determined to find a Boreal and that I'd keep coming back to the forest until the owls' mating season was over. And Stan was her brother. He knew I was the one who found Rahr, and he could've delivered the note for her in Savage.

But I just couldn't see him tossing the owl on my deck. He might be a hired gun, but he wouldn't kill a bird.

Of course, Alice could know other people in the Cities as well. She could have friends there. Weird friends. Friends who would help her harass me into staying away from the woods until . . . what? Until her brother found a Boreal before me? Until Ellis had the survey securely in his pocket?

"What about the threatening letter Rahr received?" Luce asked, interrupting my silent speculating. She was still sorting through all the information I'd given her at the hotel. "You said Knott blew it off at first, but after you told him about your threats, and what happened to you guys this afternoon, maybe he should take another look at it, or at the S.O.B. people. Maybe there really is a wacko in the woods up there who thinks he's protecting the owls by scaring off birders."

I told her that Knott was on it. Actually, he and I discussed it ad nauseum on the hike back to the car after the rifle shot. The problem, Knott told me, was that his experts at the department had taken one look at my bird feeder note and were convinced that Rahr's letter and my note were authored by two different people, based on writing style, word choice, yada, yada, yada. Short of someone claiming to have written the notes, there was no way of identifying authorship. The fact that both referred to the Boreal site was, of course, of critical interest for the investigators. However, Knott pointed out, the only information that yielded was that there was more than one person involved in making threats. And to put the icing on the resulting cake of confusion, whether either author was responsible for Rahr's death was anyone's guess.

Knott's experts also agreed with the Minneapolis detective whom Knott had consulted about Rahr's letter: people who write threatening letters about environmental concerns typically don't progress to violent crimes against persons.

Obviously my eight-word note didn't qualify as a letter because someone had certainly progressed to trying to commit a violent crime against me today.

Another deer skipped across the road just ahead of my headlights. Luckily for both of us, my lead foot never dropped at night, so Bambi had plenty of time to scamper off into the bushes. The deer community would have to steal someone else's headlights tonight.

Luce was too quiet in the passenger seat, so I decided to try to lighten the mood. "Did I ever tell you about the time my mom got accosted in the grocery store?"

She turned in her seat to face me. "The grocery store?"

I shot her a quick grin. "Yup. Right in the catsup aisle. I was there with her. I must have been about five years old. My mom had on this sweatshirt that read 'Trust me. I'm a mother.' This woman comes up to her and stands right in front of my mom's shopping cart, blocking her way. She gives my mom this really mean look and says 'I hate your shirt. The last person I would ever trust is a mother. Mine was a lying bitch.'"

"What did your mom do?" I could tell by her voice that Luce wasn't sure if she should laugh or be appalled.

"She very politely smiled and said, 'I'm sorry to hear that.' She turned the cart around and we went back down the aisle the way we had come. When we turned the corner to the next aisle, we both looked back, and the woman was still standing there, looking furious. 'Let's blow this pop-stand,' my mom said, and she took my hand and we walked out of the store—we even left the cart sitting there right at the end of the canned soup aisle with the food we'd selected still in it. When we got home, she told my dad that buying catsup was hazardous to her health."

Luce laughed.

"Bottom line," I said, "is that there are all kinds of people. But very few of them are seriously homicidal. Or at least, we hope not.

"Besides, Knott and I both have the same gut instinct," I told her, "that the scene of the crime is the key here. That's why we went up there today. The fact that I seemed to attract a bullet there confirms our theory: somebody doesn't want anyone wandering around that particular location. The threats I got are dependent on where I am, Luce, not who I am. Otherwise, why wouldn't someone have tried to kill me back home in Savage? What we haven't got, however, is the lock for the key: why. Why would anyone care so much about that particular place?"

"The owls," Luce repeated. "Someone thinks he's protecting the owls."

"From what?" I said, exasperated. Knott and I had been around this mulberry bush at least a hundred times on the ride back to Duluth, and we'd still come up with nothing in our berry buckets to show for the effort. "S.O.B. already got the DNR to make the sites off-limits to loggers. Birders—even groups of them—aren't a threat to the habitat. Of all people, birders are probably the most conscientious about leaving no traces behind them. There has to be something else."

"You know, Bob, you're wrong about your threats not being connected to who you are." Luce reached over and patted my thigh. "Whoever is threatening you must know you well enough to know how determined you can be when you're chasing a bird, and that determination of yours is what's worrying him. He's afraid you won't quit. You won't stay away from the Boreals, and for some reason, that's a very, very big problem for him. If you look at it that way, then your circle of suspects just expanded to include most of the birders in Minnesota. Your reputation precedes you, my dear."

The car rattled a little as we crossed an old bridge over a stream leading down to the lake.

Luce was right. I was well-known to Minnesota birders, as well as state troopers.

Oh, my gosh.

My license plates.

If someone knew I was going to the Boreal site this afternoon, all he would have had to do was watch for my plates to go by. I might as well have a big neon sign on top of the car, flashing, "I'm Bob White. Follow me!"

"What?" Luce asked.

Suddenly paranoid, I was checking my rear-view mirrors, but there was no one else on the road. Then again, I wasn't up in the forest. As long as I stayed away from the Boreals, I was safe. Apparently.

"So, what's there?" I continued, avoiding Luce's question. "Flora and fauna. I don't think a deer bashed Rahr's head, but could there have been a hunter, an out-of-season hunter, whom Rahr caught in the act? Then he killed Rahr to keep him quiet?"

"A poacher, you mean." Luce thought it over. "I suppose it's possible. But those are big woods. How slim a chance is it that a poacher would be in the one place Rahr would be? Or that he'd stick around to take a shot at you today? And the idea that a poacher would kill Rahr to keep from being turned in is a little extreme—remember what I said about money, revenge, and jealousy being the big motivators? It's not like deer are valuable commodities, Bobby. I can't imagine there's a thriving business in deer poaching."

I had to agree with her. This wasn't Africa. There weren't any animals roaming these woods that commanded a big price. Jason had gotten his deer hooves at a garage sale, for crying out loud. And, I had to admit, hearing Luce's thinking about the subject only confirmed my own conclusions about Stan's possible hunting status. It had occurred to me he might have been poaching with his rifle and crossbow last weekend, but, as Luce said, any poacher would be careful to steer clear of anyone else in the forest to avoid getting caught. Likewise, what killer would return to check on the body? Only a very stupid one, and I was pretty sure that was one thing Stan wasn't.

"That's why it makes more sense to think someone followed Rahr there," Luce was saying. "And now, that person is trying to keep other people away, if whoever shot at you today is the same person that killed Rahr. But why? The million-dollar question, right? We just keep coming back to that."

I nodded in the dark and took a right-hand turn into the little dirt lot next to a small building with a broad awning over the door. Beside the door, a large wooden sign in the shape of a waterfall was lit by a spotlight suspended under the eaves of the roof; in a clean script, we could read "Splashing Rock Restaurant." I opened the door for Luce, and we both ducked our heads a little as we went in—we've both been in enough places with low ceilings that it's become sort of a habit. As soon as we were inside, though, low clearance was the last thing on our minds, because the wall facing us was a floor-to-ceiling window looking right out onto Lake Superior.

"Oh, my," Luce breathed.

The hostess took us to our table, one of only about twelve in the white pine-paneled dining room. Luce had been correct when she said the bistro was new, because the scent of the cut pine was still strong in the air. Beyond the window, Lake Superior stretched into the blackness of the night sky; the only way you could tell where the lake ended and the sky began was that below the horizon, moonlight lit up gentle crests of waves as they rocked across the lake, while above the horizon, a million stars twinkled.

"Well, the view is certainly spectacular," I commented. "Let's see how the food measures up."

I ordered us both a glass of red wine to tide us over while we looked at the menu, since I know it takes Luce a long time to order. Not that she's indecisive. She's just that thorough: when we try a restaurant for the first time, she reads through every single description of every single item. I swear she's memorizing ingredients to try back at home in her own kitchen. Anyway, it takes a while, so I settled back to gaze out at the lake and mull over the events of the day. Every so often, Luce would make little noises of interest or surprise as she contemplated the menu, but for the most part, I was on my own.

The more I turned everything over in my head, the more I was convinced that Luce was right about someone following Rahr, because there was no other way to account for the murder taking place at the exact remote spot that only Rahr frequented.

Unless, of course, Rahr brought his killer along with him, but that seemed highly unlikely for several reasons: (1)

everyone Knott had talked with, from Mrs. Rahr to Alice to Ellis to other professors in the department, insisted that Rahr was a loner and that he always worked alone on-site; and (2) Rahr's vehicle was found parked at a trailhead, so if he'd brought someone along, they would have had to hitch back to town on a sub-zero day; and (3) there was no reason to hike that far into the woods to do the deed when the killer could have done it just as easily a whole lot closer to the road.

If I went with the scenario of Rahr being followed, that would better explain the location of the murder, because the Boreal site was Rahr's destination. Once he was working there, he wasn't a moving target, but—as I'd just experienced myself this afternoon—a sitting duck. Did Rahr know he was being tailed? If he did, that might explain the hammer as a weapon of defense, though that sounded like an awfully weak conjecture, I had to admit, since you'd have to be anticipating close combat to use a hammer. We're talking owl research here, I reminded myself, not commando training. So if I dumped the idea about the hammer as weapon, that left the hammer as tool—for spiking trees, apparently. And why would Rahr be doing that? According to Alan, people—make that environmental terrorists—spiked trees to keep the trees from being cut down. But S.O.B. had made sure the trees weren't going to be cut down by convincing the DNR to stay out of the forest to protect the Boreal Owls' habitat.

Luce made an "Ooh" noise and licked her lips. I assumed she was reading the dessert suggestions.

Which brought me to two conclusions: there was something sinfully chocolate on the dessert menu, and for some reason,

Rahr thought that trees around the Boreals were in danger of being cut, so he went to extreme measures to stop that from happening.

But then someone stopped him.

Chapter Sixteen

I drained my wine glass and looked around the Splashing Rock. Only two small tables were empty, including one in the corner two tables away from us. As I watched, the hostess brought another couple to be seated there. The man sat down with his back to me, and the woman sat down on the other side, facing him. I noticed she had the same wavy chestnut hair like my mom.

It was Margaret Montgomery, the director of S.O.B.

I blinked.

She was still there.

Coincidences everywhere lately.

I waited until we ordered—it was the arugula salad and venison medallions with roasted garlic potatoes for me, while Luce went for the lingonberry vinaigrette salad and pan-seared walleye with champagne sauce (having Luce for a girlfriend, I notice these things now)—before I excused myself and went to Montgomery's table.

"I'll be right back," I told Luce.

As I approached the corner table, I was struck by how much bigger Montgomery looked than my mother. I don't know that she was any taller, but she looked broader and heavier through the shoulders. Off camera, she also looked harder—less like my mom, who wanted to chase you down and cuddle you to death, and more like the kind of mom who gave you stiff kisses once a year on your birthday. Then again, I figured it probably hadn't been an easy week for her with the media hounding S.O.B in the wake of Rahr's death.

"Excuse me," I said. "I happened to notice you being seated, and I wanted to meet you." I held out my hand. "I'm Bob White. I'm a birder, so I'm familiar with your work for the Boreal Owls."

Montgomery smiled and took my hand. A lot of class, I thought. Here I was imposing on her quiet dinner, and she smiled graciously at me. "I'm pleased to meet you, Mr. White. Actually, I know your name, too."

I could feel my eyebrows lifting in question.

"The Minnesota birding community has quite the grapevine, and you're on it regularly. What was that most recent find you posted on MOU's list serve just last week? A Goldeneye, was it?"

"A Barrows Goldeneye." I was both surprised and flattered she made the connection. "I think it was as much a shock to me to see it this early in the year as it was for everyone on the list serve to hear about it." I returned her smile. "I guess it caused quite the stampede of birders to Black Dog Lake."

"So I heard. I also heard you were going to run the state fair booth for the MOU again this year. I'm hoping we can get some S.O.B. literature into your hands. Phil Hovde recommended I contact you."

"Really." This was news to me. Dr. Phil hadn't mentioned knowing the director of S.O.B. I wondered why it never came up at the board meeting when we were talking about Rahr and the owls.

"Yes," Montgomery explained. "I met Phil last summer. He and his wife were spending some time on the North Shore, and one night, they attended a dinner benefit for S.O.B. Well, one thing led to another, and pretty soon we were talking about business investments, and we realized we had some similar interests in that area. As a matter of fact, by the end of the evening, we decided to go in together on a local start-up company as principal investors."

"Really," I said again.

Montgomery's dinner partner cleared his throat.

"Oh, I'm so sorry," she apologized to both of us. "How rude of me. I wasn't thinking. This is my good friend Vern Thompson. He's a bit of a birder, too."

"Bob White," I said, shaking Thompson's hand. The man was probably in his late fifties, and his silvering hair was receding on his temples. He looked like he spent a lot of time outdoors because even in March, his skin looked tanned and weathered.

"Vern and I met last spring. We were both on one of Dr. Rahr's tours up to see the Boreals." Montgomery paused. "I suppose you've heard about Dr. Rahr?"

"Yes," I said. "I did." I would have liked to ask her if she knew of any raving lunatics in the S.O.B. organization who wanted to kill Rahr or shoot at birders, or at me in particular, but decided this probably wasn't the best time or place. I turned to Thompson. "Do you bird often?"

"No, I'm afraid not," he answered. "I started my own business six months ago, and it's keeping me pretty well occupied."

"What business is that?" I asked, glancing beyond him to where Luce had turned around at our table and was waving me back to her.

"It's a wholesale business. I'm a gardener, really."

That explained the tan. Lily has that year-round tan too. The thought of Lily made me pause.

"What did you say was your company's name?"

"I didn't say," Thompson said. "It's VNT. My initials really, but I call the company Very Nice Trees."

Very Nice Trees. What a coincidence.

"Really?" I said, for a third time.

Thompson laughed. "Yes, I know it's not the most original name for a company, but it's truth in advertising."

I remembered Lily saying something to the same effect.

"And where is your business located, Mr. Thompson?" I asked, ignoring Luce's waving, which was becoming more insistent by the moment. I figured I had fifteen seconds max before she started throwing silverware in my direction.

"Oh, it's a ways out of town," he answered. "I have an office in Two Harbors, but the actual stock is located on a piece of land that's a bit of a drive north and west of here."

I nodded and said I didn't want to take any more of their time. I returned our table and sat down. The salads were waiting.

"Spill it, Bobby," she said. "You've got that totally blank look you get after you've had on your politely interested face that covers up your surprised face."

"What?"

"Maybe 'blank' isn't the right way to say it. It's like you're at home but you're really, really far away from the front door."

"What?" I had no idea what she was talking about.

She leaned across the table towards me. Her blue eyes looked almost black in the low light of the café. Wisps of blonde hair trailed out from where she'd piled it on top of her head. She stared at me, and I felt like I was getting sucked into her eyes. She smiled very slowly.

Damn, she was gorgeous.

"Do I have your attention?" she asked quietly.

"You sure do," I said.

"Tell me who those people are, what you talked about and why you're surprised."

Did Luce really know me that well to be able to see through all my counselor faces? Even when they were layered on top of each other? I started to put on my politely interested face before I realized I was doing it.

"Bobby!" she practically hissed at me. She sounded like a Canada Goose defending its territory. I thought it was kind of cute, actually. Not that I'd ever say that to her. Especially when she had a fork in her hand.

I shook my head to clear it and started telling her about my conversation with Montgomery and Thompson.

"So, why didn't you say you wanted to see his greenhouses?" Luce asked, carefully tasting the vinaigrette.

"Because he wasn't exactly inviting me to stop by," I replied. "He didn't offer me a business card, didn't ask me if I had any gardening needs. You'd think someone who's only been in business for six months would still be marketing himself every chance he got. Thompson's not." I stuffed a forkful of arugula into my mouth. "Tomorrow we'll drive out to his place and see it. How's your salad?"

"The lingonberry is a little heavy, I think, but it's still good. I have high hopes for the walleye, though, not to mention the old-fashioned chocolate pudding cake for dessert."

As it turned out, she liked my venison more than her walleye. (She always snitches from my plate—Luce says it's her responsibility and obligation as a professional chef.) The cake, however, was excellent, and Luce begged the owner for the recipe, promising to credit the Splashing Rock when she used it at the conference center.

By the time she had the recipe in her purse, Bradley Ellis showed up in the dining room doorway. It looked like our after-dinner drink was still on. *Two points for you*, I thought. *You're either innocent or incredibly brazen.* He caught my eye and nodded.

He only took a few steps into the room, though, before he made a detour.

A detour straight to Montgomery.

"I hope you got what you wanted," Ellis told her, his voice carrying across the room.

He sounded ticked off. I tried not to listen, but it was kind of hard to miss it. The room wasn't that big, and the other diners weren't making enough noise to cancel out Ellis's volume.

"I don't know what you're talking about," Montgomery said.

"Oh, I think you do, Margaret." He placed his big hands on her table and leaned in. "Weren't you the one just after Christmas who was raising a stink about keeping birders out of Andrew's study sites? To protect the owls during mating season? Well, you got it. Nobody's going to want to go anywhere near those sites now."

Heads were starting to turn at other tables. Ellis didn't care.

"But guess what?" His voice dropped a level or two. "I'm planning to pick up where Andrew left off. That study is *mine*, and there's nothing you can do about it."

"Back off," Thompson said, standing up and stepping close to Ellis. "Margaret is sick about this whole thing. How do you think she feels? She was one of Rahr's biggest allies around here. The Boreals are her bread-and-butter. If you think she'd do anything to jeopardize S.O.B., you're crazy."

He held Montgomery's coat for her. "Let's go."

Montgomery slipped into her coat, and they were gone.

"My, my," Luce whispered. "The roux thickens."

I wasn't thinking about any roux, thickening or otherwise. I was looking at Ellis, wondering if he'd taken a shot at me this afternoon. The man certainly looked angry enough to kill someone.

I just hoped it wasn't me.

I stood up to meet him as he walked toward our table.

"Bob," he said, shaking my hand. His voice wasn't as loud, now.

"This is my friend Luce Nilsson," I said, nodding my head in Luce's direction. "She's also a birder."

Luce held out her hand.

Ellis took it.

Then he covered it with his other hand.

I expected Luce to pull her hand away.

She didn't.

The man was definitely brazen.

"Luce Nilsson," Ellis repeated. He smiled.

Luce smiled back.

I stood there, looking at the two of them. *Die, scum.*

"Put some candles in your hair and you could be Santa Lucia, the Swedish goddess," Ellis told her.

Bad move, buddy. I waited for Luce to shoot him down.

She didn't.

For crying out loud.

"She's Norwegian, not Swedish," I corrected him, since Luce had gone mute. "And Lucia is a saint, not a goddess."

"Oh, no," Ellis said, looking straight at Luce. "She is definitely a goddess."

Luckily for Ellis, Luce laughed. If she hadn't, I was going to punch the man. Not only was he unbelievably brazen, but he was making a pass at my girlfriend.

Instead, I held out my own chair for him. No way was I going to have him sitting next to Luce. "Take a seat," I told him.

He did, and I pulled a chair from the empty table next to us. I nudged Luce over closer to the window and sat opposite Ellis. I felt like a male protecting my territory.

So sue me.

"I didn't know you knew Montgomery," I said to him.

"My mistake," Ellis said. "The woman is a disaster."

"How so?" Luce asked.

Ellis gave her another smile.

Scum.

"Let me count the ways," he said. "She's manipulative, insincere, self-serving and a glutton for media attention."

"That's her job," I said. "She's a lobbyist."

"That's the problem," he replied.

"Can I get you anything else?"

The waitress was back. We ordered a round of coffee.

"Why is that a problem?"

"Because she doesn't care about the Boreals or the study or anything that's really at stake, here," Ellis said. "She's running S.O.B. because she gets paid to run it. She gets paid to champion the owls. She gets paid to look good on television. Take away her salary, and Ms. Montgomery would be out of here so fast, it'd make your head spin."

"That's a pretty cynical assessment," Luce said.

"It's the truth. Margaret Montgomery didn't even live in this state before she was hired on by S.O.B. last year. Andrew told me the owl tours were her idea. He was concerned about bringing people into the owls' breeding grounds, but she convinced him he needed the exposure to generate more support against the logging initiative. Then, two months ago, she does an about-face, telling him he's got to forget the tours for this year. Too risky for the owls, she said."

"Maybe she realized it wasn't a good idea, after all," I suggested. "Maybe she'd realized Rahr was right."

"Or maybe she was feeling the heat from some very generous, well-heeled S.O.B. supporters, who wanted Andrew in control of the study, not her."

Our coffee arrived. I looked out the big window and wondered if Dr. Phil was one of those very generous, well-heeled S.O.B. supporters. He'd known Rahr a long time, after all, and when it came to personal wealth, I'd witnessed the good doctor's largesse on repeated occasions over the years. And now, thanks to Montgomery, I also knew that she and Dr. Phil were acquainted with each other. That they were, in fact, business associates. One business associate, I supposed, could certainly have some influence on the other.

Something clicked in my head. I remembered again Rahr's complaint about sabotage and thinking that Alice's note-passing might explain it, although his reaction to me seemed a bit over the top for an information leak to one birder. Now, considering what Ellis said, perhaps it wasn't Alice's indiscretion at all, but, instead, Montgomery's insistence that he skip the tours that had fueled his anger and suspicions.

Or was it just too many cooks spoiling the broth?

The Boreal Owl study was Rahr's baby. It always had been—at least until a year ago, when the circus, as Alice had called it, came to town. Till then, Rahr didn't have to deal with anyone else when it came to his work with the Boreals. He just did his thing. Even after my short phone call with him, I could definitely see where it would gall him to suddenly have other people telling him how to run his own show.

Of course, he'd had that experience before.

With Ellis.

Luce began laughing at something Ellis said.

"So," I interrupted. "We should talk about the study. What are you thinking?"

For the next half hour, we talked about the owls. When he finished his pitch, Ellis turned to me.

"Tell me what you think. Shoot."

Shoot.

Poor word choice, that's what I wanted to tell him. Especially since I could still almost taste the mud in my mouth from hitting the ground this afternoon to avoid a bullet.

"Shoot" raised a lot of questions.

Like, for instance: was Ellis, by any chance, training for a biathlon earlier today?

But without the skis?

Yet, sitting here now, across from Ellis, I just couldn't see him taking the shots. Oh, I could imagine it. I knew he was skilled and driven and arrogant enough. But it didn't fit. He wanted the MOU Boreal study. He wanted it badly. When he'd spoken to Montgomery, he'd practically rubbed her nose in it. It wouldn't make any sense for him to try to kill the man who could give it to him—namely, me.

I'd promised my MOU colleagues that I'd make a decision about hiring Ellis for the study, and regardless of any lingering suspicions about the nature of his relationship with his former mentor, Ellis was, without a doubt, the man to pick up where Rahr had left off. Since the study was a priority for the board, and letting any more time lapse wouldn't benefit anyone, especially the owls, I put my reservations aside and decided to give him the job.

I'd leave the question of how badly Ellis had wanted the study, and what lengths he may have gone to secure it, to Knott.

"It's all yours," I told him. "I'll let the board know."

Ellis smiled. He seemed to relax. He seemed relieved.

At least one of us was.

I, on the other hand, was nowhere near relieved. I was still thinking about "shoot."

If not Ellis, who?

Who?

I sounded like an owl. For crying out loud.

And now, I had not one, but two mysteries to consider. One: who killed Rahr? Two: who tried to kill me?

I paid the check, and Luce and I got up to leave. Ellis said he'd take a look at the study sites tomorrow and hoped to start collecting data by Sunday. He asked Luce if she'd like to give him a hand, but she declined.

He didn't ask me.

I didn't offer, either.

We left Ellis drinking another cup of coffee and walked out to the car. The air was crisp, but not frigid.

"What do you say we try for the owl?" Luce said. "But not where you went today. One of the other places."

"I say yes."

I remembered my license plates.

"Let's take your car, okay?"

Chapter Seventeen

About an hour later, we parked on the side of an old logging road deep in the woods northwest of Two Harbors. It was the first place Mike and I had tried last weekend. Since it was the farthest site from where I'd been shot at, I was relatively confident that it would be a safe spot for owling tonight.

That and the fact that we'd taken Luce's car.

We got our binos from the back seat, dropped them around our necks and started to hike into the forest.

There was an old trail to follow, so it wasn't rocket science to find our way in. Last Saturday, I had timed our walk to the Boreal Owl site. All we had to do tonight was walk for the same amount of time: about forty minutes. Of course, Luce's legs are a lot longer than Mike's, so we covered more ground faster. After just ten minutes of walking, I could hear some Great Horned Owls calling in the distance.

"They're quite a ways off," I told Luce.

"Just as well," she replied. "I'm sure not interested in walking near any Great Horned Owl nests tonight. They can be just so downright aggressive when they're protecting their breeding grounds."

"Yeah, I know," I said. "My uncle Gus has a scar on the top of his scalp where a Great Horned swooped down on him one night because he was hiking right by a nest. Everyone said it was because of his thick bushy hair—that the owl thought it was a big fat rat being offered for a midnight snack."

"Ow," Luce commented.

I'd also heard of neighbors' outdoor cats permanently disappearing at night. Owls are predators and Great Horned Owls are big, strong birds who will take all kinds of prey, including small pets and other owls. If you hear a Great Horned calling close by, you need to be careful; invading their nesting areas is definitely not a good idea.

Just ask my Uncle Gus.

And Great Horned Owls were way more tolerant of humans than Boreal Owls were.

"Speaking of owls calling, a couple years ago, I went owling with a guy who had just gotten a CD of bird calls," Luce said as we walked along. "He was convinced that finding Screech Owls would be a snap with the CD."

I do that, too. You take along a CD player when you bird and play the call of the bird you're looking for and hope it attracts the bird itself, which then flies in closer to you. You keep playing the CD until the bird either flies into view or you hear it calling back. It works like a charm with some birds. Unfortunately, Boreal Owls don't respond to the recorded call, so I hadn't bothered to bring my player and CD with me this weekend.

"We hiked into this enormous county park after dark and he played the CD maybe twice, and we heard the owl call back from pretty far away. He played it some more, and the owl got closer. He played it again, and the owl got closer still. Finally, we figured it had to be just around this bend in the woods, and when we snuck up as quiet as could be, sure enough, we found it.

"But it wasn't a Screech Owl," Luce added. "It was another birder with the same CD."

I laughed and told her about the time I had the same experience but with a Yellow-billed Cuckoo. I was on a MOU trip, and we were looking for a Black-billed Cuckoo. There were about eight of us driving in two cars, and somebody in the first car saw a Black-billed Cuckoo fly by. So, the first car pulled over and was followed by the second car; we all piled out and looked through binos for the bird. While we were watching for it, our group leader suddenly hushed everyone. He said he thought he'd just heard a Yellow-billed Cuckoo, which would be a real find for all of us. We were standing on the side of the road next to a wooded area, so we figured we'd have to walk in and try to find the Yellow-billed. Our leader took out his CD and played the Yellow-billed Cuckoo call and after a couple tries, we got a reply. We zigzagged through the woods, playing the CD and moving toward the answering calls until we saw a guy approaching us and realized he was a birder trying to get a Yellow-billed, too.

"So there we were, nine birders standing around looking at each other. I think our trip guide was mortified that he'd led us on a hunt . . . to another birder." I put out my hand and touched Luce on the arm. "Stop a minute."

We both stood still and listened. I focused on the sounds of the night, filtering out the sounds of trees creaking, small animals scampering across dead leaves, an occasional whistle of wind. Although the sense of hearing is especially important for birding at night when you don't have the benefit of daylight visibility to help locate birds, it's a necessary talent for every really successful birder. When I was a young birder, my parents always commented on my eyesight. They said I could see birds they couldn't begin to see and that my skill was a gift and especially suited to birding.

Well, that may be true, but as I got older and became a more experienced birder, I realized that my real gift was my acute hearing. After I memorized all the bird calls in Minnesota—maybe 300 of them—on my CDs, I found I could isolate specific calls from among others. That means when I'm looking for one bird, I can listen for its own call even if the air is filled with the songs of other birds. At the same time, I can pick out the calls of all the other birds singing and name them off. The first time I did that with my dad along on a birding trip, he couldn't believe it.

"How do you do that?" he asked, stunned, after I listed off about seven birds calling at the same time, their songs layering over each other. I think it was during a warbler weekend, the time in May when all the warblers are migrating back through Minnesota.

"Do what?" I asked him.

"Hear each bird," he answered. "I can hear them, but I can't begin to separate their songs. On top of that, you can tell where they are. A minute ago, you said there was a Blue-winged

Warbler about a hundred yards up the trail, and sure enough, there it was."

I shrugged. "I can just do it," I said. "I know all the songs. And the distance thing, well, that's just practice. I can tell by the distortion of the sound how far it's traveled."

Like I said, experienced birders rely on their hearing to find birds, probably even more than they do on their sight. If I had to break it down, I'd say eighty percent of my birding—actually finding the bird—is by ear.

"What do you hear?" Luce asked me.

"A pair of Great Horned. A Great Gray Owl."

I was totally still.

"That's all."

We started walking again. The night was cold, but it was nothing like it had been just a week before. My breath still frosted when I exhaled, but the cold air didn't sting the back of my throat every time I inhaled. I was even starting to feel warm underneath my parka as we climbed up and down the trail that wound deeper into the forest.

Finally, after another twenty minutes of hiking, I came to a stop. Luce stood next to me, looking up into the treetops, focusing on branches to see if an owl materialized out of the shadows. Because we were so far from human habitation, there was no light pollution from artificial lights to absorb or scatter the natural light of the moon and stars; the deep patches of snow still on the ground acted almost like mirrors reflecting what natural light there was to further illuminate our surroundings. By now, our eyes were well accustomed to the darkness and given that it was about eleven o'clock at night, we could actually see fairly well, though everything appeared to be in black or varying shades of gray. Through the tops of the bare trees and pines we could see a good portion of the sky and I pointed out the North Star to Luce. It was bright and flanked by other dimmer stars you never see anywhere but out in the wilderness.

"It's almost like the night sky in the Rincons," I told Luce. The Rincon Mountains border the Saguaro National Forest east of Tucson in Arizona. Over the years, I've birded there a few times, and the desert sky never fails to impress me. Clear and clean with an almost unbounded horizon, I don't know another place with starrier skies.

Gazing now into the Minnesota night, I almost jumped when I suddenly realized what I was seeing: too much sky. Too much sky for the middle of a thick pine forest.

"I'll be damned," I breathed.

"What?" Luce asked, craning her neck to look up in the trees. "What do you see?"

"It's not what I see, but what I'm not seeing," I answered her.

Out of the corner of my eye, I could see Luce staring at me, her gloved hands on her parka-covered hips. "What in the world are you talking about?"

"Luce," I said. "Look up at the tree tops. What do you see?"

Luce looked up again. After a moment, she whispered, "Nothing."

"That's right," I agreed. "Nothing. There's nothing there where treetops should be. Someone has cut the tops off these pines."

"Exactly what I was thinking."

I spun on my heel in time to see Stan, in full camouflage battle gear, fade smoothly into the forest.

Chapter Eighteen

"It has to be illegal cutting," Luce insisted at breakfast the next morning.

The sun was well above the horizon by the time we'd taken a table at Amazing Grace, a little café near to our hotel. We'd gotten in so late after our trek into the woods last night, we'd slept in. Normally, when I'm on a birding weekend, I'm up before dawn and breakfast is a cup of coffee and a doughnut purchased at the gas station on my way out. To sit and enjoy a hot, full breakfast was a rare treat.

Except that I kept expecting to see Stan materialize next to me, just like he had last night in the woods. Maybe if I threw syrup on him, he wouldn't be able to disappear. Or if he did, I'd at least see the maple footprints he'd leave behind.

To pass the time, Luce and I had decided to hunt for sea ducks this morning. An early start wasn't necessary; the ducks would be hanging around a good part of the day as long as they found a spot along the shore of Lake Superior where the ice was out. The past two days had been unseasonably warm up here, so there was some heavy melting going on. Both yesterday and last night, I noticed some deep drifts were still in ravines and other sheltered places in the woods, but the trails themselves had been relatively snow-free. Down here, closer to the lake, the snow cover was virtually non-existent.

I took another bite of the house breakfast special—two eggs, two plate-sized buckwheat pancakes, two thick rounds of honey-cured Canadian bacon and a side of home-style hash browns—and tried again, for about the fifth time, to make plausible connections between the topped trees and . . . anything.

I agreed with Luce. The topping had to be illegal. Not only were those trees well within state forests, they were within the Boreal Owls' range, and the DNR had expressly laid down a "hands-off" policy after the S.O.B. campaign last spring. Besides, if the DNR had been involved, they wouldn't be topping trees—they would be cutting them down completely.

"Do you think it was for the lumber?" Luce asked. "If it was, I don't think the cutter knew what he was doing. You'd think that if someone wanted free wood, they'd cut the whole tree down instead of just the top. You'd get a lot more usable wood that way. Although it did seem like quite a few trees were involved when we looked around." She sighed and put her fork into her French toast. "Somebody obviously ended up with a bunch of very nice tree tops."

Very nice tree tops?

I started to choke on the bite of buckwheat pancake in my mouth as I realized what those tree tops would look like.

Very Nice Trees.

Very Nice Christmas trees, to be exact.

"Are you all right?" Luce asked, looking a little alarmed as I coughed.

I nodded and took a drink of orange juice to clear my throat.

"Luce," I finally managed to say. "We've been seeing what we already decided we'd see, but that's not what's really there."

The voices of Kim and Lindsay were suddenly tangling together in my head, and now I was making less sense than they did even on their most articulate days.

"Luce," I tried again. "We were on the right track when we said there weren't any valuable animals roaming the woods that poachers would want. But we forgot about the other half of flora and fauna."

Luce still looked confused.

"Flora," I said. "There are very valuable plants in the woods. Plants that poachers could sell for big money. Those treetops would have made perfect Christmas trees. For some enterprising thief, it was an all-profit venture. No property costs, no overhead." I winced at the unintentional pun. Luce poked my arm with her fork.

"Very funny, Bobby," she said.

I was on a roll.

"If you didn't have any expenses, and you worked alone, already owned your equipment—saws and a cherry-picker, I'd guess—then all you'd have to do is cut and sell and count up the cash. And if you sold your stock out of town to unsuspecting garden shops, they'd never question where you got so many trees. Look how much money Lily made this year from selling

Christmas trees retail. And she's got expenses to cover. The supplier makes even more, especially if his stock is . . . stolen."

Luce laid her fork down next to her plate. "Bobby, are you thinking Lily's trees were poached merchandise?"

"I don't know," I replied. "Lily told me she was thinking that VNT was making offers that were too good to be true. She said their price for stock was so low that she could make a real killing in profit when she turned it around and sold it to her customers. Even without extra markup. The profit margins were so high, it made her uncomfortable. But when she tried to check out the company, she couldn't get any details. That's why I said I'd take a look while I was here. Lily may not be big on intuition, but when it comes to business, she definitely has a sixth sense."

It was true. Lily had an unerring instinct for business matters. She could size up the requirements and risks of a potential landscaping job and make a sound judgment faster than I could choose between two new blends of birdseed. Come to think of it, Lily was the same way with business associates: only the sharpest earned her confidence, which meant that Stan had passed the test. She'd even let him help her with her books, which, for Lily, was probably tantamount to physical intimacy. Now that I was thinking about it, I remembered that she had also mentioned to me that Stan had noticed the big profit margin from the VNT Christmas trees.

Bingo.

Stan was after my sister for her business.

Being an accountant, he knew a good thing—a profitable thing—when he saw it, and he could see that Lily's Landscaping was poised on the threshold of small business success. As a partner, he could give up his "contract" work for steady employment; I could believe that even government agents (if Knott was right about Stan) got tired of job insecurity. All he'd have to do was wave an aggressive, well-researched, new business plan in front of Lily's face, and the next thing you know, they'd be sharing a desk blotter.

Unless, after he'd seen the profit margins from VNT, he'd recognized an even better business opportunity and headed north to make his own appraisal of the company. In fact, maybe VNT was the target he was referring to while we were at Park Point, and the reason he didn't want me to know was so I wouldn't tip off Lily to his true intentions. He did, after all, admit he was using my sister; he knew he was going to pay for it, and pay dearly, but I supposed he figured the financial potential was worth it.

Wrong.

Hell hath no fury like my sister deceived.

In which case, he was probably sweating in his shorts this morning about VNT; he'd seen the sheared tree tops last night as clearly as Luce and I had. If he'd planned to use Lily as a stepping stone to a hefty income opportunity and found out instead that VNT was a front for plant theft, he was going to be out of more than just a bigger paycheck. When I told my sister about the hidden agenda behind Stan's interest in her books, I had no doubt that the feathers were really going to fly.

I took another bite of pancake. I'd defend my sister's honor and deal with Stan the gold digger if and when I got the goods on Lily's shady supplier. "When we check out VNT this afternoon, I'm looking for a cherry-picker," I told Luce. "As far as I'm concerned, that would be as good as a smoking gun."

As long as it wasn't pointed at me, that is.

I paid the bill for breakfast, and we headed out of town for the shore. We drove north till we got to a little turn-off I know and after parking the car, hiked along a stream that led out into Lake Superior. It was a beautiful morning: the sun was out, the sky was clear and blue, and the air had that clean fresh smell that makes you want to fill your lungs with it and take it back home to the city, where the air never smells this good. The lake was brilliant, reflecting the sun so that the whole horizon shimmered between sky and water.

We picked our way between puddles of snowmelt and soggy earth on the shore, scanning the water for sea ducks. In particular, we were hoping to find a Harlequin Duck and Long-tailed Ducks. I held up my binos to get a better look at a dark spot on the water. Luce stood next to me with her binos to her eyes, too. Her parka sleeve brushed mine. I lowered my binos and looked at her. While she studied the waves, I studied Luce.

Her cheeks were pink from walking in the cold, and strands of her blonde hair were sticking out from under her woolen cap. She was as still as I was, perfectly content to spend a cold March morning standing on the shore of Lake Superior, squinting into the distance; I was perfectly content to be standing there next to her. It occurred to me that if someone were spotting us just as we were spotting birds, we'd look like a matching pair with our puffy torsos, capped heads and raised binoculars. We could be a pair of ducks.

Mated ducks.

Some ducks mate for life, you know.

"Luce," I blurted out. "Do you want to get married?"

She put her binos down and looked over the water, then turned to face me. She smiled and didn't say anything for a minute.

"Possibly." She paused. "Probably." She paused again. "Eventually. But not right now."

I released a breath I didn't know I'd been holding. "Just checking," I said. I wasn't sure if I was relieved or disappointed.

"Are you relieved or disappointed?" Luce asked, grinning.

I rolled my eyes in exasperation.

"How do you do that?" I asked, wondering again how it was that she knew me so well. I'm the trained counselor, after all, and I'm supposed to be better at this kind of thing, like being intuitive and being able to hide my immediate reactions.

"I'm psychic, Bobby."

"Right." First Knott, now Luce. Everyone's a comedian.

Then she laughed. "Oh, come on, your expression is a dead give-away. Maybe you can fool other people, but you can't fool me. And you know what?" She placed her lips on mine and kissed me. Even in the cold, her lips felt warm against mine. "That's one of the reasons I love you. You're never anything but honest with me, and even if you weren't, I can read you like a book. And how could I possibly resist that romantic streak of yours? I don't know too many guys who would take me out to freeze on the shore and look at ducks and find it the right moment to bring up marriage."

"They mate for life," I said by way of explanation.

"I know," Luce said. "You sweet-talker, you."

The memory of Ellis making a pass at Luce last night popped into my head. I wasn't the only man attracted to my girlfriend.

"What, by the way, did you find so . . . arresting . . . about Ellis last night?" I hoped I sounded casual, not too concerned—all right, jealous. "You couldn't even talk when you met him."

Luce thought about it for a minute.

"Well, he was certainly an attractive man, and I could say his animal magnetism was almost overwhelming."

Not the answer I was looking for. And way more information than I wanted. The wrong kind of information.

"But that's not what had me speechless." Luce laid her gloved hand on my cheek. "I was so angry, wondering if he'd taken a shot at you, that it was all I could do to keep my mouth shut in a smile and not go for his jugular."

That's my Luce, all right. Eat your heart out, Ellis.

We looked out at the water again and decided to follow the shoreline up to a place where there was a deep, rocky cove. We thought there was a good chance we might find the ducks there, where they'd find shelter from the wind. Sure enough, as we rounded the point of the land, we saw two ducks floating in the cove. We both put up our binos to take a good look.

"Long-tailed, all right," Luce said, smiling. "I haven't seen one in years."

Long-tailed ducks nest in arctic regions and typically stay out farther on the lake, so this was an excellent find for the morning. After watching the ducks for a few minutes, we hiked back to the car and drove to another spot to try for the Harlequin.

This time we didn't even have to get out of the car. We parked at an overlook and there was a very small raft of ducks, bobbing out on the lake. Luce and I both picked up our binos to look and immediately recognized the unmistakable markings of the Harlequin Duck.

"No doubt about it," I said. "They've got their white grease paint on."

Harlequins' faces have such distinctive white spots of coloring that you can't miss them on the water. They're obvious. Transparent, even.

Unlike some people I could name.

People like Vern Thompson, for instance.

Last night, he hadn't exactly been volunteering information about his company. Granted, maybe he just wasn't that good of a businessman and wasn't interested in marketing while he was out on a dinner date, but I just got the sense he was being somewhat evasive. If a stranger asked Lily about her business, she'd whip out the four-color brochure and business cards so fast it would make your head spin, no matter where she was, or what she was doing.

Unless, of course, she was at a Minnesota Wild game. Then she might wait till between periods to make the sales pitch.

I put down the binos and noticed that clouds were moving in. I turned on the car radio to listen to the weather to hear what we could expect for owling tonight.

Instead we got the excited voice of a reporter.

"Breaking news here in Duluth. In a dramatic turn of events, an unidentified man has walked into the police station and confessed to the killing last weekend of owl researcher Dr. Andrew Rahr. The man, whose name is being withheld at this time, claims that he killed Rahr in defense of the primeval forest and its occupants."

Luce and I looked at each other, speechless. After the immediate shock wore off, I shook my head and sighed. It was a looney, after all. A nut case had killed Rahr. "That sucks," I said.

"I bet he's also the one who wrote the letter to Rahr, then," Luce said after a minute. "And maybe he's the person who's been threatening you, Bobby." She reached over and gently rubbed my shoulder. "It's over. Knott can tie up the case, and you can go back to work on Monday. For all we know, this guy may have already confessed to taking the shot at you yesterday. He must have believed he was protecting the owls."

I sighed again. Luce was right: it was over. Rahr's killer was in custody. I could go back to work. Mr. Lenzen would leave me alone. Kim and Lindsay could spill their guts to me again over and over. And over.

Forget the tissues. I was going to need a mop in my office.

The fact that my life could return to normal should have had me pumping my fist in the air in jubilation, but mostly, I just felt sad. Sad for Rahr and sad for his killer and his misguided intentions. Killing people to save owls was definitely not a solution. How could anyone possibly think that? It certainly wasn't on any list I've ever seen of the top ten best ways to promote conservation.

It wasn't going to make environmentalists or bird-lovers look any better, either, and it sure wasn't going to contribute to my public relations efforts at the state fair booth, no matter how close we were to the cheese curds. Fielding questions about birder murders wasn't exactly on my agenda for enticing people to take up bird-watching.

I put the car in gear, and we drove to Two Harbors, the little town just north of Duluth on Lake Superior, where VNT was located. On the way, we listened to the rest of the news broadcast. Of course, everyone and her brother (that's my gender sensitivity showing there—just thought I'd slip that in) had a comment to make about the big news. The city mayor expressed relief to bring a shocking crime to a close and thanked everyone for their cooperation in the investigation. Margaret Montgomery echoed the mayor's comments and lamented that the confessed killer—who was definitely not a card-carrying member of her organization—chose murder as a means of voicing his conservationist convictions.

"No wonder environmentalists get a bad name," Luce muttered. "It only takes one crazy person to do something like this, and then people who really care about, and work hard for, the environment get slammed."

After Montgomery, there was a sound byte from a local psychiatrist (no surprise there—even if your market is certifiable, free advertising is still free advertising), a former colleague of Rahr's, a few random people-on-the-street reactions, and finally, comments from Knott.

Or to be more accurate, "No comment" from Knott.

No comment?

"So why isn't he dancing in the street?" Luce asked. "He's got a confession."

"I don't know," I said, bothered that Knott hadn't said anything more than "No comment." Maybe that was police protocol. Maybe he couldn't say anything else because now lawyers would get involved and who knows how it would end up. Maybe Rahr's killer would become the newest celebrity in town, especially if he could be linked to a hot issue. The media loves that stuff. I could almost see the headlines already: OWLS' AVENGER KILLS RESEARCHER OR FOREST WARRIOR ARRESTED FOR MURDER. As I thought about it, I sympathized with Montgomery big-time, because I knew that her job had just turned into a nightmare. No matter what she did or said, Save Our Boreals was going to be dragged through the mud because people would associate S.O.B. with the s.o.b. who killed Rahr.

Talk about a mess. She was going to need a mop even more than I did.

Chapter Nineteen

Eating helped.

After a burger and fries—typical birding fare, plus pie!—at north shore institution Betty's Pies, I felt a little better about the radio report. Knott and I were both off the hook now with our superiors, and Luce and I could head into the forest with impunity.

Or, at least, with our binoculars. Either way, I wasn't going to have to worry about an owl vigilante taking a shot at me or lining up Luce in his sights. I could finally focus again on getting my owl. And, for some reason, I suddenly felt lucky. That Boreal was a marked bird.

But before we could take up the chase, Luce and I had another mission to accomplish: checking out Very Nice Trees for Lily.

I had the address that Mike had left for me at the hotel (I didn't know what he'd had to do to get it and I hadn't asked) and a map of Two Harbors. We drove back toward town and took a right on Hillside Drive, which wound up a slight rise past some warehouses. At the end of the road sat a pre-fabricated building about the size of a small classroom. There wasn't any sign out front, just the street numbers mounted above a mailbox affixed to the right of the front door. There were two large picture windows, however, and through them, I could see a desk, shelves, files, a worktable, and a grouping of upholstered chairs surrounding a low table.

Nice office, I thought. I wished my office at school looked that nice or was even a third the size of this one. I had a desk, two burgundy plastic chairs and a file cabinet jammed against a concrete wall. Public eduction chic. This looked like a successful realtor's showroom; in comparison, my office looked like a broom closet at the gas station.

Come to think of it, I've probably seen nicer broom closets at gas stations.

I could also see that Vern Thompson, VNT himself, was in the office.

"The man is in," I told Luce and got out of the car. She followed me up to the door, and I opened it for her to walk through. Thompson rose from his desk as we stepped inside, and I could see surprise register on his face as he recognized me from the Splashing Rock.

"Mr.—uh . . ."

"White," I finished for him. "Bob White."

"Yes, of course. The birder."

We shook hands, and I introduced him to Luce.

"Actually, I'm here on behalf of my sister," I explained. "She owns Lily's Landscaping in Savage and asked me to look you up since I was going to be up here for the weekend."

"Lily's Landscaping. Yes, we did some business before Christmas," Thompson said. "She took a good-sized shipment of our Christmas trees."

"Yup, that's right. She was very happy with them. They were very nice trees," I couldn't help adding.

Thompson smiled. "Truth in—"

"Advertising. I know," I nodded. "Anyway, Lily wanted me to take a look at your operation, see what you've got in the way of white jack pines and, I understand, a great deal on ladyslippers."

"Won't you take a seat?" He gestured Luce and me over to the overstuffed chairs by the coffee table. "Can I get you something to drink? Pop? Tea?"

"No, thanks," Luce and I both replied as we sat down. I noticed a little display calendar on the top of the rough-cut white pine coffee table and picked it up. It had a photo of Mount Rainier on it and the words BIG TIMBER INDUSTRIES OF CASCADE, WASHINGTON, emblazoned across the bottom.

"Pretty country," I commented, replacing the calendar on the table. "Have you been out there?"

Thompson sat on the broad arm of a chair and shook his head. "No, I haven't. I'm a Minnesota boy. Born and raised outside Ely. How about you?"

"Minnetonka."

"Luce?" Thompson asked.

"St. Paul. Right on the Mississippi River, as a matter of fact."

"Near the old Ford plant?"

"Yes," Luce said. "Do you know it?"

"Sure do," Thompson grinned. "I spent ten years there in the seventies, working the assembly line. Hot, hard work. Cooped up all day around big machines and sweating buckets because there's no way to cool off inside a big plant like that. Some days, I just knew hell had to be cooler than that. But then business was bad for a while and I got laid off, so I came back north. I liked the Cities fine, and I sure learned my way around machinery at the plant, but I guess I just missed the north woods too much. Hunting and fishing, you know. And I like working outside. Ended up working in logging till last spring."

I wasn't surprised he'd been a logger. That certainly explained his muscular arms and overall good physical condition. Thompson might have been twenty years older than me, but I would have jumped at the chance to pick him for my Red Rover team on the playground.

"This," he said, spreading his arms out to include the office, "is my newest business venture. And a good one it is, too."

He laid his tanned hands on his knees. "So what can I tell you about VNT?"

"Basically, I was hoping to see your greenhouses," I told him.

Of course, what I really wanted to know was if he was stealing stock off state land, but I didn't think that was a good line for opening communications. "So, Vern, are you poaching all your product?" As strong as he appeared to be, I figured I could still take him if he threw a punch, but I wasn't itching to prove it. Good counselors don't provoke; they tactfully elicit. Another gem from one of my graduate classes.

"Well, Bob, I'd sure like to do that, but actually, we don't have greenhouses, per se. We've got plantings, and it's a little tough right now to get up to our growing property, what with the heavy snow and melting we've had this last week. The roads are mud, at best, and I've already got a couple vehicles stuck up there. So I'm going to give you a rain check—make that a sun check," he smiled, "to see it the next time you're up this way."

He stood and handed me his business card, making it clear our friendly little chat had come to a rather abrupt end.

"Sorry you made the trip out here for nothing and I can't show you anything, but tell your sister that I can deliver all the ladyslippers she wants and she won't find a better price or better stock anywhere. And if she wants those jack pine she talked about, well, I've got plenty of them, too."

"Sounds like you've got quite a piece of land for all that stock," I commented, tucking his card into my wallet.

"That I do," he agreed. "That, I surely do."

"It's not a wasted trip, either, Mr. Thompson," Luce told him. "We've already had a good morning birding and we're hoping to find one of those Boreal Owls tonight. Bob's got a line on a couple possible sites, so we're going to give them a try."

"Is that right?" He glanced at me and paused for a moment, like he was thinking that over. "How do you know where to look? Did you go on the owl trips last spring?"

"No," I answered him. "We didn't make it up here in time. I've just been researching Rahr's journal reports, and based on that information, I've narrowed it down to some probable nesting areas."

"Interesting." He ushered us to the door. "I wondered how you—I mean, birders in general—could find those sites. They seemed fairly remote when we visited them last year on the tours. It looked to me like you'd have to be pretty highly motivated to track those owls down. There's a lot of country up there."

He stepped back to let Luce go through the door first. "Well, let me know how you do. I'd be curious to know what you find. So would Margaret, probably," he added, "being as she's the S.O.B. director."

Thompson walked outside with us. I looked around the little parking area, empty except for my SUV and what I guessed was Thompson's truck—a beat-up old olive green pick-up that could have doubled for one of the trucks we used when I worked for the DNR years ago. To my complete disappointment, however, even though I wished as hard as I could, there was not a single cherry-picker to be seen, let alone one with a stolen pine top hanging over the edge of its rusty old bucket.

So much for wishing. Time for Plan B.

Or, at least, it would have been time for Plan B if I'd had one.

Which I didn't.

"So you've got a couple trucks stuck in the woods, huh?" I was back to hoping for incrimination by conversation. If he let slip that one was a cherry-picker, I was going straight to the nearest police station and asking for back-up.

"Yeah," he said, crossing his arms over his chest. "I'd probably still be stuck up there myself, too, if Maggie hadn't come and given me a ride home. She's an amazing woman."

"Maggie?" Luce asked.

"Margaret," he said. "Montgomery. She was having dinner with me last night at the Splashing Rock. Bob met her. Nice place, don't you think? All that white pine in the dining room. I supplied it. The Splashing Rock was one of my first clients—helped me establish the business."

I nodded in acknowledgment, remembering the aroma of pine that lightly scented the restaurant and trying to recall details from our conversation the night before. "That's right, she said you two met on one of Rahr's owl trips last spring."

"Do you bird?" Luce asked him.

"No, not really," Thompson laughed. "I went on the trip more out of morbid curiosity than out of interest in the owls."

"Morbid curiosity?" Luce repeated.

"Yeah. The owls cost me my logging job. I was working for the company that was counting on the DNR contract to clear the forest, and when it fell through, thanks to the owls and Maggie's S.O.B. crowd, so did my job." Thompson laced his fingers together and pushed them out palms-first in front of his chest. "But turned out, it was the best thing that happened to me. Now, for the first time in my life, I'm my own boss."

"That's quite an accomplishment," Luce said. "Congratulations."

"Thanks . . . Luce," he said.

For a second there, I thought he was going to say "little lady," but I guessed when he realized he was looking up at Luce, he figured it didn't quite fit the situation. But Luce had his attention now. "I'd love to have my own business," she told him, a note of longing in her voice.

She did?

Funny, she'd never mentioned aspirations of ownership to *me*. I slid her a glance and saw that she was gazing at Thompson with what I could only call blatant admiration. I even thought I saw her bat her eyelashes at him.

For crying out loud.

She was flirting with the guy.

What was she thinking? That a little female flattery was going to overpower his instincts of self-preservation and convince him to confess to poaching plants from government land? That her beautiful blue eyes would reduce the rugged lumberman to a pile of sniveling self-reproach? That flirting was going to get us a clue?

"Yeah, having your own business is the greatest thing in the world," he assured her, smiling. I swear he suddenly seemed taller. Not that it helped. He'd have to grow another four inches to catch up to Luce. But it did make him talkative.

"You don't have to worry about lay-offs, job security, or catching grief for coming in late," Thompson said. "I wouldn't do it any other way, now. I think it would kill me to have to go back to working for someone else."

Kill me.

All at once, previously unrelated thoughts rammed into each other in my head. Bells were ringing. Instincts were screaming. Thompson had something worth killing for.

So maybe I was a little hasty about criticizing the flattery approach.

Thompson was an outdoor guy. His livelihood was made in the woods—legally or not. Would he, I wondered, kill someone who threatened his business? Someone who could send that being-your-own-boss dream-come-true crashing down to the ground?

The topped trees Luce and I had seen last night were in the owls' range of woods; if Rahr had stumbled on Thompson cutting trees that were protected, would Thompson have threatened Rahr—or even, possibly, had him killed—to keep his illegal business secret and intact?

Was that why Knott had no comment on the man who had turned himself in as Rahr's murderer—because there was more than one person involved, and the case was far from closed?

Rahr's body, however, hadn't been found at the place we'd visited last night where we saw the topped trees. His body was at another site a long ways from there.

And then another thought crashed into what was becoming a virtual interstate pile-up in my brain. Were the trees topped where I'd found Rahr's body?

I didn't know. I sure hadn't noticed last weekend, but I hadn't been looking either. Tonight I was definitely going to check. Of course, I was feeding a huge suspicion here: Thompson was the one who had topped the trees.

And, I sternly reminded myself, even if he had, that didn't prove he had anything to do with Rahr's murder. Knott had a confessed killer in custody.

But if Thompson's "work" in the forest brought him into any kind of proximity to Rahr's research areas, then there might have been some kind of on-going territorial dispute between the men that no one else knew about. And I wouldn't have put it past Rahr to take matters into his own hands, especially if he thought someone was deliberating trying to sabotage his work.

Which, apparently, he had, judging from our phone conversation.

And that, in turn, would explain the spiked trees.

If my emerging theory was correct, Rahr must have discovered that trees around his Boreal study sites were getting cut, and so he spiked the trees himself in an effort to stop the harvesting. In addition, he must have suspected the tree cutting was specific to his research locations. Being the secretive researcher he was, he didn't want the DNR and the attendant media circus invading his space and disturbing the owls because of it, so he didn't call in any complaints to the authorities. That left just one question: why, in that big forest with all those trees, did he think it was only his Boreal sites that were being targeted?

The answer was obvious: Rahr must have found a pattern of poaching at his research locations.

I knew the location of only three of his sites; certainly he had others I didn't know about. But of the three I did know, one was topped and one was spiked. What about the third site?

Suddenly, I was anxious to get going. I wanted to see the third site while it was still light and see whether it fit a pattern—spiked or topped. I took Luce's hand to pull her to the car, but she and Thompson were still talking.

"I have to say, though, if it weren't for Maggie, it probably wouldn't have happened," Thompson was saying. "She's the one who suggested I start my own business. Use your expertise, she said. Think creatively, she said. She'd been through job changes, too, so she knew what she was talking about."

"What job changes?" I asked, and almost simultaneously thought, *Crap! Why did I do that?*

This is, I've found, one of the occupational hazards of being a counselor: you form a habit of encouraging people to talk. Even when you really don't want them to talk anymore, when what you most want is for them to shut up, go away and leave you alone, you can't help yourself—you ask them to keep talking. Unfortunately, this same habit makes people think you're a good listener and that you're really interested in them when it's really nothing more than an automatic reflex. I used to think I had invisible words—invisible to me, at least—painted on my shirt that read "Tell me your life story. I really want to know," because people I hardly knew would tell me all kinds of personal, intimate details I wouldn't dream of sharing with my closest friend, let alone a virtual stranger.

Judging from the eager monologue that was now pouring from Thompson's mouth, the invisible message on my shirt must have been flashing like a theatre marquee on opening night. Without any encouragement at all from me, he was spilling his guts.

Or rather, he was spilling Montgomery's guts.

"Maggie hasn't always worked in Duluth, you know," Thompson was saying. "She's from the West Coast. That's where I got the Seattle calendar you were looking at—from Maggie. She was a hot shot lobbyist for the timber companies out there back in the late 1980s." He started shaking his head. "But things went from bad to worse for logging people after the owl thing, and she said she'd had enough. That's when she landed in Minnesota."

Thompson paused and chuckled. "Funny, isn't it? She moves out here and ends up on the other side of the fence."

"What fence?" Luce asked, totally confused.

It hit me like the proverbial ton of bricks. All at once, I understood what Thompson was telling us.

Before she came to Duluth to defend the habitat of the Boreal Owls, Margaret Montgomery had worked for the logging industry in the Pacific Northwest . . . as an opponent of preserving the habitat of the Northern Spotted Owls.

In her current job, as the director of S.O.B., she was the champion of owls.

In her previous life, she had been the enemy.

Chapter Twenty

So what?" Luce said as we drove back into Two Harbors. "So she switched jobs. And perspectives. People do that."

I knew she was right. Again. People make changes for all kinds of reasons. It doesn't necessarily make them bad people if they make a complete reversal in the causes they defend. Sometimes it's a simple matter of convenience. Sometimes it's a matter of enlightenment. Or, like Luce said, it's a change in perspective.

Although at times, I was sure, it was pure self-interest.

Regardless of the reason, though, whatever lay behind Montgomery's switch of allegiance was none of my business. For all I knew, Montgomery's lobbying work and environmental activism were just her job, simply something she was good at, that earned her an income, and not something in which she had a personal emotional investment. I was the one who had made that assumption, and you know what they say happens when you assume—it makes donkeys out of all of us. Or, at least that's the cleaned up version I tell my students. Maybe what really bothered me was that she looked like my mother, but this was definitely not something my mother would do: posture for pay. It felt cheap and dishonest. To my way of thinking, it gave S.O.B. a bad name to have, basically, a soldier of fortune for its director.

Okay, so maybe I should reword that.

Not the soldier of fortune part. The bad name part.

I mean, how could you get a worse name than what it already had—S.O.B.? Anyway, as far as I was concerned, this little bit of biographical revelation about its director didn't exactly cast a glow of confidence on the credibility or sincerity of its leadership in the area of conservation.

But, as Luce proceeded to point out to me, that wasn't my problem.

"Bobby, we didn't come up here to validate the work of S.O.B.," she reminded me. "We came up here to find a Boreal Owl. And check out Very Nice Trees. And the Splashing Rock. Two down, one to go. Get over it."

"Hey!" I said. "I'm dealing with a crisis here. I'm experiencing a major paradigm shift. What I assumed was true and good isn't necessarily so. A little sensitivity might be appropriate."

Luce rolled her eyes. I drove in silence for about—oh—thirty seconds.

"Okay, I'm over it," I said. I looked in my rear-view mirror and seeing the road clear, I pulled a fast U-turn in the road.

"What are you doing?" Luce grabbed the dashboard to steady herself against the sudden turn.

"We're going up to see that third Boreal Owl site I know."

"But it's not dusk, yet. The owls won't be calling now."

I gave Luce a quick glance. "I'm not looking for the owls. I'm looking for a pattern."

"A pattern?"

"Topped trees. Spiked trees."

Another body?

I sure hoped not. One was already more than enough.

At which point, one last thought plowed into the still-smoldering wreck of my mental demolition derby. If I'd been shot yesterday, *I* would have been another body near a Boreal site.

Did two bodies a pattern make?

In the middle of hundreds of acres of deep woods, yet within calling distance of established Boreal Owl study sites—I'd have to give that a big thumbs up, buddy.

And then I flashed on the hillcrest where I had been a sitting duck.

It was unnaturally open. No trees.

At least, there weren't trees there anymore.

Because they'd already been harvested.

Now, in my mind's eye, I could clearly see the hillcrest again, and what I had consciously missed seeing at the time: tree stumps. While I was lying on the trail, waiting for Knott to reach me, I'd scanned around myself at eye level and seen ground-level stumps lining the trail.

Stumps of white pine.

A tree cutter had been there.

"Bobby?"

I glanced at Luce. She looked concerned.

"Are you all right? You looked kind of . . . glazed . . . for a minute."

I breathed deeply. "I'm okay." I reached over and patted her thigh. "Some pieces of the puzzle just fell into place. I think Rahr was on to something that had nothing to do with the owls."

Then again, maybe it did.

In fact, maybe it had everything to do with the owls.

The location was the key, just like Knott and I had figured.

Whoever was cutting the trees had deliberately selected the remote spots where Rahr did his research, specifically because the spots were so difficult to locate, which was almost a guarantee that the poaching there would go undetected.

Unless you knew exactly where to find them. Was that why Rahr had jumped all over me in our phone call? Did he think I was directing poachers to his sites?

"Luce," I said, getting more excited as other pieces of information now made sense to me, "someone was cutting at his study sites, and Rahr knew it. That's why he spiked the trees—he was trying to scare off the poacher. He didn't know who was doing it, but he suspected it was someone he had trusted. He said as much when he yelled at me on the phone that someone who was supposed to be on his side was sabotaging him."

"Someone on his side?" She shook her head. "That's a cast of thousands, Bobby. Colleagues at the university, S.O.B. members, the Minnesota birding community, anyone who'd gone on his owl tours. That's not exactly a small bunch of suspects."

I had to agree, but I doubted that many of them had logging connections, because that was what it would take to pull off this poaching. We needed to make two lists, I decided: who had logging connections and who knew the location of the sites. Without hardly thinking, I could name one person for the top of both lists: Thompson.

On the heels of that name, I realized I knew another: Montgomery.

And another: Alice.

Alice had said she'd been on a first-name basis with the logging industry people who'd lobbied Rahr. Could she have inadvertently—or not—leaked the site locations to someone looking for a lucrative, albeit illegal, sideline? Was that the person to whom Rahr caught her passing his research data, and not to Stan as I had assumed?

Ouch. There was that donkey thing again.

I tried to think of a way I might be able to whittle down the list of possible people who had not only access to the sites, but who had actually visited them in the last few months. I could only think of one way.

"I sure hope he's home," I said under my breath.

"Who?" Luce asked.

"It's time to call in the cavalry," I told her. "We're going to Crazy Eddie's place."

We followed the county road west out of Two Harbors and wound up and down for about twenty-five miles. I made a right turn onto a dirt track and stopped the car in front of a rickety wire and post gate. I honked the horn twice, then tapped it three short blasts, then two more long ones.

"ONLY NORWEGIANS PAST THIS POINT," Luce read off the enormous hand-lettered sign attached to the gate. "OTHERS WILL BE SHOT. HAVE A NICE DAY. What is this, reclusive Scandinavian militiaman meets Minnesota nice?"

"This," I said, "is Crazy Eddie's place. He likes his privacy. He'll be out in a minute. You'll see."

Sure enough, a couple minutes later Eddie came rolling up to the other side of the gate on what looked like a brand-new ATV. Even though he was driving slowly, every time he hit a bump in the track, the woolly ear flaps on his winter cap jumped, looking for all the world like little wings getting ready to take off. He was concentrating so hard on watching the track, I was afraid he was going to drive right through the gate, instead of opening it in a more conventional way. His long white beard drifted down his chest, and his cheeks were rosy with the cold. He was wearing an open down vest over his trademark flannel shirt, his red suspenders stretched across his rather expansive belly. At the last minute, he made a sharp turn and braked next to the gate. He flashed me a big grin and waved, then leaned over and unlatched the gate to slide it open with one hand while he had the ATV in reverse. I drove through far enough so he could close it behind us, and then I turned off the engine.

"Oh, my gosh," Luce whispered. "It's the North Pole and we've caught Santa Claus out of uniform. Where are the reindeer and elves?"

"They're on spring break in Cancun," I said. "Come on. You have to meet Crazy Eddie."

I got out of the car and waited for Eddie to pull up next to me. "What's with the ATV, Eddie? Where's the Mercedes?"

Eddie laughed a big belly laugh and punched me in the shoulder. “Hit a deer. Again. This time it took out the radiator.”

I could relate. Luckily, I’d only lost the headlight.

Luce came around the front of the car, and I introduced her to Eddie.

“Luce, this is Eddie Edvarg. Eddie, Luce Nilsson.” They shook hands, and I noticed him giving Luce a very obvious once-over.

“Eddie and I worked together one summer for the DNR up here,” I explained. “We were tracking the movements of moose and documenting their range for a survey. Eddie’s a whiz with electronics and spreadsheets. He could predict where those moose were going to be ten days out if he wanted to.”

Eddie laughed again. “Hell, I could tell you what they were thinking if I wanted to. Come to think of it, anyone could, because moose don’t think real hard.”

He stroked his bushy white beard and addressed himself to Luce. Like a lot of men, he had to look up at her to make eye contact; at just over five feet tall, he’s not the most impressive in the height department. Unlike a lot of “vertically challenged” men, however, he’s not self-conscious about it. He insists his short stature makes him “accessible,” though to what, he’s never quite spelled out.

“Moose have got to be the dumbest hoofed beasts on God’s green earth,” he told Luce. “I’ve heard of young bulls charging trains to prove their dominance. Guess who loses? And did you know they’ve been known to walk out onto a frozen lake, get their hooves frozen to the surface and instead of trying to pull ’em off, they’ll just stand there and freeze to death? Swear to God. So, are you Norwegian? You look like one. I am, you know."

Luce nodded. "Minnesotan Norwegian all the way."

"That's good," Eddie nodded, too. "Then I don't have to shoot you. Bob here, though, he's a problem. I've tried for years, but I just can't get him to eat the lutefisk. I've got a bottle of aquavit around here somewhere." He twisted on the seat of the ATV, sticking his hands in all of his pants and vest pockets searching for a bottle of the traditional Norwegian liquor. "Can't welcome a Norwegian properly without a toast with the aquavit."

"Eddie," I said. "Can we cut across your land to that Boreal Owl site Mike and I visited when I was up here last weekend? It saves about an hour of driving. Otherwise I have to take the long way around."

"Sure you can," he said, giving up on finding liquid refreshment. "Aren't you here kind of early for owling?"

"Actually, I'm not looking for the owls right now," I said, climbing back into the car. "I just want to scout the place."

"Oh-ho, scouting! I like the sound of that. You need any surveillance equipment? Tiny cameras? Hidden microphones? Need help securing the area?"

"Ah, no thanks, Eddie. I just want to look at the trees."

"What's with the trees, anyway? Back in November, that DNR guy was up here almost every day clearing out timber on that state land next to mine on the north side, and now he's been back a couple times in the last week. I thought the DNR gave up that idea because of those owls."

"They did. What DNR guy?"

"The one with the truck like we used to use for our surveys. You know—beat-up, ugly green pick-up, standard issue. I stopped him once and asked what he was doing up there, and he said he had to thin out some young trees. He even had the DNR jacket. I got him on video if you want to look."

"Video?" Luce asked.

"Yes, ma'am. It's been a long winter up here, and my satellite dish crapped out in January, so I rigged up motion sensitive cameras along the front gate here to watch the world go by. Cheap entertainment, basically, but it beats the monotony of watching the snow fall." Eddie pointed to four tiny cameras mounted along the gate that I hadn't noticed before. "Usually, all I get is the deer, an occasional bear and lots of coyotes and raccoons. But this month was busy, between the DNR man, those two gals and Dr. Rahr. And that guy in camos. In fact, last weekend it was a regular parade up here."

Last weekend? Eddie had Dr. Rahr on tape? Along with four other people?

Before Luce could ask, I explained to her that Eddie's place wasn't just a convenient short cut to one of the Boreal Owl sites. The road it sat on, the road we'd taken up here, actually led eventually to two of the sites: the one we wanted to see now and the crime scene where the trees were spiked. I knew Eddie was living up here, so when I was doing my research to pinpoint possible birding locations and I realized his land butted up against owl territory, I'd called him and asked if I could use his place as a short-cut. He'd said sure.

Then when I was up here last Friday night with Mike, I also realized that the road Eddie lived on hooked up to a long back route to the other site. When we went owling again on Saturday night, though, we hadn't come this way first, but took a more direct route up to the site where we found Rahr. Eddie's location on the road to the sites was the real reason I'd wanted to see him now, on the chance he might have some recollection of people or vehicles traveling by. To find he had video was a stroke of luck I couldn't have even imagined. Maybe Luce had been right—yet again—and Eddie really was Santa Claus.

"Eddie," I said, "could you get me a copy of that video? There's a detective in Duluth who would want to see it. He's investigating Dr. Rahr's death. You may have gotten a picture of a killer."

"What?" Eddie asked, his bushy eyebrows rising with surprise. "Wait a minute. Dr. Rahr's dead? When did that happen? I just talked to him last Friday morning. He went up to his site where you're going now, and then he said he was going to drive on to that other research spot he has way out there in the woods. Said he had some preventative maintenance to do."

Eddie cast a disgusted look towards the satellite dish sitting near his cabin. "Damn dish," he said. "I don't know what's going on anymore. I moved out here to get away from it all and damned if it doesn't seem like the world still comes after you." Eddie shook his head.

"Actually, my friend in Duluth—a detective with the name of Knott—arrested someone this morning for Rahr's murder, but I expect he'd still want to look at those tapes. Maybe it would give him some hard evidence." I put the car in gear while Luce buckled her seatbelt. "How about we pick it up on our way back out? Say in about half an hour?"

"You got it, Bob," Eddie said. He revved off to his cabin set back in the woods, his beard flying and his earflaps flapping.

I took off down the track across Eddie's property.

"So why is he Crazy Eddie?" Luce asked as we bumped along the soggy road. "I don't know that he's any crazier than anyone else I've met. My great-aunt Vivi always carries a flask of aquavit with her. Just in case, you know."

"He's filthy rich," I said. "Eddie and his wife won the lottery about twelve years ago. They'd lived in this small town down in southern Minnesota for years, but they had to move because they were so swamped with phone calls and strangers showing up at their door asking for money. They could have gone anywhere: Hawaii, Florida, Europe, the Riviera. And they could have lived in luxury, but they love the north woods, so they moved here. Eddie doesn't have to work—he's got plenty of money—but he loves tracking for the DNR. You saw how he is about electronics. So when I got to know him when we worked together that summer on the moose survey, I told him he was crazy, that he ought to go lay in the sun somewhere and drink piña coladas instead of freezing up here for six months of the year. My name for him stuck."

"Does he really have a Mercedes?"

"No, he doesn't have a Mercedes."

I gave her a grin.

"He has *two*—at least."

I stopped the car at the edge of Eddie's land. We got out to hike just a short way beyond the state forest marker to where I'd located the Boreal Owl site. When Mike and I had come last weekend, there had still been good-sized drifts of snow, but today, the snow was rapidly melting into the earth. We came to a slight rise in the forest path and saw a wide clearing up ahead. When we entered the clearing, Luce and I both looked up . . . at a huge circle of topped trees.

Chapter Twenty-One

By the time we got back to the hotel, it was late afternoon. We wanted to start our drive up to our last Boreal Owl site before dusk, so we planned a quick stop for clean-up and to pick up the cooler Luce had packed for us yesterday afternoon at her place. I tossed Eddie's video on the dresser and debated calling Knott about it. We'd taken a quick look at it before we'd left Eddie's place, and, frankly, I wasn't sure now what good it was.

The recording was stamped with dates and times, so it had been easy to find the footage we especially wanted to see.

"Now here's last Friday morning," Eddie had said, kicking back in his recliner while Luce and I sat on the sofa in front of the television set. On the screen, a beat-up truck neared the camera.

"Isn't that the truck we saw this afternoon at VNT?" Luce asked, leaning forward to get a better look.

"Definitely a resemblance," I answered, although I had to admit that it could just as easily have been any DNR vehicle—the agency must have had a corner on the world market for ugly green pick-ups. But then the driver's face came into view, and if it wasn't Thompson, then it was his identical twin.

"That's the man," Eddie said. "Same DNR guy who was up here in November carting out trees. Thought it was kind of odd they were doing that kind of work so late in the year, but when they've got the budget for a job, they do it no matter what the season, I guess."

"He's not a DNR employee," I told Eddie. "He owns his own garden supply company, and last November, he sold a big shipment of Christmas trees—very nice Christmas trees—to my sister Lily. Based on what you're saying, Eddie, it sounds like those very nice trees were also very hot, as in stolen."

"Poached, you mean," Eddie said.

"Poached and then sold," I added.

"This was last Friday, right?" Luce asked, still studying the tape as it played.

"Sure was," Eddie replied. He nodded toward the television screen. "See, I told you it was a parade."

Luce was looking at the next vehicle approaching the camera. It was a jeep we'd never seen before, but as it neared the gate, we got a clear view of the driver.

It was Margaret Montgomery.

Luce and I looked at each other. Margaret Montgomery had been up here last Friday? Close on the heels of Thompson, it appeared. Eddie forwarded the tape to the next vehicle. This one also we didn't recognize, just as we didn't recognize the driver.

"That's Dr. Rahr," Eddie commented. On the tape, Rahr stopped his truck at the gate and waited. A few seconds later, the gate opened and the truck drove through.

"That's when he came to take the shortcut back to the site you just visited," Eddie explained, hitting the pause button. "It was when he left that he told me he had some maintenance to do at the other location."

A sudden idea hit me. Did Eddie have tape showing when Thompson—and Montgomery—had returned? It was hoping for a lot, I knew, but it couldn't hurt to ask. The idea that they'd both been using a road in the morning that led to the Boreal site where Rahr was killed later in the day opened disturbing doors of possibility. Had they seen anything—or anyone—suspicious along the way, either going in or coming out? Could they possibly be witnesses, unaware that they had information that could help Knott tie up his case?

Or were they witnesses and knew it, but had kept that knowledge to themselves?

I remembered my earlier suspicions about Thompson. If he was the poacher—and Eddie's comments seemed to confirm that—and he had tangled with Rahr, he'd probably be happy to have Rahr out of the way. As in permanently. Who did it or why wasn't his worry. As long as he could keep poaching in peace, he was happy to let the police continue to run into dead ends. The last thing he'd want to do was show up at the station with information that would lead Knott directly to his place of "business."

As for Montgomery, she'd have no reason not to report any suspicious activity along the road. What her reasons were for being in the area was anyone's guess, though I had to admit that her association with Thompson made her a little suspect in my mind. What were the odds she'd be out for a drive just minutes behind Thompson?

Another possibility reared its ugly head. What if Thompson hadn't stumbled upon the killer, but instead, had deliberately gone to meet him that morning? What if Thompson had hired a killer, and his trip past Eddie's place had taken him to a rendezvous during which he led the killer to Rahr?

And what if Montgomery, then, had chanced upon the two of them?

My stomach lurched.

Was Montgomery in danger from Thompson? If she'd seen her friend meeting with a man in the woods near Rahr's research site and then learned about the subsequent murder, she'd have to be terrified of Thompson and what he might do to her if she went to the police. At the same time, since she hadn't already come forward, but had joined him for supper at the Splashing Rock, she could possibly be arrested herself as an accomplice after the fact. An accomplice to murder.

Probably not something she'd want to include on her next job application.

Unfortunately, the video couldn't tell us Thompson and Montgomery's final destinations that morning. Whether they had actually gone to the far site, met anyone, or just looped around Eddie's property to the site Luce and I had just visited, was all conjecture. For all we knew, they'd each been out for a winter day's drive through the forest and never had stopped anywhere at all. But it did seem that this was a very popular part of the forest, apparently.

I turned to Eddie.

"Before he left here last Friday morning, did Dr. Rahr say he'd seen anyone at the site here?"

"No," Eddie said, bringing his recliner upright. He put his hands on his knees. "He didn't mention anything like that."

"Eddie," I said. "Does your surveillance tape show Thompson and the woman returning that day?"

Eddie looked me in the eye.

"No."

"So they must have taken another route back out," Luce concluded. "And that might indicate they went out by way of the other Boreal site."

"Don't know that," Eddie said. "But I got tape of them driving by the next night, too."

That was the night Mike and I had discovered Dr. Rahr's body.

"Both of them?" I asked.

"Both of them," Eddie confirmed. "Except that time, they were driving together in the truck."

Bottom line was that despite its visual definition, Eddie's video couldn't prove a thing. It couldn't tell us where people had gone or why. Unless it showed Thompson hauling trees—or meeting with the man who had surrendered to Knott—I had nothing to support any of my suspicions.

Luce and I got up to leave, but Eddie wasn't done with the tape yet.

"Wait a minute," he said. "There were three more cars that came by after Dr. Rahr left. I forgot about it until I looked at the tape again. Maybe you ought to see."

Eddie hit the play button, and another vehicle approached the gate. We got a clear view of the driver as he went by.

It was Bradley Ellis. That was odd. Last Friday he'd been preparing to go to Michigan to be with his father. Or so he said. Why was he up here?

"Did he come back later?" I asked Eddie.

"No tape of it," he answered.

The video was still running and I had to blink when I saw the face of the next vehicle's driver.

Alice Wylie.

"Do you recognize her?" Luce asked when I made a choking noise.

"Yes. I do. It's Ms. Multiple."

And then, bringing up the rear a few minutes later, was a third car. I could have sworn that Stan looked right at the camera and smiled.

Eddie was right—there had been a parade up here last Friday morning. But of all the participants, only Rahr never made it back.

Chapter Twenty-Two

"Call him, Bobby."

I turned to see Luce watching me as she took the last items from the room's mini-fridge to put into our cooler for supper.

"It's going to bug you all evening if you don't call Knott and tell him about the video. I want to get that Boreal, and we won't get it if your mind is still on that tape."

"But it doesn't prove a thing," I reminded her. "Except that Eddie is a frustrated surveillance expert."

She narrowed her eyes at me and shook her head in warning. I picked up the phone and placed the call.

"Knott here."

"Are too." I was going to miss this.

"You're a smart-ass, White," he laughed.

I laughed too. "Congrats, Detective. I don't suppose it's every day the killer you're looking for walks right into the station."

The laughing stopped. "You're right," he said. "It isn't every day. And it wasn't today, either."

It took me a split-second to register what he'd said. "What?"

"Our resident nutcase didn't do Rahr," Knott said. "This guy—the one who walked in today—shows up every year or so and takes credit—or whatever you want to call it—for the unsolved crime of the day. He's a publicity addict. The veteran reporters know him, so they don't fall for it when he calls in the tip that he's about to make a confession at the police station. The new kids on the media block aren't wise to him yet, so they're the ones he calls, and they're the ones who jump."

Well, I'll be damned. Score two points for me, I thought. My counselor's instincts must have been working subconsciously earlier when I first heard the radio announcement of the arrest. For some reason, I hadn't felt the closure or relief I'd expected. Instead, I'd felt adrift or frustrated almost, like something was missing. Sure, I'd been impressed that the local media was on top of developments so quickly, but I hadn't questioned that what I was hearing was accurate. Oops. My naiveté must have been showing.

Again.

First, it had been the truth about Montgomery's pose-for-pay, and now, the integrity of broadcast news. I was beginning to think that nothing was what I thought it was. Even so, I couldn't suppress a little twinge of triumph. Somewhere inside me, I'd known it wasn't over, that Rahr's killer wouldn't just waltz into the station and everything would turn up roses. Hearing the news from Knott was bad, for sure, but it also gave me some affirmation, along with confirmation. Yes, those counselor instincts were still sharp, all right. And, more importantly,

I definitely wasn't ready to let Mr. Lenzen put me out to pasture.

Or to job hunt, either.

Which brought me back to the matter at hand.

There was still a killer at large, and my job was still on hold.

On hold.

Like a paused frame of video.

Like a paused frame of Eddie's video.

"I have something to show you," I said. "How soon can you get here?"

Ten minutes later, Knott was sliding the video into the player on top of the hotel room's television. I explained to him how Eddie had played it for Luce and me after we had discovered the topped trees and driven back to Eddie's house.

"I don't know if it can tell you anything concrete except who was where at one point last Friday morning," I warned him. "Eddie can testify that he caught Thompson red-handed last fall with some illegally cut trees, but there's nothing on the tape that can verify any poaching. As far as Rahr's murder goes, the video might be useless for you, John, but I wanted you to take a look at it." I socked him gently in the shoulder. "See? I meant it at lunch yesterday when I told you I'd learned my lesson about withholding anything connected with a case."

"Good call, Bob. I knew there was a reason I didn't wring your neck yesterday." His gaze fastened on the television screen. "We'll go after Thompson, I promise. And if this tape can give us anything to work with, I'll give you an honorary detective badge. How's that sound?"

"Keep the badge, John. Just get me back in my office chair on Monday."

Luce and I watched the video again while Knott jotted down names and times. When Stan appeared on the screen, Knott paused the tape.

"Who's this?"

"This is Stan Miller," I informed him. "Just another guy in full camouflage gear out for a drive in the forest. You know the type. Stealthy, well-armed, non-existent. Doesn't play well with others."

Knott leaned closer to the image on the screen and said nothing for a moment or two. "Son of a gun," he finally whispered, "I wondered what had happened to him."

Luce and I traded a look of total disbelief.

"You *know* Stan?" I asked him.

"His name isn't—wasn't—Stan. Yeah, I know him. University of Minnesota, Class of 1984. An expert marksman and a brilliant mathematician. Got snapped up by the CIA for field work shortly after graduation." Knott grinned. "He was my college roommate. Almost my brother-in-law, until my sister couldn't take his three-word sentences anymore."

"He's up to five words, now."

Knott laughed and looked back at Sam's face frozen on the screen. "Son of a gun," he repeated, then whispered to the screen, "What in the world are you doing in this?"

I breathed a sigh of relief. Well, at least my sister wasn't involved with a mob hit man or an escaped lunatic. Thank God for small favors, right? I wasn't sure about the CIA part, though. That could be good or bad, depending on which part of the CIA he was working for. And then I remembered the MOU rumors about him.

"Is he still working for the CIA?" I asked Knott. "Do you know?"

The detective pushed the eject button on the tape player and grabbed the tape as it slid out.

"Last I heard, he was on some kind of rehab leave. The grapevine said it was permanent, that he'd come home to Minnesota and set himself up as an independent contractor, working jobs for the government." He snagged his jacket off the back of the desk chair in the room and headed for the door.

"So your gut was right, Bob," he said, smiling. "You can definitely trust Stan Miller on this one. Whatever job he's doing, it's for Uncle Sam, not Uncle Guido, and if you want to go owling tonight, there's no one better to have watching your back."

He stopped just before leaving the room. "Thanks for the video. And the poaching angle. Like we said, Bob, it's all about the location. I'll be in touch."

Only after I closed the door behind him did I realize he hadn't told us Stan's real name. "How about that?" I asked Luce. "Scary Stan really *is* a former CIA agent. I guess that means I don't have to worry about Lily being safe with him anymore." And although I still didn't know what he was using her for, or what "contract" he was working on, I decided that if Knott could vouch for Stan's character, then it was okay that the man was dating my sister.

Scary, but okay.

"So, do you still want to try for the Boreal tonight?" I asked Luce. The idea that Rahr's killer was still out there somewhere, along with the still-too-fresh memory of my close conversation with a bullet yesterday, had me thinking more than twice about resuming our chase for the owl.

Luce, however, was steady as ever.

"You know what they say about getting right back up on the horse that threw you," she said. "I know Knott said we need to be careful, but there'll be the two of us, and I'm totally willing to give this a try. Besides, this is our night to find the owl, Bobby. I can feel it."

Funny thing was, so could I.

"But," she added pointedly, "let's take my car, just in case. My license plate isn't quite the advertisement that yours is."

I had to agree. Traveling incognito had a definite appeal to it tonight.

As I pulled the hotel room door closed behind me, Luce was already in the car, checking to make sure we had our night binos as well as our regular ones. I asked her what was in the cooler, and she described the menu for the evening: a wild rice and sesame chicken salad, crusty French rolls, marinated snow peas with carrots and for dessert, fudgy brownies. A perfect feast for a night of owling. Or for anytime. Alan was right. I'd better marry this woman.

Eventually.

"I hope Eddie's video helps," Luce said as we pulled out of the lot. "It sure seemed to cheer the detective up, at least."

"At this point, I'm sure he's grateful for any leads. His job is on the line, too. He needs to catch a killer pronto, or he'll have the whole community, as well as city hall, on his tail. In comparison, I've only got Mr. Lenzen."

"Oh, Bobby, I'm sorry."

"Not your fault. I'm the one who found Rahr and got involved in a murder investigation." I flashed her a smile. "The least I can do is get the owl out of it."

We drove to an overlook that provided us with a panoramic view of Lake Superior. Luce dished out our supper, and we sat in the car, eating and admiring the big lake that was beginning to wake out of its winter sleep. Even from this distance, we could see the rhythmic roll of its surface and silvery glints on wave crests as they slowly slid to shore. The sky above had cleared again and was beginning to dim with the approaching night. We cleared our laps of empty food containers and repacked them in the cooler. I got back on the road, and we headed west.

Somewhere ahead of us, the owl was waiting.

Chapter Twenty-Three

We drove for about an hour. To alleviate my own anxiety about returning to the place where I'd barely avoided a bullet, I decided that we'd take a different approach to the Boreal site, one that skirted around that neck of the forest. On this route, there wasn't much to break up the scenery; mostly it was trees and trees and trees. Occasionally, we'd pass a mailbox, most likely for someone's summer cabin. The road wound in and out of national forest, and we could see old logging roads trailing off along fences that marked park boundaries. The sun was definitely setting as we got closer to our destination. In the growing dusk, we could just make out a few stars.

I parked in an old trailhead access lot, and Luce and I geared ourselves up for the hike to the site: we pulled on our woolen caps, looped binos around our necks, grabbed our small flashlights and tucked a couple of water bottles in our parka pockets. Then we started walking.

We followed an old trail that I assumed Rahr had used in the early years of his research; every quarter-mile or so there was a wooden marker nailed onto a tree at just about shoulder height. On the markers, dates and notes were jotted in permanent ink and covered in yellowed plastic. Next to a date, there were either dashes (lots of those) or the word CALL. My best guess was that this was some kind of record of where and when he heard the owls calling—as we went deeper into the forest, the CALL notation appeared more frequently on the markers. Using my flashlight, I checked each marker for the notes. When we came on one that noted CALL, Luce and I would stop walking and listen.

After our second stop, we both took a drink of water and looked around the darkening forest. Somewhere off to our right, we heard a shuffling noise. It sounded like a fair-sized animal; I guessed it was a deer.

At least I hoped it was a deer. And that was because I hoped it wasn't a bear. Coming face-to-face with Smokey once in this forest had already been one time too many. And as far as I could tell, Stan wasn't around this time to scare it off for me.

Luce moved closer to me.

"Do you think there are moose up here?" she asked in a quiet voice.

I was worried about a bear. Luce was worried about a moose. Were we brave birders, or what?

"We don't have to worry about moose, Luce," I assured her. "They aren't predators. They eat grass."

"I know that," she said, making that almost-hissing sound again.

Luce the Goose, I thought. I could feel myself smiling. Oh man, she'd kill me for that one for sure.

"I'm not worried that a moose would eat me. I just don't want to run into one," she explained, a note of annoyance in her tone. "They may be dumb, but they're big. And strong. Not a great combination, if you know what I mean."

I knew exactly what she meant. I did, after all, work with big, strong adolescent males every day. Not to infer that they were dumb, but sometimes you had to wonder what in the world they were thinking . . . or not. So far, none of them—to my knowledge—had tried to take down a train, but in a high school counselor's office, you learned to be ready for anything.

Luce took another drink of her water. "Once, when we went camping in Wyoming one summer, we were up in the mountains outside of Laramie, and we hiked into this big meadow. We were about to lay out a picnic when I read a posted warning that said 'MOOSE RELEASE AREA. PLEASE USE CAUTION.' Well, I was petrified. The only moose I'd ever seen in the flesh was a stuffed one, and that had scared the bejeebers out of me." She capped her drink bottle and looked at me.

"It was this huge stuffed dead moose with an enormous rack of antlers that stood in the lobby at the lodge we stayed in when we went to Thunder Bay in Canada when I was six years old. My mom wanted to take a picture of me with the moose, so I stood in front of it. I didn't know my dad was hiding behind it, and just as my mom snapped the picture, my dad shoved it up against my shoulder and made a moose sound. I screamed and jumped about a foot straight up, hit the underside of the stuffed moose's neck and fell back on the floor."

"Poor baby," I said, putting my arm around her shoulder and hugging her close. "No wonder you don't like moose."

Luce started laughing. "My mom was so furious with my dad that she hardly spoke to him the rest of the day. She was afraid I'd need therapy to get over my fright."

"Did you?"

"Heck, no. I just learned to stay away from moose. Although I suppose it might have contributed to my obsessive habit of immediately scanning my surroundings wherever I go so I don't get taken by surprise."

"That's true," I said. "I've seen you do that scanning thing every time we go somewhere new. You did it last night at the Splashing Rock, didn't you?"

"Yup. No moose."

I gave her shoulder another squeeze.

"But I bet I noticed something there that you didn't," she said.

"What's that?"

"Thompson's jacket hanging on the back of his chair. When I was motioning to you to come back to our table, I noticed the lettering on the right shoulder of his jacket."

"What did it say? 'VNT'?"

"Nope. It said 'DNR.'" She looked up at the sky, looking for stars. "And, Bobby, did you also notice the truck parked in the VNT lot today?"

I wasn't sure where she was going with this, but suddenly I got a feeling that I wasn't going to be happy when she got there.

"Yes," I said slowly. "It was an old pick-up like the one I drove for the DNR."

Luce laid her gloved hand on my cheek. Even in the dark, I could see the lines of concern on her face. "You told me that yesterday, when you and Knott drove up here, an old DNR truck flew past you, and you saw the DNR patch on the driver's jacket shoulder. His right shoulder. Bobby, you and I both know that the DNR doesn't use that emblem on the right shoulder; it's on the left. We also know, thanks to Eddie, that Thompson tried to pass himself off as an agency employee while he was poaching trees."

I waited for her to spell it out.

"I think Thompson was sitting in that truck waiting for you to go by, then when you did, he raced ahead of you and got himself into position to watch that cleared area." Her eyes glimmered in the night. "He had a trophy for marksmanship in his office, Bobby. It was sitting behind his desk. He shot at you to keep both you and Knott out of his poaching territory."

"And all he had to do to identify me was watch for my license plate," I filled in for her. "Which means that Thompson knew I was going up there yesterday afternoon, and that I was someone he needed to keep out." I shrugged in my parka. "But I didn't even meet the man until last night, Luce. So how could he plan to get rid of me before he knew me?"

In the distance, an owl hooted. A moment later, another owl answered.

"Great Horned," I said automatically.

Luce hugged me tight. "I think there's someone else involved, Bobby. You said yourself that both Ellis and Alice heard you say you were on your way up there."

"It's not Ellis," I said. "He wants the study. And because of that, I can't imagine that he'd be mixed up with someone who was destroying the habitat. So that leaves Alice." I patted

Luce's back and held her away from me so I could look in her eyes. "I honestly don't have a clue what Alice is capable of, Luce. But I want to think that if she were really dangerous, Stan would have done something about his sister before now."

"All right, let's think that, Bobby," Luce agreed. "But let's also remember that someone in the cities delivered a note and a dead owl to your deck. Maybe that someone also knew you were coming up here to owl and contacted Thompson to keep an eye out for you and make sure you stayed out of the Boreal sites."

"You think Thompson has a partner in the cities?"

She nodded. "It makes sense, doesn't it?"

"Yes," came a voice from behind me. "It does."

I rubbed my hand over my eyes. "I swear, you're going to give me a heart attack." I turned to peer into the camouflaged face. "What took you so long, Stan?"

Luce pointed to the crossbow slung across his back. "What are you doing with that? It's not bow-hunting season."

"I'm not bow-hunting."

Luce and I waited for him to continue, but he didn't.

Instead, I heard another sound. But it wasn't an owl.

It was the sound of machinery, off in the distance. Machinery grinding. Like gears.

The sound I'd heard last Saturday after finding Rahr's body.

I tried to visualize the maps I'd studied when I was trying to locate Rahr's sites. Where was a road close enough that I could hear a vehicle from here? On the maps, there hadn't been any roads marked at all, for the simple reason that Boreal Owls don't nest anywhere near places where there might be traffic. They liked their seclusion. Like Eddie, they wanted distance from the rest of the world, but no matter what, it seemed like the rest of the world was determined to come after them.

Including me.

Damn.

The last puzzle pieces fell into place.

The grinding engine I was hearing wasn't on any road. It was on an abandoned logging trail. A logging trail that cut right through the owls' habitat. And given the sloppy thawing conditions this year, the vehicle had to be mired in mud—hence, the sound of grinding gears. Last week, when I'd found Rahr, someone had also been trying to move a vehicle somewhere nearby. That was the sound I'd heard. And who would be so desperate to attempt to gun a big vehicle out of the forest in March mud?

Someone who was using it to poach trees.

Someone who had to remove evidence of illegal harvesting before some birders came looking for Boreals on their own private owl tours and stumbled across said poaching operation.

Someone like Thompson who had told Luce and me he had two trucks stuck up in the forest.

Someone like Thompson, who'd been captured on Eddie's tape heading into the woods on both last Friday and Saturday.

Location, location, location.

And what was the one thing that had tied all those poaching sites together? The owl tours, of course. Before Rahr conducted the tours last spring, who else knew how to find those particular places? Ellis, perhaps, though it had been a long time since he'd been working with Rahr, and Alice, probably, though I expected her knowledge of the sites as Rahr's longtime secretary was more clerical than first-hand. So, basically, the owls had had the forest to themselves.

Until Thompson, the unemployed logger, signed on to take the tour and noted the isolated locations, at which point he recognized an untapped gold mine of lumber and native plants, both of which could command high prices as building supplies and landscaping stock. And though the locations were remote, they were perfect—because since no one knew exactly where the owls were, the whole territory had been placed under the protection of the DNR. As long as a poacher cut trees in November, no one would even know he'd been there, because no one—not even Rahr—was in these woods then. Rahr only did his research in March and April when the owls were mating. S.O.B. had made sure people stayed away thanks to all the publicity about preserving the integrity of the Boreal Owls' habitat. And because the DNR had banned any logging, there wouldn't be any timber people nosing around, either. So an enterprising poacher could have the place to himself—a protected, virtually unlimited supply of Very Nice Trees, and, come spring, ladyslippers—that could yield him a very nice profit.

Rahr, then, must have discovered the topped trees on his first foray back to his research sites earlier this month, figured someone was cutting the trees and decided to put a stop to it before it scattered the owls. He spiked the trees, not realizing that the tree topping was a seasonal thing for Christmas and that his sites were no longer in danger of cutting. At least not during the owl mating season.

"So you think Thompson killed Rahr to protect his poaching business?" Luce asked after I laid out my theory to her and Stan.

"Either that, or hired someone else to do it," I said, sliding a glance at Stan, wondering exactly what his stint as a CIA field agent had entailed.

"Not me," he said. "I don't do that. Anymore."

"Good to know," I told him. "Not that it helps."

"Your threats," he added. "It's all about the vehicle. They didn't want you to find it."

"If it's Thompson," Luce said, "he must have heard that you were the one who found Rahr's body, Bobby. And then he heard about your reputation for finding birds, and he was afraid you'd be back for the Boreal and find his stuck truck instead. It was never about identifying Rahr's killer or protecting the owls at all—he was afraid you were going to destroy his business."

We all stood there for a minute or two, trying to process our conclusions. If we were right, Thompson was a murderer, and I'd almost been his second victim. Luce and I had sat in his office just hours ago.

"I've got to sit down," I said, and dropped to the ground.

"Near death does that to you," Stan said.

I looked up at him, a dark ghost in the night. "What the hell are you doing here, Stan?"

"Birding."

"No!" I shook my head and caught his eyes. "I mean really. What is this 'contract' you're working on? Because every time I turn around, there you are. What's the connection, Stan? Even though that's not really your name, is it?"

He blinked. "Knott."

"I know it's not!" I almost shouted.

"No," Stan said. "Knott. The detective. He told you about me."

"We had a video recording," Luce explained. "You were on a surveillance tape from a road."

Stan nodded. "Crazy Eddie's place. I smiled at the camera."

"Stan!" I was losing what little patience I had left after a very long, very frustrating day. "What is the contract?"

He nodded in the direction of the grinding gears, which were now silent. "VNT. Tax fraud. Lily's books tipped me off. I really am an accountant," he added. "A forensic accountant. For the government."

"So now what do we do?" Luce asked.

I looked at Stan and then at Luce.

"Find the Boreal."

Chapter Twenty-Four

We crept through the forest, stopping every few yards to listen. Twice I thought I heard part of the Boreal Owl's flute call, but each time, it broke up before it finished. We were getting close to where I'd found Rahr's body, and little shivers were racing up my spine as I remembered the arm popping up in front of me. Then, from out of nowhere, something Thompson had said popped into my head.

"What about Montgomery?"

Luce turned to look at me. "What about her?"

"Thompson said she gave him the idea to start his own business. We know they went on the owl tour together. Maybe she's the one who came up with the poaching idea. I don't know—maybe it was her revenge against owls in general after she lost her job with the lumber companies in the Pacific Northwest."

"Bobby," Luce said. She stared me straight in the eye. "I love you, honey, but get a grip."

"Yeah, you're right," I said, shaking my head. "Momentary insanity."

"Maybe not," Stan's voice floated behind me. I'd followed Knott's advice and asked Stan to bring up the rear of our little march. No reason to deny the man's expertise. An ounce of prevention, you know.

"From the sparse financial data I've managed to obtain on VNT, there's obviously another partner involved. Just like you suggested earlier, Luce."

"I'm impressed," I said, my voice tinged with awe. "That was a pretty complex sentence for you, Stan. Are you all right?"

"Eat dirt, White."

"No thanks," I replied. "Been there, done that yesterday."

"So you think Montgomery might be the partner, Stan?" Luce tried to continue the conversation.

"Good probability. She has access to money. Some I can't trace. And she and Thompson seem pretty tight."

We stopped for a moment and listened again. The air was colder now, the night completely black. We caught a glimpse of stars through the pines, and the trail was easy traveling since so much more of the snow had melted since I had walked last weekend. I stuck my hand in my parka pocket and pulled out a little gadget Eddie had pressed on me.

"To be honest, I'd wondered if perhaps Montgomery might be afraid of Thompson," I said. "After seeing that tape, I wondered if she might have seen her pal meeting with Rahr's killer, and she was afraid of what he might do if she went to the police. "

"What's that?" Stan pointed to the tiny recorder in my hand.

"A toy from Crazy Eddie," I said, turning it over in my palm. "He said it's the highest resolution recording device on the planet Earth. I don't know if that's true, but he's pretty skilled with this stuff, so it's probably better than most. He said I should record the Boreal when I hear it. Kind of like a trophy, he said." I put it back in my pocket. "We'll see."

We walked for another ten minutes in quiet. Great Horned Owls continued to hoot, and once more, I thought I heard the Boreal, but again it didn't complete the call. Luce thought she saw movement in the trees off to our left and raised her night vision binos to her eyes. She didn't move for a full two minutes, so I lifted my binos, too. I didn't see anything nearby, so I adjusted the focal distance out.

"I'll be damned," I breathed.

"Yup," Luce breathed back.

"Money in the bank," Stan said, his binos up, too.

We were looking at a cherry-picker.

Standing on the hillside across a ravine, the picker looked like part of an oversized preying mantis, partially draped in camouflage cloth. Covered in snow from last weekend, the machine would have disappeared into the forest because no one would have been able to distinguish it from the landscape around it. It tilted at an odd angle.

"It's stuck," Luce said. "I bet it was on its way to the Boreal site to do some harvesting and got stuck in the snow back in December. That must be one of the old logging trails it's sitting on."

"Which Thompson knew about because he used to log up here," Stan added.

"And if it was sitting there when Rahr made his first trip up here earlier this month, he would have been convinced he needed to do something to protect the habitat." I thought again of Eddie's comments. "Eddie said Rahr told him he was going to do some preventative maintenance. I guess he was referring to the tree spikes."

We crossed down and through the ravine, then slogged back up the hill to take a closer look at the stranded cherry-picker. Definitely sitting at a tilt and definitely stuck, it was splattered with freshly churned earth along its sides. I put my hand on the hood over the engine.

Still warm.

This was what we'd heard less than an hour ago. Someone had been here, trying to move the truck.

Behind me, I felt, rather than heard, Stan melt away into the night.

"Luce," I whispered. I reached out for her hand and pulled her next to me. "Do you have your cell phone with you?"

"Yes," she whispered back. "Why are we whispering?"

"Because. Humor me. Give it to me, please."

She pulled it out of her jeans pocket and handed it to me. I looked around us, but I didn't see anything moving. Stan was gone. I glanced into the cab of the cherry picker to make sure no one was hiding on the floor of the cab. Nobody there.

I pulled out my flashlight and aimed it at the seat. A parka, heavy gloves, and a wool cap were laying on the bench. Clothing you'd wear in the woods on a frigid day. Clothing that would keep you from freezing.

Clothing that Rahr's body hadn't been covered in.

I punched in Knott's phone number.

"Knott here."

I let out the breath I hadn't realized I was holding. "John," I whispered, my voice barely audible.

"Really, I'm not here," the recorded message ran. "I'm unable to take your call, but if you leave a message at the sound of the tone, I'll get back to you."

This is why I hate answering machines.

"Allow me," Margaret Montgomery said, stepping out of the darkness from behind the machine. She reached up to take the phone from my fingers. At the same time, she raised her other hand. In it, she held a gun.

Chapter Twenty-Five

This was not what I wanted to see.

For a second, I had that same feeling I had when the deer materialized in front of my car that night and I swerved to miss it: like I had been instantaneously transported into another universe where things just randomly appeared out of nowhere and completely altered your experience.

Except that the deer hadn't been holding a gun.

Nor had it looked like my mother.

Stupid, stupid, stupid, I told myself. If I hadn't been so intent on finding the owl, I would've realized that the gears we'd heard earlier was not a good sign—that someone else was in the vicinity. Someone who might not be totally thrilled to see us traipsing down the trail. But somehow I'd convinced myself we were safe: the grinding had stopped, the forest was silent and there were three of us. Safety in numbers. I gave myself a mental kick in the head. There were two of us yesterday and somebody still took a shot at me. Obviously, safety in numbers failed to kick in until you got past three.

At least.

"Step away from the truck," Montgomery said, waving the gun slightly to my right, indicating to Luce and me where she wanted us to move. "Further."

Obediently, we moved together, practically joined at our hips. As we shuffled, I felt Eddie's recorder that I had dropped back in my pocket dig against my leg. I carefully slipped my hand in and hit the record button. Someday, I reasoned, inquiring minds might want to know.

Like maybe the police when they found our bodies.

Montgomery walked us further away from the vehicle, then she slowly backed up to the cab, holding the gun on us all the while. She took a quick glance into the cab.

"Looking for something?" I asked.

There was enough moonlight filtering through the tree limbs that I could see expressions chasing each other across Montgomery's face: expressions like frustration, calculation, resolution. Gee, isn't it great that I can recognize these things? Too bad it didn't count for squat at the moment.

"Yes," she replied, her sarcasm thick. "I'm looking for a way out of this mess."

"And which mess would that be?"

Crap! I was doing it again, asking counselor questions when what I really wanted was for Montgomery to stop talking, go away, and leave us alone.

"Where should I start?"

A memory flared in my brain. I was in the girl's bathroom at school one morning, about a year ago. A petite brunette stood at the sink, shaking, holding a razor blade just above her wrist. Calmly, I talked with her, using every trick I'd learned in Crisis Intervention 692 in grad school. I empathized, I gained her trust, I directed her attention, I listened. In the end, she had folded and dropped the razor.

I just had to do the same thing here. Except that this wasn't about wasn't a teen with a razor at her wrist. This was a desperate woman with a gun . . . aimed at me.

I looked Montgomery in the eye. "I'm listening."

"For starters, I need to get these clothes out of this cherry-picker."

"Why's that, Margaret?"

I couldn't be sure, but I thought her gun hand wavered a little. Even though my eyes were well adjusted to the darkness, there were too many shadows to make my vision completely reliable. I tried to quiet myself even more and focus completely on her so I would know the moment she lapsed, either mentally or physically. And the second that happened, I'd push Luce to the side and make a dive to tackle Montgomery, and we might be able to get out of this situation alive, even if a little worse for wear.

And then it came.

Not the lapse I was waiting for, but something else.

The cry of an owl.

Rising, flute-like notes. A fast series of seven tones.

For crying out loud, I thought. *Not now!*

Ruthlessly, I shut it out. I needed to concentrate on Montgomery. My life, and Luce's, were riding on my paying attention. Very, very close attention.

"I have to get the clothes out of here," she said again, "because we can't get the cherry-picker out. It's stuck. I just tried again a little while ago. Damn weather. Either the ground is too soft from the snow, or too hard from the freeze, or too slippery from the thaw. I hate the weather here. You can't depend on a thing."

She was right about that, but I didn't think this was the opportune time to compare meteorological notes. Then again, everyone likes to talk about the weather. Especially in Minnesota.

"Is the weather different in Seattle?" I asked, grasping at the slim hope that she'd been living in the state long enough to want to talk weather. The truth was, I needed a conversational distraction, and this was going to have to be it.

She smiled and nodded. "Vern told me you stopped by today and that you were heading up here. That's why I came up tonight to try to get the picker moved. He thinks it's hidden well enough, but I know about you. You find the birds no one else does, and I was afraid you'd find this. I was right. And now I can't let you tell Knott, about the picker or the clothes."

Montgomery shifted her weight, still holding the gun steady. "Vern also said he told you that I encouraged him to start his own business."

"VNT is going well, isn't it?" I tried for a soothing tone. "Was the poaching your idea, too?"

"Of course not. That's illegal."

She sounded offended that I would even think it, but at least she was getting engaged in the conversation. That was good, in my favor. She shifted her weight again. Her arm definitely relaxed a fraction.

"I just mentioned there were a lot of woods up here that nobody even knew about. Trees and flowers no one would ever miss. I was a lobbyist for the timber industry, Bob. I believe we should use our natural resources wisely, but that we should, indeed, use them."

"I'm familiar with that sentiment." I hoped that Eddie's gizmo was picking up every word. "So when the Pacific Northwest logging companies got clocked by the spotted owl . . ."

Montgomery visibly stiffened. Suddenly, anger radiated off her in almost tangible waves.

Uh-oh. Ixnay on the owl-ay, I told myself. Somehow, I'd hit a nerve. A very big, very raw nerve.

"They didn't just get clocked, Bob," she snapped. "They were shredded. They were ground through the mill just like the wood they harvested for paper. Families were ruined when there were suddenly no jobs, no income. Children went hungry. Communities disappeared. No one was prepared.

"But that wasn't the worst of it," Montgomery almost spit, she was so angry. "Not for me, at least."

"What happened?" I asked. I kept my eyes locked on Montgomery's face. Beside me, I could feel Luce tense, and I carefully placed my hand on her arm, willing her to be still for just a little bit more.

"My brother was killed." Montgomery's voice went flat. "He worked for the lumber company. He was a logger. He cut into a tree that was spiked. His chain saw snapped, and the blade flew back into his chest. He was dead when I got to the hospital."

I heard Luce's quick inhale next to me, and then silence filled the night. Montgomery was still holding the gun on us, though it was definitely shaking in her hand.

"It was an exchange," I offered. "You lost your brother to the woods, so you figured the woods owed you something in return. Vern was the middleman."

Montgomery took a deep breath, and the gun steadied. "Yes, I guess you could say that. We made good partners. He needed capital to get the business off the ground—literally, with the cherry-picker—and I knew where to find it. It was the perfect enterprise—free stock and minimal expenses. Fat profits. Our investor couldn't be happier. And the Boreal sites were ideal. Vern could get in, cut, and get out with no one ever being the wiser."

"As long as it wasn't March or April," I added.

"We were doing really well with just the lumber last fall," she continued. "But then, as the holidays approached, we saw the real money-maker: Christmas trees. You wouldn't believe how much money that generated."

"Actually, I would," I said. "My sister made a killing."

My eyes dropped to the gun in her hand. Maybe that wasn't the best word choice under the circumstances.

"And then it started snowing," Montgomery went on. "The roads got so bad, we decided to just leave the picker here till spring. We covered it with the tarp, and the snow just piled on."

Montgomery stopped to catch her breath. I was pretty sure she was tiring, because she clasped her other hand over the one holding the gun and raised it just a little higher.

And then the owl called again.

This time it was closer, and there was no mistaking the rising flute call. Despite having a gun pointed at me, I could actually feel a smile on my face. Here I'd finally gotten my Boreal, but I wasn't sure I was going to live long enough to put it on my list.

My life list.

Which, unless I managed to disarm Montgomery pretty soon here, was going to be significantly shorter than I had hoped.

"Margaret," Luce said, her voice cutting through the silence that had formed around us. "It's so cold. Let's all just go home."

Montgomery laughed bitterly. "Don't you think I want to? But you're both a liability now, and I'm going to have to fix that."

Another hoot of the owl filled the clearing.

But this time, it came from directly above us.

We all looked up automatically, but before I could lunge for Montgomery, she had the gun aimed at my heart.

"I hate owls!" Her voice rose. "They killed my brother. When I heard Rahr pounding in those spikes, all I could think of was that chain saw flying into my brother's chest."

"You heard Rahr spiking the trees?"

"Yes!" she shouted, suddenly raging. "He was spiking the trees! We were trying to get the damn picker moved out of here before anyone found it, and I heard the pounding echoing from over the rise, and I knew what it was!" The gun was vibrating in her hands. "I saw him! I couldn't help it! He was making such a racket, he didn't hear me come up to his back. There was a big branch. I picked it up and swung it as hard as I could. I slammed him into the tree!"

Montogmery was a big woman. With all her effort behind the blow, I could well imagine that it would have knocked Rahr out.

And then a blur of movement flew out of the night. Montgomery went down, hard, her gun flying off into the darkness.

I blinked. Stan already had Montgomery's arms twisted behind her back and was pulling handcuffs out of a pocket.

I drew in a long breath. "What took you so long?" I asked him, for the second time that night.

Beside me, Luce squeaked and abruptly jerked away from me.

"Move a muscle, and she's going to have a heart attack."

Completely stunned, I turned. A man was holding Luce in a headlock, a hypodermic needle to her neck. Lit by the thin moonlight that filtered through the pines, he looked tanned and fit, but even in the dimness, his trademark silver toupee gave him away.

"Dr. Phil?"

Chapter Twenty-Six

I advised you to stay home, Bob," Dr. Phil reminded me. "Repeatedly. But you just couldn't stay away, could you?" His hand steady at Luce's neck, he nodded toward Stan, who had rolled off of Montgomery. "If he moves, Luce gets the shot. It'll stop her heart."

"I'm not moving," Stan said. "What do you want?"

"Get up, Margaret," Dr. Phil ordered. "We're going to do it right this time."

Montgomery sat up, obviously dazed from her impact with Stan and the ground.

"This time?" My voice rasped.

"If you want something done right, you have to do it yourself," the doctor said, exasperation plain in his tone. "First Andrew and now this."

He turned his attention back to Montgomery, who was now on her feet, though somewhat shaky. She took a step or two and stopped, then bent over to catch her breath, her hands on her knees.

"Margaret, there's a cord here behind me," Dr. Phil instructed her. "Take it and tie Bob up first. Tightly. We'll get Mr. Commando there in a minute. For now, I just want him to lie there where I can see him." He tightened his grip around Luce's head. "Don't try it, Luce. The needle's faster than you."

I had to look away. The feeling of complete helplessness, seeing Luce immobilized in Dr. Phil's hold, a deadly needle at her neck, was making my head spin and my vision blur. On top of that, I couldn't believe that Dr. Phil—a man I'd known and respected for years—was the one with the needle, and somehow involved in Rahr's murder. In desperation, I glanced at Stan, flat on his back, staring straight up into the trees.

He didn't look desperate at all. In fact, he was grinning, his teeth shining white in his camouflaged face.

I followed his gaze.

About thirty feet above the ground, a Great Horned Owl was poised on a limb, looking down and weaving back and forth, a behavior that allow him to pinpoint his prey all the better. He was about to grab tonight's dinner.

And I suddenly knew why Stan was smiling.

Tonight's dinner wasn't a rodent.

Tonight's target was Dr. Phil's bush of a silver toupee. Dr. Phil was about to join Uncle Gus in a very exclusive club.

The owl spread his wings, ready to launch himself in a silent, deadly attack.

I felt the surge of pure adrenaline in my legs.

Margaret was coming toward me with the rope, but that wasn't my concern at the moment. I prayed that both the owl and I were faster than the needle.

Another heartbeat, and the owl and I were both flying through the night.

I dove straight for Luce, wrenching her out of Dr. Phil's grip at the very moment the enormous owl reached the doctor's head. With a vicious swipe of his powerful, inch-long talons, the owl raked the man's scalp, capturing the tempting toupee and leaving bloody gashes on the dome of his bald head. By the time Dr. Phil could even realize what had happened, Stan had chopped him on the neck, knocking him out, and once again had Margaret pinned to the ground.

Shaking and gasping for air, I lay in a pile of wet leaves, holding Luce as close as I could, waiting for the tremors of the post-adrenaline rush to subside. Against my neck I could feel her breath warming the chilled skin between my woolen cap and my parka collar. I wanted to hold her right there forever.

"Are you all right?" she asked, her voice barely a whisper.

"Yeah," I told her. "Never better. I'm having a great time. How about you?"

She took a deep breath. "I'm okay. A little shook, maybe. I've never been very fond of needles, and I don't think that's going to change in the foreseeable future."

I stroked her back in understanding. "I can appreciate that. I'm not especially crazy about them, either. So, I guess we're not going to take up needlepoint, huh?"

And then Stan was looming above us. "I called Knott. He's on the way." He pointed towards Dr. Phil and Montgomery, who were both face-down in the earth, their hands tied together with the cord Dr. Phil had pointed out to Montgomery. "They're not going anywhere."

"Thanks, Stan." I pulled myself to my feet and helped Luce up. Then I offered my hand to him. "You can chase birds with me any time, buddy."

He clasped my hand with his own. "Ditto."

"Ssh," Luce hissed at us. Slowly raising her hand, she pointed up into the branches over our heads. It took me a minute to see it, but once I found the intense yellow eyes staring at me, the rest of the little owl's body became distinguishable from the surrounding blackness.

"You little devil," I whispered.

Because, if nothing else, it had been one hell of a chase.

Chapter Twenty-Seven

It was very late on Saturday night when I finally turned the key in my front door.

These weekends up north were killing me.

I really needed to rephrase that.

Since I'd had a gun aimed at my heart not even twenty-four hours ago, *killing* was not a word I could consider using frivolously at the moment. To be honest, I was so exhausted, I didn't think there were any words I could use at the moment, frivolous or not. I dumped my overnight bag, parka, and binos inside the door and collapsed on my living room sofa.

Luce, Stan, and I had all given statements, I'd handed over Eddie's recorder (which did, indeed, have almost-miraculous powers of audio reproduction—we could hear every one of the Boreal Owl's calls on it, along with every word uttered by Montgomery and Dr. Phil), and finished all the paperwork Duluth's finest could possibly push at us. We did, however, decline to buy any tickets to the policemen's ball as it was scheduled for next month. By then, I would be too busy with girls' softball to make it up for the big event, and Luce had a conference to cater. Stan's excuse was something about tax returns and April 15.

He was, after all, an accountant. Among other things.

About halfway through our stay at the station, Knott had joined Luce and me in his office. Stan had already migrated down the hall to talk to local officers about the results of his own investigation into VNT's illicit operation. Apparently, now that his covert assignment was over, Stan wasn't worried about anyone on the force interfering with his investigation. For a while, he could actually play well with others again.

"So, do you want to press charges against anyone?" Knott asked us. "You can take your pick Montgomery, Thompson or Dr. Hovde. Of course, you'll have to stand in line behind the state and Rahr's widow, not to mention the litigation we may have pending the VNT garden business."

"I just want to go home," Luce answered.

I agreed. Filing charges, giving testimony, listening to lawyers and being hassled by the press was not the way I wanted to spend even the next ten minutes of my life, let alone the next twelve months. Stan might have been an ace when it came to disappearing, but I wasn't going to fool myself that I could pull off a similar vanishing act in the face of a media spotlight. Besides, I didn't want to vanish. I had a great life back in Savage. And now, thanks to Knott's arrests, I could have my great life . . . back.

I took Luce's hand and gave it a squeeze. She looked worn out, and I expected I wasn't going to be winning any fresh-face awards with my tired mug, either. Nor was Knott.

"Tired?" I asked him.

"Absolutely." He sprawled in a chair and tipped it back on its hind legs. "I like you, Bob, but this is two nights in one week that you've kept me up way past my bedtime. I'm sort of hoping you'll stay in the Twin Cities for a while now. You know? Away from here?"

"That's the plan," I said. Now that I'd scored the Boreal, I was planning to stick close to home for the immediate future. Like, really close. As in my backyard. Maybe I'd venture out for birdseed, but that was about it.

Which reminded me of Lily's Landscaping and VNT.

"So where does Thompson fit in?" I asked. "I mean, besides running a poaching business? Did he help Montgomery remove Rahr's clothes? Montgomery told us they were trying to get the picker out last Friday when she heard Rahr pounding the spikes, so I assume he knew that she had killed him."

Knott brought his chair back to the floor and reached for his cup of coffee on the desk. "Actually, Thompson didn't know a thing about the murder until he learned about it on the radio Sunday evening."

"No way," I said. "How could he *not* know? He was right there trying to get the picker moved."

Knott took a sip of the coffee. "No, he wasn't, Bob. When Montgomery told you that *they* were working on the picker, she wasn't referring to Thompson."

"It was Dr. Phil," Luce said.

Of course. At the MOU meeting, I'd even commented on his early return, and what had he replied? That he had business to attend to. And that would also explain how my mysterious threat-maker tracked me down so fast: Montgomery must have heard about the discovery of Rahr's body on the radio and called Dr. Phil, who only had to check the MOU email to confirm that I was the birder who was planning to hunt Boreals that weekend. "He was the investor that Montgomery mentioned," I said now. "She said they were doing some business together."

"Did he know it was poaching?" Luce asked Knott. "I can't believe he'd get involved in something like that. He had plenty of money."

"*Had*, Luce. According to Montgomery, Dr. Hovde lost a bundle last summer on the stock market, so when she offered him the big returns of VNT, he didn't quibble over details." He took another sip from the cup in his hand. "When I explained to Montgomery that it might be a good idea to cooperate—maybe reduce prison time, for instance—she had all kinds of information for us. Including the fact that Hovde had stopped in to talk with Rahr last Thursday afternoon at the university, in hopes of getting him to suspend the study this season. The good doctor was angling for time to get the picker out of there."

Which was why Rahr was so defensive on the phone with me later that evening. It hadn't just been Alice's disclosing site locations to Stan that had alarmed Rahr; it had been Hovde's pressuring him to drop the research.

"When Montgomery couldn't get Thompson to retrieve the picker," Knott continued, "she panicked and called Hovde in Florida, because she knew Rahr would find it, and she didn't have anyone else she could turn to. Hovde hightailed it up here, tried to reason with Rahr, and when that failed, drove up to the forest with Montgomery to try to get the picker out of there."

At which point, things really deteriorated: Montgomery heard the hammering, went crazy and attacked Rahr.

"It was Hovde's idea to remove Rahr's outer clothing, Bob. When he saw what Montgomery had done, he had to make a choice: try to save Rahr's life or try to salvage his cash cow. He was a doctor; he knew the freezing temperatures could finish the job on Rahr and no one would have to know about the poaching. He tossed the clothes in the picker since they were wet with snow and told Margaret to pick them up later." Knott stood up to leave. "Hovde didn't want to risk even a DNA trace of Rahr to show up in his car trunk."

"But Eddie had tape of Thompson—" I started to say, then remembered again that the tape could only attest to which drivers passed by the gate, not their destinations.

"Montgomery said he was checking on ladyslippers on the other side of Eddie's property," Knott explained. "And that he almost got caught in a shouting match between Ellis and Alice."

In all the excitement, I'd forgotten about Ms. Multiple and our newly-appointed Boreal researcher. But Knott had the scoop, thanks to a very late night conversation with Alice and Ellis a few hours earlier at the station. Determined to make peace with his former mentor before he left town to visit his ailing father, Ellis had learned from the department office on late Thursday that Rahr was heading out for the Boreal sites on Friday morning. Eavesdropping as usual on the office line, Alice decided to tail Ellis up to the sites to try to make her own reconciliation with the younger professor, who'd repeatedly rebuffed her attentions. As it turned out, Ellis missed Rahr, but ran into Alice instead. Steamed by both her eavesdropping and persistent pursuit of his affections, Ellis gave up on trying to track down Rahr and took the long way back home, as did Alice.

"You know, Bob, if you hadn't found Rahr's body when you did, it's possible no one would ever have known what really happened," Knott said. "I think you must have beaten that bear to Rahr by only a matter of minutes. If you hadn't, there might not even have been a corpse left to stumble over. Without the body, we would have had just another missing person case, not a murder."

And I wouldn't have gone home to find a threatening note on my bird feeder, a dead owl on my deck and the definite possibility of my career going down the drain. Not to mention the chance to get shot in the forest or trailed by a former CIA agent. Gee, all that in exchange for chasing a little Boreal Owl.

Who says birding is boring?

Another detective leaned into the doorway and handed Knott a clear plastic bag with something in it. Knott thanked him and turned back to me, smiling.

"Remember when I asked you if you knew if Rahr wore reading glasses?"

I remembered.

"These are the ones we found under his body," he said, holding up the plastic bag for Luce and me to see its contents.

I looked at the item for only a second or two before I recognized what it was.

"Those are my mom's reading glasses," I said.

"They're Montgomery's reading glasses," Knott corrected me. "We found them beneath Rahr's body when we cleared the scene last Sunday morning. My guess is that they slipped out of Montgomery's pocket while she and Hovde were removing Rahr's outerwear."

Looking at the glasses, I remembered seeing an identical pair in Ellis's hands as he returned them to Alice. I glanced up at Knott.

"Yes, I know," he said, reading my mind. "Alice had the same kind. When I saw her using them when I went back to talk with Ellis after our lunch, I thought I had an inside track for finding Rahr's killer. Then, when you got shot, I was convinced that Ellis and she were working together, since he'd left our meeting early and had ample time to track us up there. I was in the middle of grilling them both when our local publicity hound turned himself in, but until you gave me the tape, I didn't have a shred of evidence to connect them to last Friday when Rahr was killed."

"But then you thought your suspicions were confirmed?" Luce asked.

"That's right. I knew Ellis had been nervous every time I talked to him, and the tape proved to me he wasn't telling me everything. So when I pulled him in again last evening after I saw Eddie's tape in your hotel room, I let him have it. I showed him the tape. I told him about someone shooting at you, Bob, and how we knew that he was a crack shot. I asked him if he wanted to tell me anything before I arrested him for Rahr's murder."

"A little hardball," I commented.

"That's right," Knott agreed. "And it worked. He couldn't wait to give me a play-by-play of his drive up to the site last Friday morning, including his confrontation with Alice. Then I got the full story of his less-than-happy history with Rahr and their differences of opinion when it came to research protocol. He also told me he'd been devastated to think that he'd been the last person to see Rahr before he was murdered, but he was terrified to tell us about it, because he figured he would be nominating himself as the killer. He even thought that you, Bob, were an undercover detective trying to pick up information to build a case."

"Oh, yeah, that's me," I interrupted. "Amateur sleuth extraordinaire. I thought he was going to punch me in the mouth when he found me in his office."

"But you didn't arrest him," Luce pointed out. "What made you believe him?"

He lifted the plastic bag containing the glasses. "He had a big head," Knott explained. "His face was too big for the red glasses to fit."

I started to laugh, remembering what Jim had said about Rahr's opinion of Ellis when he was a grad student.

He had a big head, he'd said.

Maybe the truth did hurt, sometimes.

But sometimes, it saved your little caboose.

Chapter Twenty-Eight

"Oh, Mr. White, like, you were so right!"

Music to my ears. I love it when my hard-earned wisdom is validated by the experience of hormone-driven teenagers.

"Lindsay wasn't jealous at all!" Kim squealed. "She knew what a jerk Brad was, and she was trying to protect me by keeping him away from me. I was just not, like, seeing him for what he really was. And even though I got mad at her, like, Lindsay stuck to her guns!"

I flinched just a little. I didn't know if I'd ever hear the word *gun* again without feeling an invisible finger of ice sliding down my spine. It had been five days now since Luce and I got home from the North Shore, but I still dreamed of a gun at my heart every night.

Lindsay showed up at my office door, and she and Kim threw themselves into each other's arms. "You are so my very best friend!" they shrieked at each other. The noise level was a bit intense, but at least they weren't crying. My tissue budget had already become a thing of the past.

"All's well that ends well, right, ladies?" I said, knowing full well this was by no means any kind of end, just an intermission. I mean, really, what's a drama queen without her drama? Just another student.

Heaven forbid.

Behind Lindsay and Kim, I could see Mr. Lenzen walking into the counseling office area and making his way over to my doorway. The girls shuffled off, still wrapped around each other, emitting little squeaky sounds. Dressed in his three-piece uniform, Mr. Lenzen (I don't think I'll ever be able to think of him as Lenzen—it seems too familiar for him, I guess) reached out his hand and, with his linen handkerchief, dusted off the seat of one of my ugly burgundy chairs. He sat down and folded his handkerchief back into his pocket.

As I watched him, I tried to think especially charitable thoughts, which I'd noticed myself frequently attempting since I'd gotten home from Duluth. As Stan might have said, "Near death can do that." Anyway, I now found myself thinking that perhaps I had misjudged the man. Maybe I should give him a second chance. Maybe he wasn't really anal, but had good reasons for his strict adherence to school rules and policies. Maybe he'd been right to threaten me with suspension out of concern for the students' safety and their ability to concentrate on their studies. Maybe his concern for the public image of the school was justifiable.

Maybe he was going to apologize.

Not.

"Mr. White," Mr. Lenzen said. "I see you still have these deer hooves in your possession."

I looked at Jason's hooves on my desk.

"Yes," I said. "I do."

"You will make sure they are removed by the end of the day. Their presence in this building violates school policy, and we must set an example for the students. I'd hate to have to make a public reprimand."

So much for my charitable feelings.

The man really was anal.

"I'll be sure to take care of it," I assured him. *When pigs fly,* I mentally added.

Apparently satisfied that I was properly contrite, he got up and left, never once mentioning my almost-suspension or my contribution to the solution of a murder.

"Are you being a bad boy again?"

It was Alan. He dropped into the chair vacated by Mr. Lenzen and put his booted feet up on my desk. "So what's on your plate for next week? It's spring break and all us chickens get sprung from the coop."

"Alan," I said. "I'm impressed. You're talking birds. Okay, maybe chickens are domestic stuff, but it's a start."

Though I've been inviting him to go birding with me for years, Alan always turned me down. He says the nature thing is just not his style. He likes indoor plumbing, room service, and a hospitality suite at Timberwolves games.

Alan laughed. "It's being around you, White-man. Despite my best efforts, you're starting to rub off on me." He picked up a hoof from my desk and tossed it in the air, then caught it. He studied it for a moment in silence, then looked at me, suddenly serious.

"You know, Bob, a lot of the old people on the reservation believe that birds are omens, that, because they can fly, they're closer to the spirit world and can bring us messages. Owls, in particular, are supposed to be connected with death."

I was silent for a minute, too. Thanks to Rahr's murder, I'd had enough of death to last a very long while. Even worse, I couldn't help but wonder if the memory of that death would somehow haunt all my bird hunts in the future. I sure hoped not. Birding was in my bones. I wasn't about to give it up because one trip went really, really bad.

Alan tossed the hoof up again. "And deer hooves, they're supposed to be connected with assistant principals who are anal."

"Now that's the best reason I've heard yet to get them out of here." I took the one hoof out of Alan's hand and picked up the other that was sitting on my desk. "And I know just where to put them."

I dropped them in Alan's lap. "Don't ever say I never give you anything."

The phone rang before Alan could respond. It was Lily.

"I've got a pallet of birdseed for you. Payment for helping me with Mrs. Anderson's landscape plan. She loves the white jack pine and cranberry bushes idea."

"Good," I said. "She'll get all the birds she can feed. Sorry about losing the big score with the ladyslippers, though. I know it would have made you a ton of money."

Alan mouthed "Later" to me and left.

"No big deal," Lily replied. "It probably would have been too much of a good thing, anyway. In landscaping, sometimes you want less of a particular plant, rather than more because that way it stands out, and you can really appreciate its individual beauty."

"Lily," I said. "You're a romantic!"

"Hardly, Bobby. I'm just practicing how I'm going to tell Mrs. Anderson she should be thrilled with ten ladyslippers instead of hundreds. Got to run. Pick up some of this birdseed on your way home, okay?"

"Lily—wait." I wasn't sure how to broach the subject, but I wanted her to know I was sorry about how she'd been used by Stan in his investigation. "About Stan . . ."

"What about him?" Her voice was brisk.

"Despite what you may think of him, he really is a good man. He saved my life, Lily."

"I know. And I thanked him before I told him to never walk into my shop again."

"Maybe you should give him another chance."

"Bobby, he suspected I was taking bribes from VNT. That's why he was seeing me—to grab a look at my books. I have no interest in developing a relationship with a man who, upon meeting me, assumed I was dishonest."

I winced. After all, I've always said that Lily knows a good bribe when she sees one. But I've never said that she herself would take one. Of course, there had been no way for Stan to know that; he'd just been doing his job, and when her name popped up on VNT's customer list, he had to do his investigating gig. In the background, I heard Lily saying something to one of her employees in the shop, and then she came back on the line.

"Besides," she said, "Stan has too many other irons in the fire to suit me. Did you know that along with his private accounting practice and his government jobs, he also field tests crossbows? I'm sorry, but I don't have time for a grown man who wants to spend what little free time he has pretending to be Robin Hood. I'm no Maid Marian."

That was an understatement.

"So, stop being a protective little brother. I'm a big girl, you know."

I smiled. "You'll always be a shrimp to me."

She hung up.

I set the phone receiver back in its cradle, but it rang almost immediately. I picked it up again.

"Bob, I just saw on the list serve that there's a Ross's Goose in Winona on the Mississippi."

It was Mike and his excitement practically vibrated through the phone. "I've never gotten a Ross's Goose this early in the year before," he said. "What do you say? Saturday? Do you want to chase it?"

I'd never gotten a Ross's Goose this early, either. It would be a real score. On the other hand, was I ready to go back in the field? Elusive birds, professional rivalries, secret poaching operations, murder and mayhem . . .

But even as the question lingered in my mind, I knew it would take a lot more than one birding trip gone bad to keep me away from chasing birds. Like I've already said, birding is in my bones. Besides, the route to Winona was already forming in my head. On the way, we could swing by Black Dog Lake and see if any other early migrants were showing up. If a Ross's Goose had turned up in Winona, chances were good some other birds might be passing through. Given a good wind and climbing temperatures, there was no telling what we might find.

"Bob? Can you make it?"

Though Mike couldn't see it, I could feel the smile spreading across my face.

"Do birds fly?"

Bob White's *The Boreal Owl Murder* Bird List

Northern Hawk Owl
Greater White-fronted Goose
Canvasback Duck
Junco
Bald Eagle
Red-tailed Hawk
Pileated Woodpecker
Great Horned Owl
Snowy Owl
Barrows Goldeneye
Screech Owl
Black-billed Cuckoo
Blue-winged Warbler
Long-tailed Duck
Harlequin Duck
Boreal Owl